Praise for Bill Granger
and the November Man Series

THE NOVEMBER MAN

"Chilling...seems to move with the speed of light."
—*Pittsburgh Press*

"Should keep you reading to the end...an engrossing book about the world of computers, treachery, slow or sudden death, and 'doing things wrong for all the right reasons.'"
—*Chicago Tribune*

"Crisp style, well-mannered prose, and inexorable tension characterize this worthy addition to the successful November Man series. Granger once again displays his winning talent for manipulating traditional elements of intrigue...highly recommended."
—*Library Journal*

"Granger's November Man series has been consistently entertaining and interesting, far-surpassing much of the work done in the espionage genre. This addition to the list maintains that consistency...builds almost perfectly to an exciting finish...on the mark."
—*Publishers Weekly*

"First-rate...This gripping novel provides further proof that November Man has grown into one of the most complex fictional spies on the current scene."
—*Booklist*

CODE NAME NOVEMBER

"Mr. Granger has combined Ian Fleming, John le Carré, and Trevanian in a heady mix...He handles all the elements with real virtuosity."

—*New York Times Book Review*

"Granger is one of our premier spy novelists. His Devereaux is the perfect spy for these less than perfect times."

—*People*

"A novelist of superb talent who has mastered the genre and brought to it a distinctly American viewpoint."

—*Chicago Sun-Times*

"A serious American writer of the first rank...Like Hemingway, Granger learned the technical aspects of his craft through newspaper work. The result is lean and uniquely American."

—*National Review*

SCHISM

"An intelligently crafted thriller...lean prose and intricate plotting."

—*Los Angeles Times*

"The mysteries and motives here turn out to be suitably momentous...all of the characters are vulnerably likeable...solid entertainment."

—*Kirkus Reviews*

"True and dramatic and entertaining...*Schism* stands on its own."

—*Chicago Tribune*

THE SHATTERED EYE

"*The Shattered Eye* is a page-turner of the first order."

—*Denver Post*

"It catches you on the first page and propels you through to the end at an accelerating speed."
—Chicago Tribune Book World

THE BRITISH CROSS

"Sharp and suspenseful . . . A fine piece of work."
—Chicago Sun-Times

"Never lets readers relax. This one belongs on the top shelf." *—New York Daily News*

"Granger handles all the elements of real virtuosity."
—New York Times

THE ZURICH NUMBERS

"An invigorating thriller. Granger is a fine, serious story-teller . . . His simple, meaty prose is a perfect complement to the intricacies of the plot." *—Publishers Weekly*

"An ingenious, imaginative plot . . . The November Man has a steely, indomitable quality that raises him to Bond's superstar status." *—Kansas City Star*

HEMINGWAY'S NOTEBOOK

"Granger writes like a shooting star. His plots and characters and dialogue are so good . . . It's chilling stuff . . . a single page will grip the reader with an impact that other writers would use a chapter to pull off."
—Chicago Sun-Times

"Fast-moving, action-packed, violent, and ultimately very satisfying." *—Christian Science Monitor*

"This lean, suspenseful tale, peopled with compelling characters, has a drive and signature all its own."

—*Publishers Weekly*

THE INFANT OF PRAGUE

"Fascinating...compelling...Devereaux, the November Man, is back, and we're all a little richer for it."

—*Chicago Tribune*

"The characters are lively; the plot is as rapidly and smoothly paced as it is complex; the humor arrives without warning, and Granger continues to juggle the pieces while producing a unique spy thriller."

—*Richmond Times-Dispatch*

"Colorful...wonderfully complex...readers will delight in Granger's deft unraveling of the skeins in this terrific page-turner."

—*Publishers Weekly*

HENRY McGEE IS NOT DEAD

"The plot moves smoothly...Granger writes crisply... Devereaux provides a satisfactory ending."

—*San Antonio Express-News*

THE MAN WHO HEARD TOO MUCH

"The action is swift and brutal...his sense of characters is powerful. As ever with Granger, the prose is the opposite of the bloodless stuff of techno-thrillers."

—*Chicago Tribune*

"Granger's plots can be as intricate as the best le Carré... Granger is a master of fooling the unwary reader."

—*St. Louis Post-Dispatch*

THE
NOVEMBER
MAN

BILL GRANGER

GRAND CENTRAL
PUBLISHING

NEW YORK   BOSTON

Copyright © 1986 by Granger & Granger Inc.

Grand Central Publishing
Hachette Book Group
237 Park Avenue
New York, NY 10017

www.HachetteBookGroup.com

Printed in the United States of America

OPM

Originally published in hardcover as *There Are No Spies* by Warner Books.

GCP mass-market paperback edition: July 2014
10 9 8 7 6 5 4 3 2 1

Grand Central Publishing is a division of Hachette Book Group, Inc.
The Grand Central Publishing name and logo is a trademark of Hachette Book Group, Inc.

The publisher is not responsible for websites (or their content) that are not owned by the publisher.

If you think we are worked by strings,
Like a Japanese marionette,
You don't understand these things:
It is simply Court etiquette.
Perhaps you suppose this throng
Can't keep it up all day long?
If that's your idea, you're wrong.

—W. S. GILBERT

Author's Note

This book reflects a struggle going on in the world of intelligence between those who deny the usefulness of agents, contractors, case officers, and all the other personnel involved in the business of espionage and those who defend the worth of HUMINT (human intelligence and analysis) in the face of the technological revolution.

The *New York Times* gathered estimates by intelligence officials, who agree that 85 percent of all information gained by the various U.S. intelligence agencies comes from ELINT (electronic signal intelligence), SIGINT (signal intelligence), PHOTINT (photo intelligence), RADINT (radar intelligence), and all the "hardware" sources, opposed to the information gained by spies (HUMINT).

Intelligence analyst Walter Laqueur noted in *A World of Secrets* that "the need for HUMINT has not decreased, but it has become fashionable to denigrate the importance of human assets because technical means are politically and intellectually more comfortable. On the other hand, the opportunities for hostile intelligence agents operating in democratic societies are incomparably greater than for their Western counterparts."

In 1985, there was a furious exchange of spies between East and West before the Reagan–Gorbachev summit. In every case of a mole's "defection" to his true side, another agent in the field was picked up by the side sinned against. In one bizarre case, a Soviet KGB agent who "defected" West later "redefected" to the Soviet embassy in Washington, claiming he had been kidnapped. Central Intelligence Agency denied his claims. In 1986, a Chinese double agent buried inside CIA claimed he had worked for China for two decades to improve relations between the countries and not for monetary gain—though he had to take the money to convince the Chinese he was a legitimate traitor. He committed suicide, according to official reports, by putting a plastic bag over his head in his cell and voluntarily suffocating himself.

These things are all true; these things are all reflected in this book.

—Bill Granger
Chicago, 1986

THE NOVEMBER MAN

PROLOGUE

THE EDGE OF THE WORLD

In a little while, she had to go away. There were assignments in the East, in the Philippines, then back to
Washington…She gave him the itinerary, she fussed
about him. It was a way of making love to him.

This was the other way. Rita moved beneath him and
her belly bumped his belly. They were tangles of arms,
they were tastes and smells; they mingled with each
other. Devereaux was never so lost as when he made love
to her. Never so abandoned. There were no cold places
in him when he made love to her. He cried out like a lost
child when he came. She held his shuddering body with
legs, arms, hands, pressed him into her. She closed her
eyes very tight to feel the wonder of this very common
act they shared with nearly every other member of the
species.

Let me be lost in you.

They shivered in pleasure in each other and then fell
away like flowers thrown on a still pond. They never
spoke when they made love; lovemaking was too true for

words. He didn't trust words. Words lied. You could say anything.

And they both heard the telephone ringing from the next room, though it was in the middle of the morning, in Lausanne, at the edge of the world they had fled from...

1

HANLEY'S DISCOVERY

Tired," Hanley said on the third Tuesday in February. He repeated the word several times to himself, alone in his windowless cubicle that was the office of the director of operations. He blinked, looked around at the white walls of the cold, bare room, and said the word again. It was as though everything familiar to him had drained his life away.

He said the word again to Miss Smurtty in the outer office and by then he had his hat on. He shrugged into his overcoat as he walked along the hall to the elevator bank on the sixth floor. He repeated the word to the security policeman at the elevator bank. The policeman said nothing.

Hanley said the word like a man searching memory for words to a song at the edge of the mind.

He went home and it wasn't even noon yet.

He took to his bed.

Each morning thereafter, he called in by nine. He talked to the same woman in personnel and recorded his absence. He said he was ill because he felt so tired. He explained to the woman in personnel how tired he felt.

And he stayed out sick the rest of the month of February. It was the first time in twenty-one years that Hanley had missed a day of work.

He was the good civil servant. As director of operations for R Section, he had a love for the Section that transcended mere identification with a job or mission.

The tiredness colored all his thoughts. He would lie in bed at night and listen to the roar of traffic beneath his apartment windows. He lived on the third floor of a large apartment building at the juncture of Massachusetts and Wisconsin avenues in northwest Washington. The rooms were large and airy but all the light was gray because it was spring in Washington and always raining.

Hanley sat by the window in his apartment in the afternoons and looked down at the cars climbing up the hill from DuPont Circle and around the Naval Observatory grounds where the Vice President's white house sat in splendid isolation. Hanley thought too much. He thought about the Vice President having a better view and neighborhood to live in than the President trapped in the tangle of the central city. Hanley thought the traffic was very thick and very loud; it was like undergrowth around a neglected house. The weeds had grown and grown until one day there was nothing to be done but burn them off and tear the old house down and start again.

Hanley wept when he thought such things.

He had been growing more and more tired for weeks before he decided to take sick leave. Dr. Thompson's pills did not seem to help him but he took them with precise faithfulness. He was a man of habits. He was cold and thin and his voice was flat as the Nebraska plains he had come from.

He thought of the child he had been. He wept when he thought of himself.

Once in a while he thought he would have to get better. He was director of operations for R Section and that meant he was director of spies. The master of the marionettes. But he was ill now and the spies were being left to dance without direction. This couldn't go on. It mustn't go on.

On March 1, the doctor came.

Dr. Thompson was vetted twice a year. He had taken his annual lie detector test in January. He was thirty-four years old and very nearly incompetent, which is why he was only employable by a government agency. Before joining the Section, he had nearly been stripped of his license to practice in his native Oregon because of some damned business involving surgery on a woman where the wrong organs had been removed. It had not been his fault.

Thompson carried a top secret clearance and had access to secrets to the level of N. He was a jolly young man with a pink face and a hearty, almost English manner. He slapped his hands together when he talked; he resembled Alec Guinness in early films.

Hanley allowed the prodding. It was government procedure. Thompson talked and poked and made Hanley cough; he tapped at his back and asked him to urinate into a jar and took a blood sample and talked about the Washington Redskins and laughed too much. Hanley endured it. He wanted not to feel so tired.

For no reason, Hanley began to weep. Thompson stared at him and asked him why he was crying. Hanley excused himself, went to the bathroom, wiped his eyes, and looked at his thin, cold, old sallow face.

"Why are you crying?" he asked himself.

When the ordeal was over, Hanley buttoned his pajama shirt and slipped the gray bathrobe over his thin shoulders and resumed his seat in the large chair by the front windows.

There were books strewn on the floor around the chair. He had been reading Somerset Maugham. He had been reading autobiography disguised as fiction in which Maugham, who had been a British agent in the First War, describes himself as "Ashenden, the secret agent." And Ashenden takes a ferry one day across Lake Geneva, from France to neutral Switzerland, and...

Hanley had read the story over and over. He didn't understand why. He didn't understand why he was so tired.

"You need rest," Dr. Thompson said. "You need to get some sun, get some color into those cheeks. Stop moping about. You took the pills I prescribed?"

"They seem to make me more tired."

"They're supposed to relax you," Thompson said. "Listen to your doctor." Smiled. "Go to Florida. Get some sun. Plenty of sun down there. Shouldn't mope around here."

Hanley thought of Florida. He had never been there. He blinked and looked out the window at his city, a place he had used and grown to love through use. They were going to tear down the café down on Fourteenth Street where he had gone to lunch every working day. Every working day of thirty-five years of work and they were going to tear it down.

He blinked and his vision was as wet as the rain-streaked windows. Thompson was talking to him. The voice droned.

Hanley thought of all the places he knew so intimately

and had never seen. Like Number 2, Dhzerzhinski
Square, Moscow. That ugly gray building—the headquarters of Committee for State Security. KGB. He knew it as
an old enemy. It was nearly the same as knowing an old
friend.

"What do you say to that?"

Hanley looked up and Thompson was beaming his
professional beam.

"What do I say to what?"

"Hospitalization. A complete rest cure."

"No." Hanley's voice was quick. "No. If I'm sick, I'm
sick. If I'm not sick, I don't need a hospital."

"You need rest."

"You can't get rest in a hospital."

Dr. Thompson frowned.

Hanley turned away, stared at the street below, stared at
the traffic. The goddamn traffic. The noise pounded at his
thoughts day and night. No wonder he was tired. Where
were all those people going to? Did they live in their cars?

Hanley blinked and felt his eyes moisten again. He had
never noticed the traffic before. His thoughts seemed to
go in circles. What had he been thinking of—he had to
get well, get back to Operations, see to the delicate business of Nutcracker.

He thought of Nutcracker.

He thought of the toy nutcracker from Germany he
had owned as a child. Given to him one Christmas by a
long-ago great-aunt. A child's toy. Fierce and bristling in
guard's uniform, with a mustache and horrible large teeth.

He smiled as suddenly as he wept. He felt warm. He
wanted Thompson to go away. The warmth of memory
filled him. He had to get back to Section, back to seeing

what was wrong with Nutcracker. Director of spies. To play the great game as he saw it in his mind.

"...medication," Thompson concluded.

Hanley nodded, said nothing. He took the prescription sheet and looked at it. He waited for Thompson to leave.

Yackley listened to Thompson, asked him two questions and dismissed him.

It was the same afternoon. It had stopped raining. The sky was full of clouds and warm winds billowed along Fourteenth Street, cracking the flags on government buildings. Yackley's office on the sixth floor of the south Department of Agriculture building had a large window that looked across the street at the dour Bureau of Engraving building.

Yackley was not pleased by anything Thompson told him about Hanley.

Yackley was director of R Section. Hanley worked for him. Hanley was letting the Section down.

Yackley stood at his window, looked down at his view, and thought about his Section. He was a political appointment from the early Reagan days. He was an attorney, a Republican, wealthy enough to work for the government. He took a Level Four polygraph examination once a year to maintain his Ultra clearance. He had access to level X in security and in the computer system called Tinkertoy.

Yackley was called the New Man by his derisive subordinates, including Hanley. They thought he was an ass; he knew that. He had replaced Rear Admiral Galloway (USN Retired) as head of Section because Galloway had stubbed his toes badly in some Section business in Florida. Galloway had been the Old Man.

Thompson had told him: "He won't go."

"Damn. He won't go. Did you talk to him?"

"He wasn't listening to me."

"This was important, *Doctor*." Yackley had put heavy emphasis on the last word, as though he didn't believe it. He could have saved the sarcasm; Thompson was immune.

He would have to do something else.

Yackley felt nervous when he had to do something. Something on his own. Maybe he needed advice. Maybe he should consult his "rabbi." Maybe he didn't have to act right away.

The thoughts flung themselves one after the other through his mind. Yackley went back to his rosewood desk and sat down in the $455 leather swivel chair. He swiveled and put his hands behind his head to aid thought. He frowned. He thought about Hanley and the goddamn agent Devereaux and the business in Florida in which Galloway had stubbed his toes and been fired. It had been Hanley's doing. And Devereaux's. Hanley wanted to be head of Section. That's what Yackley thought from time to time: A goddamned civil servant wanted to be head of Section.

Scheming. Hanley was scheming and it was all against Yackley because Hanley hated Yackley's success. Yackley had issued a directive saying that, in order to "downtrim" the budget of Section, "cutbacks were needed in every sector" and that the effort would succeed only "if we all realize we are in this boat together and help pull each other's oars."

There had been any number of obscene drawings on Section bathroom walls showing Yackley pulling the oars of others.

It wasn't funny. And Hanley—that was something Hanley would have dreamed up. To undermine his authority.

So Yackley had tapped Hanley for six months. Home and away. The taps were designed by the National Security Agency, which is the "hardware" supplier to the other intelligence services, including R Section. The taps were perfected and installed by Richfield, the Section's own ELINT man and resident "hardware" genius. As well as the supreme loyalist.

Yackley squinted at the words of the transcript of the taps. Damned good thing he had tapped Hanley; should have done it years before.

February 21, time: 1:02 A.M. Electronic count indicates the telephone number is: Country—Switzerland; City—Lausanne; Number 28-23-56.

HANLEY: Hello?
    (Silence for five seconds.)
HANLEY: Hello? Hello?
    (Silence for two seconds.)
HANLEY: Hello? Someone say something.
VOICE: What do you want?
HANLEY: There's a problem and I think I am beginning to understand it and I have to tell someone. I've discovered—
VOICE: I don't care. I'm not in the trade. (Pause.) There is no November.
HANLEY: That's just it. No November. There are no spies. I think I can tell you. I need to tell you. And did you know that your duplicate November is on his way to Moscow?

(Silence for five seconds.)

HANLEY: Hello?

VOICE: I'm not in the trade, Hanley. That was our agreement. I don't exist. November is some man running away from a wet contract.

HANLEY: A wet contract from Moscow. And now the man you tagged November is running right into the arms of the Opposition. Why is that?

VOICE: I don't care. Don't call me anymore.

(Broken connection.)

February 23, time: 1:13 A.M. Electronic count indicates the same country, city, and telephone number as previous conversation.

HANLEY: Hello?

VOICE: I'm not interested in talking to you.

HANLEY: Listen. For just one minute. I've got to tell someone this, I've got to talk it out to someone who understands. Who understands what's going on in Section. Someone who isn't in Section anymore.

VOICE: Are you drunk, Hanley? Has the one-martini lunch finally gotten out of control after all these years?

HANLEY: (garbled) has to be at the highest levels. Do you understand?

VOICE: I am not in the trade. That was our agreement.

(Garbled)

HANLEY: The pills. I stopped taking them and I don't feel as bad. Are the pills...something wrong? I sleep all the time and then I wake up and I can't sleep. I never knew there was so much traffic, all day and night, you can't sleep. Where are all those people going?

VOICE: Home. You go home, too.

HANLEY: I am home.

VOICE: Then have a drink and go to sleep.

HANLEY: My lunch. They are going to tear down the place on Fourteenth Street. I went there every day of my life. A martini straight up and a cheeseburger with raw onion. One martini. I knew all the people there. And Mr. Sianis said to me, "Mr. Hanley, I have to sell the place because they are going to put up a trade center."

VOICE: Why are you calling me? Leave me alone. Everything is over.

HANLEY: Damnit. You never leave the service. You know that. You're in for life. And I've told you that.

VOICE: November is going to Moscow. You said it. November does not exist.

HANLEY: (portion missing) the secret, the point of the thing, when it comes down to it, it might just be that simple.

VOICE: What are you talking about?

HANLEY: I read Somerset Maugham over and over. *Ashenden.* About the secret agent in World War I, he reminded me that you were in Lausanne and that you probably took the same ferry boats between France and Switzerland that he did. All those years ago. When it was accepted finally. The need for spies. Reilly. Maugham. The people in BritIntell—I thought about you when I read those stories. Because of the location. You took that ferry.

VOICE: Yes.

HANLEY: I am not insane. I am not going insane. I am tired and I have time to think about things. I mean, sanity is understanding where your feet are planted, isn't it? But I'm off my feet, I don't have perspective anymore.

VOICE: Seek professional help.

HANLEY: Sarcasm. You have to help—

VOICE: —no.

HANLEY: (interrupted) secret. I think of one thing and think of another. I had a nutcracker when I was a child and—

VOICE: Good-bye, Hanley.

HANLEY: Wait. There are no spies. That's what it means. There are no spies at all. But that's not true. That's the one thing I realize now. That's not true. (Disconnect)

February 28, time: 10:13 A.M. (Incoming call; location uncertain.)

HANLEY: Hello? Hello?

LYDIA NEUMANN: This is Lydia Neumann, Hanley. You're still ill. I wanted to see how you were. Can I get you anything? I'm worried about you and we need you in Section.

HANLEY: So we can pull our oars.

NEUMANN: (Laughter)

HANLEY: I need rest, that's all I need.

NEUMANN: Should I come over?

HANLEY: . . . sleep at night. Traffic. Where are those people all rushing to?

NEUMANN: Have you seen a doctor? Not Thompson. Don't use Thompson.

HANLEY: Thompson? He doesn't know a damned thing. I understand his little game. Pills. I know all the secrets, you know, Mrs. Neumann. I know everything. You let me fool myself but you were onto the secret as well, weren't you? This is a game in a computer and you're the master of Tinkertoy. The mistress of Tinkertoy. So I'll ask you: Where is my Nutcracker?

NEUMANN: Hanley? Hanley? Are you all right?

HANLEY: My Nutcracker. New Man knows, New Man (Neumann?) knows—

NEUMANN: Hanley, I don't know what you're talking about.

HANLEY: Spies, Neumann. I am talking about the whole business of spies. Of moles and sleepers and agents who come awake, of doubles and triples, of dogs who bark and dogs who bite, covert and overt, going into black and black bag operations, and the business of the trade. I am talking about goddamn bona fides and about software and I am telling you, I am going to get to the bottom of the whole damned business.

NEUMANN: (garbled)

HANLEY: Oh, you believe that. I know you do. There are no spies. But I have my spies and you have a bunch of circuits. I have the spies. There are no spies?

NEUMANN: Hanley, my God—
     (Disconnect)

Three telephone calls, except the call from a woman asking Hanley to subscribe to the *Washington Post*.

Yackley's frown was deep and sincere. His skin was burned brown by January's sun in St. Maarten; his eyes were blue and quite empty. But the frown spoke for his thoughts.

The room was lit by a single green-shaded banker's lamp. The soft light framed the two photographs on his desk. His wife smiled crookedly at the photographer; his daughter smiled at Daddy. If they only understood all the secrets he had and was privy to. If they only could understand the nasty business that had to be done.

There are no spies.

Hanley told Devereaux that. And he told Devereaux about Colonel Ready, tagged as November, now making his way to Moscow to try to arrange a defection. A damned mess, all of it. And what was the real November going to do now? Except plot with Hanley.

There are no spies. And the New Man knows.

Yackley considered the matter for a moment. He knew exactly what he was going to do; he was working up an argument in conscience to sanctify it. But it had to be done in any case, even if it was going to be dirty.

2

THE *FINLANDIA* INCIDENT

Alexa was quite beautiful in the way of a certain kind of young Russian woman. Her eyes were coal-dark and deep and it was difficult to describe their color. Her eyes were also set sharply in the paleness of her strong features. Despite the generous width of her mouth and her very high cheekbones that seemed to stretch her skin, despite her coal-black hair that severely defined the edges of her pale features, her eyes held you. Her merest glance compelled you to stare at her, at her eyes, in total fascination.

Her eyes were her only drawback, from a professional point of view.

She might be able to change the color of her hair or disguise her slender figure by flattening her full breasts or by stooping to seem shorter or older than she was. But she could never disguise those eyes.

Alexa turned from the bar in the warm green room on the third deck of the *Finlandia* and gazed across the room at the man she was going to kill.

The trouble with Alexa's usefulness as an intelligence

agent for the Committee for State Security was that she was very good at those assignments that called for action—immediate, brutal, violent—and very bad at those assignments that called for mere intelligence gathering.

She was intelligent; but she was too visible. She was very beautiful and she was noticed wherever she went. Her Moscow accent was slight when she spoke English; her Moscow manners might have made many people mistake her for a New Yorker or a Parisian. She had the right mixture of rudeness and grace.

But it was no good having your informant fall in love with you or having your network of agents desire you sexually. Or have the watchers from the other side find it too agreeable to watch you. And suspect you, even as they fell in love with you. Besides, she could never change her eyes.

She stared at the man with graying hair who sat at the wide window, gazing into the gloomy night of the Baltic Sea. Alexa was the death-giver. It was not so bad, it was over so quickly, it was part of a large game. She never felt bad afterward. In fact, she had felt bad just once, when her victim had lived.

Two years ago. She was sent up through the Soviet embassy in Mexico City, which was the usual route of spies working on the West Coast of the United States. In that area south of San Francisco called Silicon Valley— where they made computers and invented wonderful things—she had seduced a somewhat shy, certainly amoral security guard who was twenty-four years old and made $7.23 an hour guarding the great secrets of M-Guide Computer Laboratories in Palo Alto.

His name was Tony. Poor Tony. He was now in the very harsh maximum security prison at Marion in southern Illinois. He was kept in a narrow cell most of the time and his only recreation was reading and working with weights. She felt bad afterward not because she had loved Tony at all—that had been business—but because she thought of herself caught in a cell for the rest of her life. She pitied herself. It would have been a merciful thing to kill Tony. She had considered it, the night he put his face between her legs and she had the Walther PPK under the pillow and she thought about it because Tony was very close to being caught. But he had pleased her and she had been merciful. Too bad for Tony.

Better to die like the man at the window in the bar. She studied his face, his lean chin, his glittering eyes. Dead man, she thought.

The *Finlandia* slid down the open sea passage between the islands that are flung out in a stream east from Stockholm, almost to the coast of Finland. In the bright moon of the starry night, here and there, above the snow, poked roofs or sticks of summer homes on the islands. The islands were the perpetual retreats of middle-class Swedes in summer; the islands, some no more than an acre or two in size, promised summer even now at the end of the long Scandinavian winter.

The *Finlandia* was a huge ship, the largest car ferry in the world. She might have been an ocean liner but was trapped in the dull passage every day between Stockholm and Helsinki. She always passed at night because the trip took exactly thirteen hours. It was midnight and the ship was halfway to the lights of Helsinki.

The man at the table was Colonel Ready. He had been

chased for 400 days. He had killed three "contractors" sent by KGB. He had disappeared in Copenhagen five months ago and despite the large network of Soviet agents working in that city he had not been found.

Until he surfaced four weeks ago. With messages to the Soviet courier. He wanted to sell secrets; he wanted to sell himself. After all, the KGB knew he was an agent of R Section called November. He had many secrets.

The bartender was in love with her. He was a large blond Swede and he spoke good English. He thought his good looks impressed her. When she treated him with reserve, even coldly, he adored her. Her eyes always lied; her eyes always told of passion and unbelievable lust. The coldness of her manner only framed the passion promised in her eyes.

"Please, another drink for you?" he said, not sure of himself, fawning. He was too large and handsome to fawn.

"Perhaps," Alexa said, as though deciding. "Yes, I think," she said, deciding, giving him one small smile as a reward. "Glenfiddich." She had her preferences: single-malt Scotch whisky, and the Walther PPK, a very small automatic with a deadly accurate field of fire at short range. She worked in very close because she was not afraid of killing or feeling any passion at the act of giving death.

It was just as well that Alexa was so good in the matter of wet contracts.

She had been contracted to November four days ago. There had been confusion for a long time inside KGB over who November was. He was supposed to be the man who kidnapped KGB agent Dmitri Denisov six years ago in Florida; who had wrecked the IRA plan to kill Lord Slough in his boat off the Irish coast; who had caused enough troubles and embarrassment—all outside the rules of the trade understood by both sides—that Gorki had "contracted" him. He had to be killed. Which is why he wanted to come to the Moscow side. Gorki said it was too late. Gorki said November—who was this man, Colonel Ready—had to be killed because he could not be trusted.

Alexa thought of Gorki, head of the Resolutions Committee. Her mentor. A gnome with yellow skin and sandpaper hands. He had used her; the only man who had truly used her. When he was finished with her—in the dacha, long ago—she belonged to him. He knew that and never made great demands on her again. She was a painted wooden doll upon his shelf. He had opened her and found the doll within and the doll within the third doll and so on. He had gone to her core. She had shuddered at his touch and needed it. She had danced naked for him.

Gorki was not his name. Alexa was not her name. They were named by computers and codebooks. They were puppets, all of them. But some puppets danced naked for the others.

Alexa had been at Moscow University when KGB approached her. She had been afraid at first and then curious. What if she ended up in the translation pool that worked in one of the buildings adjacent to KGB headquarters in Dhzerzhinski Square? She knew what the pool was. She would be plucked from the pool as though she were a piece of fruit, by some KGB major to serve as his mistress, to feed his ego and maleness, to be discreet so that when he had to escort his plain, quite fat official wife she would understand and say nothing. She would be taken to Paris by him but not to the Black Sea because the Black Sea was for the family. She didn't want that to happen to her, not at all. And it had not happened. She had been placed inside the Resolutions Committee and her superior, who was not permitted to make love to her, an obnoxious man named Mikhail, had said of her: "Women cannot kill, except in fury."

She had proven him wrong in a brilliant bit of business in Finland. She had attracted the attention of Gorki.

She thought of Gorki now and shivered as she drank the Scotch. The Scotch flooded her with warmth. Her loins were warmed. Gorki commanded her.

And she was very good at what she did.

Which is why he had full confidence in her to wet contract the annoying American agent called November.

November had limped and left a trail until he disappeared in Copenhagen. Then he made contact with the Soviet courier chief in Copenhagen. His code name was Stern. He played November along until he got instructions. They came from Gorki. The wet contract was still in force, Gorki said. Tell November we will negotiate with him—but in neutral Finland. Give him money to get to Finland. Tell him the running is over. And I will send Alexa to intercept him and to kill him once and for all.

November had no choice but to believe them.

Alexa had flown to Stockholm for the intercept at eight in the morning. She had spent the day in the splendor of the Birger Jarl, which was a warm hotel. In the afternoon, she took a walking tour through the narrow old streets of the Gamla Stan, the island of Stockholm that contains the oldest parts of the city. She had never been in Stockholm and found it charming. She bought a pair of leather boots at a shop in the Old Town. The clerk had very dark hair and an innocent face. He knelt before her to put the boots on her legs. She had felt the warmth build in her then and nearly considered it. But there was business to take care of. She had no doubt the clerk would have obeyed.

She had not seen boots like the ones she purchased even in the special stores in Moscow. They fit her well. Everything she wore fit her well. She always got a second-hand copy of *Vogue* each month from the Paris courier. She dressed in fashion.

The *Finlandia* had sailed at six from the grimly modern terminal on the southeast coast of the city. The terminal was as sullen and cheerless as a bus station and she had sat at a table in the cafeteria, eating a stale cheese sandwich, watching November enter the place, look around, wait in line with the others. She had boarded the ship at the last moment.

She had watched him at dinner in the vast dining room. She would have preferred to dine alone but agreed to be seated with a middle-aged woman from Malmo who spoke no English. They smiled to each other with the wary grace that only women display when meeting other and unknown women. The woman from Malmo certainly saw how much more beautiful and better dressed Alexa was.

The dining room had been cheerful, full of small lights and small tables and a quiet orchestra at one end. Everything was made very intense by the presence of the Baltic Sea all around them. We are alone in the world, Alexa had thought with pleasure.

The American agent dined alone across the room.

Their eyes met once and held.

He had not smiled at her.

He did not turn his eyes away. It was she who broke contact.

She had followed him after dinner. He had gone on deck, he had visited one of the smaller bars, he had looked in the duty-free shops. She followed him and he knew it; it was what she had wanted him to know. The advantage was hers.

He was handsome in a rugged sense. Perhaps he believed she followed him because she desired him.

There was a trick to killing him on this ship, in the middle of the night, in the middle of the winter of the Baltic Sea.

Alexa would use the obvious approach and he would stop it; he was smart enough to have eluded Moscow for 400 days of running, so he would see the obvious. But the obvious way sometimes worked when a man had grown lonely or careless or dejected or had been lulled into the belief that Alexa merely wanted to go to bed with him.

Alexa had backups. When the obvious did not work, the backups would.

She decided to cross the room.

She carried her glass and sat down across from him in the overstuffed chair. She put her glass on the table and stared into his blue eyes. He was smiling at her.

He wore a ragged red beard now, perhaps to cover the scar that was on his cheek. He looked a little different from the descriptions given her, but then, anyone on the run for more than a year undergoes changes.

She let her eyes lie to him. Her eyes, she knew, glittered with lust. But Alexa was calm, without any feeling at all. She stared at him and let her eyes do the trick. Then she said, in precise English: "I have seen you and I want to go to your cabin and make love to you. Tonight. Now. Or you may come to my cabin."

"All right," he said. Just like that.

They did not speak or touch again until they reached his cabin door. He turned the key in the lock. The carpeted passageway was empty. He smiled at her with perfect white teeth. There were pain wrinkles at the corners of his eyes. He had lost weight in 400 days of running. She thought he might be thin beneath the loose shirt and that his ribs would press out against his skin. But it wouldn't come to that, Alexa thought.

He kissed her very suddenly at the door to the room and reached for her purse with one motion.

He pushed her away a little.

It was in the purse and they both knew it and it seemed to relax the tension between them.

He produced the shining Walther PPK and unsnapped the safety and pointed it at her. She wore a short fur jacket and a black silk blouse and a dark wool skirt that came to the top of her boots. The darkness of her clothing accentuated her paleness. She wore no jewelry and her lips were painted lightly. Her eyes were wide and deep and November stared into them. She was smiling.

"You know who I am. I wanted you to know so that there would be no trouble—"

"You're a little obvious," he said.

There, Alexa thought. There. That made it better.

"Come in," November said.

"All right."

She smiled—a properly small smile of acknowledgment of his superior instincts in this matter—and brushed past him through the narrow cabin opening into the room. There was a single bed made up. There was a small dresser and a porthole. In the front was a shower and a toilet.

"Strip," he said.

She turned and he smiled at her.

"Please," she began.

"Strip," he said. And he smiled.

She took off her coat.

She looked hesitant.

He was grinning at her. He put the pistol on the purse on the dresser.

"You want help? I could take off your clothes for you. Not as carefully as you might do it."

"I am KGB," she said.

"I know exactly what you are. Right now, you're a woman and I want you. I saw you get on the ship, I saw you at dinner, I guessed we would meet. Do you think I'm crazy? I know there's going to be a setup along the way. You're the setup; but if I overcome it—overcome you— they'll have to talk to me. I'll have you and then we will talk some and then maybe I won't kill you," he said.

Gorki had emphasized the brutality of the man and his cunning. He had lectured her about him. Alexa had taken precautions.

She began to unbutton her blouse. She undressed slowly, watching his eyes watching her.

November stood still, fully dressed, watching her, smiling.

She took off her blouse. Her brassiere fastened in front. She opened her brassiere and her large breasts sank a little against her slender frame.

She sat down then, on the only chair in the room, and removed her boots.

She reached beneath her dark skirt to remove her nylons. She blushed now because it seemed a good idea to her. "Really," she said.

"Come now. Only a few more things."

She blushed furiously. She reached for the top of her panties and panty hose.

The weapon contained two plastic bullets encased in a plastic firing device that was eighty-nine millimeters in length. She pulled down her hose and panties and the device, between her legs, fastened by the elastic of the panties, was in the palm of her left hand.

The device—it could scarcely be called a pistol because the principles were not the same, all the firing parts were electronic—popped loudly once and there was a sudden and large dirty hole in the middle of his forehead.

It was over that quickly. It amazed both of them.

He was quite dead, though it takes the brain some moments to realize that the flicker of images in mind and eye are terminated, rather like a reel of film still spinning after the screen has gone blank.

There was no need to fire a second time—there were only two charges in the plastic device—but Alexa was a woman of carefulness. It was why she had risen in a bureaucracy that might be described as not very progressive in the matter of respect for the talents of women.

The second opening in the skull came very near the first. Alexa was a professional and played a top game.

She had to step aside to let his body fall between her and the bed.

She went through his pockets. He had a few notes of

Swedish money on him; also a Danish passport and a credit card issued by a Danish bank; also a passbook with a canceled account from Credit Suisse in Geneva.

She opened his shirt out of curiosity. He had a very nice chest, she thought. If there had been time to arrange the matter differently . . . well.

She dressed again. She put the device in her purse. As a precaution, Alexa buried the Walther under his mattress.

She lifted the body onto the bed and covered it with blankets and buried a pillow over the face so that the holes could not be seen clearly.

She went to the door and opened it carefully and looked up and down the empty corridor. She flicked off the lights in the room. The engines of the ship chugged serenely below decks. The night was clear and the waters of the Baltic Sea were gentle and shining beneath the full moon.

3

Breach of Security

It was the fourth of March. The day was filled with sun and blustery winds down the broad avenue that connects the White House with Capitol Hill. In the dark corner office of Frank L. Yackley, there were four chairs around the big rosewood desk. The illumination in the room had not improved. The light from the green-shaded banker's lamp made the faces of the four arrayed around the desk dark and indistinct. Frank L. Yackley's face seemed large and unreal, as though he might be the Wizard of Oz. It was the effect he desired.

"The problem is Hanley," Yackley said.

Lydia Neumann felt the chill again in the pit of her stomach. She counted as Hanley's closest friend in the Section, though "friend" might be too strong from her point of view and "friend" might be too weak from Hanley's. Hanley had no friends and pretended not to want them. He trusted Lydia Neumann as he trusted no one else. He had been a bachelor all his life, he was sexually indifferent; he was a bore, in fact. But Lydia Neumann with her raspy voice and Ma Joad manner had liked him in the way that some people favor the runt of a litter of farm dogs.

But she knew there was a problem as well. She squirmed in her chair and the leather squeaked protest.

"He needs help," Yackley continued in his careful voice, slowly rubbing the side of one hand up and down the palm of another, as though playing his hands.

There was no sound in the room. The other chairs were occupied by the director of signals, the director of translations and analysis, the director of research. Lydia Neumann, the only woman at this level, was director of the computer analysis division. Since her duties overlapped those of Franz Douglas in TransAn (slang for translations and analysis), they were rivals in the fabric of the bureaucracy. Naturally, Franz Douglas would oppose Neumann on the matter of Hanley. It was the way things worked.

"We are all aware of his illness. We are also aware of his extraordinary response to Mrs. Neumann's call of... sympathy. I have talked to him as well. I am afraid that Mr. Hanley has suffered some severe shock."

That was a giveaway, Lydia Neumann thought. She narrowed her eyes. *Mr.* Hanley. He was getting the setup.

She was a large woman and huddled for a moment in her even larger loose sweater, her hands on the lap of her cotton dress. She might have posed as a farm-woman from another era. She was a Midwesterner as Hanley was; perhaps that explained their attraction to each other.

"I am not competent medically to make a judgment," he continued. "I have sent for Dr. Thompson to make a report."

"He said Hanley needed rest," Lydia Neumann said. "He's been overburdened."

"Yes, Mrs. Neumann," Yackley said. "But there is rest and there is rest."

"I don't understand—"

"Neither do I. I consulted with Dr. Thompson, who agrees with me that some evaluation needs to be made of Mr. Hanley. Perhaps at a different level than that afforded by Dr. Thompson. Who is, after all, concerned with the ills of the body."

"The mind," said Franz Douglas. "There's something in what you say."

"Acted peculiar," chimed in Claymore Richfield, director of research, a white-gowned scientific sort who never noticed anyone or anything. He had developed a large budget because he agreed with everyone in the Section and then went off and created miracles. Like the wire of the innocent copper bracelet worn by field officers and used to garrote the unsuspecting. Like Marcom One, which not only analyzed photographs from the spy satellites but automatically coordinated them in computer memory so that the face of the Soviet Union from ninety-seven miles up was captured fresh from morning until night by photos that could sense the change of traffic lights in Moscow. Claymore Richfield was not of this world, Hanley once observed; he did not see things on a human scale but as a god might. Hanley had imparted this observation to Lydia Neumann once as they got drunk at the Christmas party held in the translation pool. "Intelligence is a mountain to be climbed," Hanley had intoned. "It is not a mountain to be descended to."

The fifth person in the room, Seymour Blyfeld, was director of signals and the upper-level liaison with NSA. He didn't count.

"Whether there is or not, we are faced with difficult

decisions," said Yackley, quietly picking up the consensus. "The trouble with Hanley is that he has Ultra clearance, he can be very dangerous to us, to the Section, to the country. He has secrets."

"He's not a traitor. You're not calling him that," Lydia Neumann said. "He's ill—"

"I am not diagnosing him, Mrs. Neumann," said Yackley in a stiff voice, grinding the walnut words into powder. "I am suggesting that there must be an evaluation. A psychological evaluation."

"From which he won't return," she said in a stubborn voice. "No one ever gets a clean bill of health in a psychological evaluation—"

"And no one is ever recommended for one unless there is something wrong with him," Franz Douglas said in his thin, snippy voice.

"We have a problem, Mrs. Neumann. In the past three years, FBI has uncovered thirty-two traitors, thirty-two spies who have—"

"FBI? What does that have to do with us—"

"Traitors," said Yackley. "What if it were proven by one of our dear sister agencies—let us not name the agency, let us just assume it is one of our Competition—that the director of operations division was not only off his head but that he was babbling secrets to outsiders?"

"Has that happened?" Lydia Neumann said.

"Yes. He has made contact with a former agent. A former agent who no longer exists. He is babbling over an open line—"

"How do you know this?"

"Because the line has been tapped for six months. At my directive," Yackley said. Richfield looked innocent.

Lydia Neumann's face went red. "What about us? Are we tapped as well?"

Yackley smiled at that. "It wouldn't do to tell you if you were, would it?"

"I wouldn't mind being tapped," said Franz Douglas. "I have nothing to hide."

Mrs. Neumann ignored him. "Who is the agent? The ex-agent? What did he say?"

"That's not really your concern, Mrs. Neumann."

"What secrets did he—"

"Mrs. Neumann. I have called this meeting for the purpose of gaining a consensus for a course of action in the matter of Mr. Hanley. I think the course of action is obvious. I will recommend to the director of National Security that Mr. Hanley be examined at the facility at St. Catherine's."

Mrs. Neumann knew. She felt the ice grow as a real thing in her belly, press against the warm skin from the inside and freeze it, grow up into her chest and make the breath come short.

"That's wrong," Mrs. Neumann said at last, choking.

"It is the only solution of the moment," Yackley said. "St. Catherine's is secure. St. Catherine's is a perfectly respectable private institution with a government contract and they have served us well over twenty-five years. The Claretian Sisters—"

"This is not about the nuns, that man has some say in this, some rights—"

"Mrs. Neumann, this is a matter of grave national security. Mr. Hanley is a sick man, he needs treatment." The voice had stopped grinding walnuts. There was the balm of healing. Yackley looked at the photograph of his wife on his desk for a moment, at the crooked, good-natured grin.

He smiled at his wife. He smiled at them all. He felt a string of reassuring clichés coming on. "This is a matter of security at every level of government, at the level of secrecy in our private agencies. The government has become a sieve intelligence-wise. There are Soviet agents on the prowl—"

"And we know it," Lydia Neumann said in her barking whisper. "We know everything."

"Only God knows everything," said Claymore Richfield in his vague and scientific way, as though he might be on intimate terms with the Almighty. "We *guess* we know."

"We know who they are. They know who we are. We trade our agents from time to time. A long time ago, we had a field agent, he said there was so little worth knowing and so many people bent on finding it that it mixed us up. We had too much information."

She thought of an agent called November, long buried now in dead files.

"I'm not going to let the Langley Firm or the Sisters make us dance to their tune. I am not going to be embarrassed by discovering the first Section agent who has gone over to the Opposition," Yackley said. He was using the voice he used on Capitol Hill during the budget hearings in the clubby privacy of the ornate Senate Conference Room.

"So this is about politics, not about Hanley's mental health—"

"It is about reality."

"Hanley didn't give up his human rights when he joined the Section. And I add he joined it a long time ago, before any of us."

"This is not a matter of depriving him of his rights," Yackley said. With patience. "It is a matter of helping him. Of restoring him. Of finding the best way to treat him."

"But he's committed no crime—"

"Indiscretions—"

"But how can you order an evaluation, a psychiatric evaluation—"

"—done all the time—"

"But he's not crazy—"

"—we're not talking about crazy. The word is meaningless. People aren't crazy, people have psychological problems they have to become aware of to solve—"

"—Hanley has the right—"

"That's it, Mrs. Neumann." Yackley never spoke in a loud voice. The room was jarred to silence. Yackley's face was as round as that of a wizard; he thundered and spoke fire:

"It is done. It is going to be done. Hanley is a security risk until further notice. He is a problem. We are going to resolve our own problems. Until I make a further decision, I will take over active directorship of operations, pending selection of a successor. To Hanley. The rest of you remain at your posts, carry on as before. We are all going to have to bend to the oars to make this work. The loss of Hanley diminishes us."

Franz Douglas said, "We understand, sir."

Claymore Richfield mumbled assent. Richfield was working on an equation that might be able to link Comp-An with Translations, eliminating an entire division inside the Section. It was fantastic, and it was being worked out right now on a sheet of paper during a long and tedious meeting in the office of the director. Richfield never looked up, even when the others filed out of the room in silence. Yackley left him alone because it was obvious that Richfield was lost in thought, on another plane. Not of this world, as poor old Hanley had said once.

4

ONCE IN A BLUE MOON

She was not allowed back into the Soviet Union. The message had been left for her at the dock by a seaman in a dark-blue pea coat and stocking cap and full blue-black beard. The message puzzled her. There was a dead man on the *Finlandia* who would be found in time. Alexa had wanted to be back in Moscow in time for dinner.

She took a taxi to the Presidentti Hotel in the center of Helsinki, near the bus depot and down the street from the red granite walls of the imposing Central Railroad Station. There was a train every day from Helsinki to Leningrad. The journey took eight hours because of the procedures at the border crossing. It was the route that Lenin had taken in 1917 to return to the Soviet Union and lead the Revolution.

Alexa waited in the lobby for a long time. She amused herself by playing the slot machines and watching the herds of Japanese tourists check in after their numbing flight over the polar cap from Tokyo. They all appeared to be dressed in thin clothes with cameras and a need to bunch together, chattering like birds.

She drank Scotch at the bar. It was very expensive. After a while, an American began to talk to her but he was rather old and portly and she pretended to be French. It worked because she knew Americans never spoke foreign languages.

At noon, the contact arrived. He was a man called Alexei. She had worked with him once before and he had presumed too much based on the similarities of their code names.

He was a large, bluff man and carried the accents of Georgia. Like all Georgians, he was rather brutal, loud and crude, and Alexa worked around him carefully until she was in a position to explain her independence from him and his goodwill. He had been reprimanded, that last time, by Gorki himself.

They sat in the inner lobby of the hotel. It was a place of dark woods and square architecture and large spaces.

He had to have a drink. He sipped the chilled Stolichnaya like a thirsty man.

Alexa watched him drink with her deep, dark, glittering eyes and noted it. That would be useful sometime as well. Everything was useful to a careful woman.

"It is too late," he began.

"Everything went all right," she said. The responses must be kept at a minimum.

"All wrong," Alexei said. He had thick eyebrows that bridged his nose and hostile blue-gray eyes and the overwhelming smell of cologne of the sort smuggled into Moscow in attaché cases.

Alexa had never worn perfume. Her body was clean and pure. She drank a little Scotch whisky at times and, at dinner, wine. She ate vegetables. She did not smoke.

Her breath was sweet. Her body smelled like fields of flowers and she thought the smell of her body was more beautiful—even to herself—than the appearance of it.

She waited, attentive, her hands on her lap, her legs slightly apart because it was amusing to sit in such a way and no less comfortable to her.

"You have taken care of the wrong man."

"No," she said. "I was certain."

"I have information from the Committee. They could not reach you on the ship. In any case, it doesn't matter."

"What doesn't matter?"

"You killed a man named Ready." He pronounced the name with a long *e* sound and spoke it again. "He was not November."

"I killed November—"

"Like a blue moon," Alexei said suddenly and she saw that he was smiling. "Gorki is embarrassed."

"What embarrassment?"

"The wrong man. There were two men called November. One was the shadow of the other. But the man we were to have killed was not the man on the *Finlandia*. He was another man. Your task, my dear, is not over."

"I am not at fault—"

"You know how it is," Alexei said, still smiling. "Everyone must share responsibility."

"I was sent to fulfill a contract. I fulfilled a contract."

Her voice was absolutely clear and chill, chips of arctic snow on a tundra at the edge of the world. It was without mercy. It had no anger in it because she could hide anger. Or fear. Or desire. She was very good at what she did.

"Like a blue moon," said Alexei. "You were in London Station? The English have a saying for this, it is very amusing. It is the second moon that comes in a month. Two full moons in one calendar month. It is called the blue moon and because it is rare, the English—they call this rare thing, 'once in a blue moon.' It is rare. But it happens all the time in nature."

"I don't know English expressions. I prefer the sayings of my own country. There is no more rich language than Russian." She was annoyed by the situation. "Besides, why do they call the moon blue? Does it become blue? Of course not. I am Russian; speak Russian."

"Russian spoken by a Muscovite," Alexei said with sarcasm.

"Certainly," she said. She might have been a Parisienne or New Yorker, she might have been a Chinese Mandarin or a London chartered accountant forced to share a first-class coach from Victoria with two Irish businessmen.

"Two moons of November," Alexei said in a voice of poured gravel. "So the other one. It begins for you now. A long journey. You find him and resolve him."

"Another contract," she said in a dull voice. She felt tired. She had felt tired after killing the man in the compartment of the *Finlandia*. It was her reaction to death. "All right. Who is he and where is he?"

"That is a problem," Alexei said. He was enjoying this. "The details are very few. A man with gray hair."

"Like the man I killed—"

"Yes. But he was not the man. A man with gray eyes. A man last seen twenty-six months ago in Zurich—"

"That's no information at all," she said, moving the iceberg of her voice. "This cannot be serious."

"I do not understand this matter." Alexei suddenly confessed it. "There will be more information. Into your

mission, they tell me. Information along the way, that is
the expression used. You are to go to Zurich first, there
will be more information—"

"This is absurd, like a children's game—"

"In two days' time. The problem is with the information. I have an instinct. They are developing the information as you travel. They want you very close to the target
when they have it certain."

"Like the spy satellites," she said.

"Yes. I suppose that is where we must now borrow our
imagery from. Spy satellites. Is that what we are, my dear
Alexa? This matter with two Novembers—why does it
come up now? Why didn't we know this before? I don't
understand it at all."

"Of course not."

"Money," he said, handing her a packet. She opened
the packet. There were Swiss francs, dozens of pieces of
the colorful bits of paper engraved with stalwart drawings of stern Swiss heroes. The largest objects on Swiss
bank notes are the numbers; the numbers can never be
misunderstood.

"All right," she said with a little note of defeat. It seemed
fantastic to her; and wasteful. "I will need a weapon."

"At the time," he said. "Now, you have two days. Enjoy
yourself. You will stay here tonight?"

"I don't know—"

"Please, I would take you to dinner—"

"No. I don't think so."

"My dear cousin," he began.

"We are not related," she said, rising out of the soft
chair to lift herself from her note of defeat and tiredness.
"I told you that a long time ago."

"Please, cannot we be friends?"

"Of course. We are comrades," she said. "But I have much to do. I have to leave you now, Alexei."

"One more message. From Gorki. He said that this one, this second November, was as dangerous as the first. Perhaps more dangerous because he has survived so long."

"I am not afraid of anything," she said.

"He said that I should tell you this," Alexei said.

"Thank you, Alexei," she said. She turned. The American was at the bar, staring at her. Because she was beautiful and she knew men had to stare at her, it had not annoyed her for a long time.

She smiled a smile of pity at Alexei, who had scrambled to his feet to be polite. It was so difficult. "Comrade," she said. She took his hand. She let him kiss her on the mouth as he had wanted to do and felt his large hand on her back, pressing her body to him as he kissed her. She endured it for a moment. Then she broke the contact with a slight body movement and she was free. She really pitied them sometimes.

5

St. Catherine's

Hanley offered no resistance although they came prepared for resistance. It was a matter of following standard procedure. They placed the restraints on his thin, gray body and took him downstairs on a stretcher. He complained loudly about the treatment. So the second one, who rode in the back, gave him a heavy dose of sedation. He slept as he left the city he had lived in for thirty-five years.

The ambulance screamed its way through the heavy afternoon traffic. The ambulance prowled through the maze of traffic northwest along Wisconsin Avenue, to Old Georgetown Road where it turned west, along the road to the Beltway. The ambulance was orange and white and the lights on the roof were orange, red, and white. Across the hood was painted the word *ambulance* written backward, presumably for terrified drivers ahead who would glance in their mirrors and see a beast of a vehicle approaching with lights and flashing headlamps and not be able to guess that it was an ambulance.

Hanley slept in the early March afternoon. The trees

were forming buds along both sides of the parkway. The buds stood out like embroidery on the bare limbs. The clouds floated as brightly as sailing boats in warm waters. The wind was blowsy and voluptuous. The first garlic was growing in the shade of the forest; and the first blades of grass. There were mushrooms springing up in the soft soil beneath the elm trees.

The ambulance siren was turned off ten miles north of the capital. The lights continued to flash. The interstate journey continued for nearly two hours, through Hagerstown and the little towns once strung like garlands along the old National Route, which had been Route 40, now replaced by the prosaic Interstate 70 that forgot everything the old towns could have taught the new road.

Hanley saw none of these things. He had a long and strange dream he could never recall, except for the feeling of being lost in the dream, of being so lost to the world that he could never find home again.

The ambulance turned off at Hancock and then the journey was slowed down by fog in the deep valleys that begin west of Hancock. At the top of the road entering the second valley the ambulance began its wail again and the scream echoed back and forth across the valley. The people in the small city at the bottom of the valley who were on the street, feeling their way through the fog rolling down the hills, knew that sound.

Someone was going up to St. Catherine's.

Sister Mary Domitilla had taken her adopted religious name from a Roman woman who lived in the fourth century, was martyred for her faith, and became the patron saint of cemeteries. In 1968, it was decided at the Vatican

in Rome that the saint had never existed. It was a blow
to Sister Mary Domitilla at the time but she had learned
to live with it. She had a round face and sharp faith.
Her hands were always clean and she had no protruding
fingernails—she clipped them nearly every night, so that
the edges of her fingers were always sore. She offered the
small, useless pain to God.

Sister Mary Domitilla waited at the entrance. Mr.
Woods was usually on the gate, but for special cases he
was replaced by Finch, the government agent. Finch operated the gates, and the ambulance, its siren now muted,
slid through on wet gravel.

"I have the key to Ward Seven," she said to the driver.
She got into the passenger side of the front seat. She
glanced back at the man on the stretcher.

"Violent?" she said.

"He put up a fight," the driver said. He slipped the GMC
ambulance into drive and came around the turning circle,
the tires crunching the gravel.

"Is he all right?" she said.

"Yes. He's all right."

"Did you give him?"

"Yes."

"He'll be dopey."

"We gave him less this time. The last one. Whew." He
sighed, remembering the last time.

"Sister Duncan is there."

"That's good. He'll sleep it off. He's all right," the
driver said.

Ward Seven was detached from the pile of old red
brick buildings that formed St. Catherine's. Ward Seven
was built of cinder blocks and had very small windows. It

was two stories high and there were bars on the windows because the patients were violent. That's what everyone in the town in the valley believed, when they thought about St. Catherine's at all. St. Catherine's had always been in the valley and always apart from it; it had been there so long that people in the town could remember when it was called the Insane Asylum. That was before a more humane time.

The buildings of St. Catherine's were done in a neo-classical style popular at the end of the nineteenth century. There was a small church called "the chapel." Ward Seven was located at the rear of the property, near the electrified fence that ran through Parson Woods. The ward was isolated in another way as well. There was a fence within the fence, so that there was a space between the outer electrified fence, so that there was a space between the outer electrified fence and the inner nonelectrified fence. This was useful on days when there were visitors to St. Catherine's. The power to the fence was shut off and three Dobermans ran in the alley between the fences instead.

Sister Mary Domitilla fed the Dobermans. She called one Victor, after a childhood dog; the second was Spot, after a childhood book; the third was St. Francis of Assisi, after a saint whose reputation had fared better than her namesake's.

Hanley awoke in darkness, sweating. He was in a bed like a hospital bed. He wore a hospital gown, open in the back. He felt uncomfortable and he had a headache. He realized his feet were manacled to the sides of the bed. His eyes were wide in the darkness.

The room was furnished like a motel, save for the bed.

There was a pressed-wood dresser done in walnut veneer with a mirror. There was a straight chair. Above the desk was a portrait of sunny Spain complete with Man of La Mancha with pike. On the opposite wall was a couch. It depressed Hanley to see the couch; wherever he was, they expected him to remain here for a time. Above the couch was another bit of factory art, this time a watery portrait of a Paris street.

He saw clearly in the darkness. The door to his room was closed but there was a light that came from a built-in neon tube above the Paris scene and ran the extent of the wall. The tubing was shaded but it gave enough light for someone to check on the guest in the hospital bed from the square of window in the door.

There was a thin small window high on the third wall to Hanley's left. It was protected by three vertical and two horizontal steel rods that might be considered bars.

The headache overwhelmed him for a moment with nausea. He blinked, gagged, held his breath. The nausea passed. He waited and let the sweat drop down his face, blinding his eyes with salt.

He blinked at the harshness of his body sweat.

He felt very dry. He found he could move his hands. He reached for a table lamp to his left and turned it on.

On the table was a remote control device for a television set. He glanced up and saw the set was on a platform between the wall to his left and the wall opposite that carried the bad painting of Paris. He turned on the set. The set crackled for a moment in darkness and then flicked on. It was the David Letterman show. So that's what time it was.

He flicked through the channel selector to get some idea of where he was. The network program flipped to a movie, flipped to a second movie, flipped to a religious program, flipped to a station off the air. No identification. He might be in any place in America; he was lost.

He remembered the two men now. One with rimless glasses and the other with a blue stubble of beard. It was important to remember what they looked like. The trained operative in the field was an observer of insignificant details.

The trained operative.

All of it a charade. Meaningless. There are no spies at all.

Hanley groaned and turned off the television set. The image of Victor Mature evaporated. The peculiar sickness came over him again. It was a sense of déjà vu with a physical reaction in his stomach; it put his brain out of control. He sweated. His body felt cold. He closed his eyes to get out of it. His brain stopped, filled with light, then colors, then triangles built within other triangles. He opened his eyes. He shivered.

He thought of November. And he saw an image of a nutcracker, the one he had owned as a boy, the nutcracker with outrageous teeth set in that fierce mouth. *The better to bite you with, my dear.*

He had to reach November.

He stretched out his hand and felt a water pitcher on the table next to the bed. The pitcher was made of plastic; so was the glass. He sniffed the water in the glass before he drank it. It tasted like water to him. He was very thirsty and drank another glass; and then another.

He could not move his ankles. They had cuffed him. He tried to move against the restraints.

They couldn't do this to him.

He wept again.

When he was through crying, he looked at the table again. There was a call button on it. Also, a plastic toilet used in hospital situations.

He would not stand for it.

If spies ceased to exist, nothing mattered. Then why torture him like this?

Nutcracker, he thought. He had to keep Nutcracker in his brain and tell them nothing. He had to reach November.

But his mind was drifting again. He was a child. He was back in Nebraska and he could smell the earth. It was summer and he stood in a Fourth of July cornfield with the stalks knee-high all around him. The corn smelled sweet and tempting; it even smelled of growth in the rich field. The child saw the bees above the stalks where they kept their nests. All was alive, all was nature, all was part of one single great sense that was seeing and hearing and smelling and touching. The touch of corn silks tickled his palm. The farmhouse was white. A red Ford pickup truck with flared fenders stood in the soft brown earth of the long drive that wound up to the house from the country road. The child saw and heard the world in that moment and understood perfectly.

Hanley wept.

6

DEAD AGENT IN LAUSANNE

Lausanne is a wonderful city. It is in the French-speaking part of Switzerland, beneath the mountains, above the shores of Lac Leman, which is also called Lake Geneva in honor of its principal city at the southwest corner of the lake. It sprawls up the hills on several terraces. The lower town is connected to the upper by a system of funiculars (called the Metro) and elevators. Lausanne is an easy place to live in. There seem to be no strikes, no graffiti, no intolerance, no rudeness, no hustle (though enough commerce to satisfy all who wish to be satisfied by commercial transactions), no crime, no cuisine. They serve the same *poissons* from the lake in Lausanne that they serve 7.5 miles across the lake in Evian, in France, and they are satisfying without being as good. Everything in Lausanne is old shoe. It is a city with a university and a cathedral, some good restaurants and some solid hotels, some intrigue (though not as much anymore as one might think), and a place where a man named November shed his identity as an American field officer with R Section and went to ground.

His name was Devereaux. It was his surname when he had not been in the Section. It did not matter what his Christian name might have been.

He did not know, on the fifth of March, that a woman called Alexa was on her way to Switzerland to kill him.

He did not know that the man who had been his control for nineteen years in R Section—a cold and close-pursed man with a flat voice and bare manners named Hanley— was residing in the violent wing of a private hospital that once had been called an insane asylum.

He did not know about Ready. He did not know that KGB and an agent named Alexa had killed the agent mistakenly called November.

Four hundred days before, he had laid a careful trail to move the wet contract against him to a man named Colonel Ready. He had reason to hate Ready, enough to kill him. Ready had been his enemy. Ready had raped Rita Macklin. Devereaux had cut his Achilles tendon and tagged him November in the eyes of Moscow and the world of spies and sent him limping down the trail, trying to get away from the killers sent after him. It was the cruelest thing Devereaux had thought to do; and it still did not make up for his violation of Rita Macklin.

In the long list of things he did not know, the last item—the death of Ready—might have amused him. It was what he had wanted: to be retired, to acquire anonymity at the edge of the world of spies, to go to "sleep" in the terms of the old trade. November was dead; long live the man who had been the real November.

It was a curious thing that he had never questioned the wet contract put out against him. KGB had its reasons. He had been an agent who had played outside the rules of the game. Hanley had once pointed that out. Hanley had once said, "There are procedures to be followed."

Devereaux had replied. Usually, he said nothing because he thought Hanley was a fool, a petty bureaucrat to be endured and not trusted. But he had replied once: "There are no procedures to be followed; there are no limitations; there are no rules."

"But that is chaos," Hanley had said.

And Devereaux said nothing more.

Devereaux had retired because he could force Section to let him go to sleep.

Three people knew of his existence: Hanley, Mrs. Neumann, and Yackley. They had to know, to make the scheme work. They had disinformed files and reports on Colonel Ready to make it seem he was really November. The reports and files had fooled the KGB into shifting its focus on Ready. Ready could protest but he did not have anything but the truth on his side and the truth was rarely enough.

And the three in Section would keep the secret because they had to.

That was what Devereaux believed on the fifth of March.

He was a man alone. He had always been.

He had been a child of the streets in Chicago and had killed a gang member when he was twelve. He had grown tired of the trade long before he could leave it. He had never wanted a thing in his life except Asia—except the view of blood-red suns over morning paddies and farmers squatting in their pajamas to tell stories to one another. He had loved the idea of the East and joined Section to find the East and, because of the trade, lost the East forever. After that, he had found Rita Macklin.

She was thirteen years younger than Devereaux She had red hair and green eyes and a face of openness that was beautiful. She was very tough because she thought she was tough. She spoke the beautiful lilting accent shared by some people in Wisconsin and Minnesota. There was a song about her presence that always made people smile.

Devereaux had met her; used her; slept with her; left her. And all the time, he fell in love with her more deeply than he had loved anything or anyone else in the world. Because of her—because it was possible—he had quit the trade and gone to sleep at the edge of the world.

They lived together in Lausanne. They slept together. They went everywhere together and shared silences with each other. When she was away on her long assignments in far places, he was truly alone: The cold thing in him came back as before. When she was away, he was transformed back into what he had been.

He walked the crooked streets of Lausanne every day and saw everything and filled his mind with the images of the trained spy. He saw too much, as a spy will if he becomes good at the trade.

He walked down the hills of the city to the train station where he bought the newspapers every day from the same kiosk just inside the entrance. He was there nearly every day at ten in the morning—though he had not noticed he was now a man of fixed habits.

He was tall, rugged, with deceptively large shoulders and flat, large fingers. His square face, creased with care lines, suggested the cold thing inside him. His hair was gray mixed with dark brown. He wore an old corduroy jacket most days now and shoved his hands deep into the pockets when he walked. His gray eyes watched and watched and saw too much; and saw nothing because the world held no consequences when you were withdrawn from it.

He bought *Le Monde*, the *Herald-Tribune*, the European *Wall Street Journal*. Sometimes, because it was so well written, he bought *Libération*. He thought he should interest himself in the world for the sake of Rita Macklin and for the child they had taken in, Philippe.

It was hard work. He was a man of silences who preferred the world to be a separate place. He read books that others might find gloomy, the kind of works of philosophy that are never fashionable. He felt solace in them. He had not expected much from existence for a long time. And then Rita had changed that. So he read newspapers to learn about the world.

Philippe was the third member of the ménage. He was black and very tall for his age, which was now thirteen. He attended boarding school near Lugano, by the Italian border. He loved snow and he knew how to ski. He said he wished to be a sailor when he grew up—but he said it in the way of boys who are being boyish to please their fathers.

Devereaux had taken him off the island of St. Michel at the last moment, almost by instinct, as the boy stood in the waters and pleaded to leave that place of hell. It had been another business in another time. Rita had understood that gesture, though no one else would have. Philippe did not love Devereaux because Devereaux did not expect love, not even from Rita Macklin. It was enough to love her.

Rita was now in the Philippines. There was an election

to cover, a riot and an assassination. It was an old story but Rita told him that all the stories were old ones. "Everything has been written before," she said.

"Shakespeare's advantage," Devereaux had replied.

"Yes. Something like that. A cliché is only something well said in the first place."

He had been alone for three weeks; she would leave the Philippines for America then, to see her mother in the city of Eau Claire, in Wisconsin; and then to Washington, to see Mac, her old editor at the newsmagazine; and then back to Paris. They would meet again in Paris in four weeks' time.

He sat in the bar of the Continental Hotel and drank Kronenbourg poured into a cold glass and tried to understand the world according to *Le Monde*. It seemed that France was at the center of this world, just as it seemed the United States was at the center of the world portrayed in the *Herald-Tribune*.

Devereaux said once to Rita Macklin that Switzerland was never at the center of the world. It was a good place to be.

He spent his days like this: Walking, reading, seeing as much as he could, playing chess with the old man in Ouchy who came down to the chess pavilion on good days. They moved the large pieces around and walked on the board and considered all the moves and problems from the perspective of almost being participants. The old man said that he and Devereaux were the two best in the world because they had so much time to practice.

Devereaux wondered if he could do this for the rest of his life. He had buried himself by making someone else assume his identity. He was safe, detached from

R Section. He read and read and read, absorbing the worlds of Montaigne and Kierkegaard and Hegel. He read Dickens all the time because it represented a world more real to him than the one he was in.

On Sundays, he would drive down to the school near Lugano and take Philippe out for the day. They might go to Italy and they might, in good weather, rent a sailboat on Lac Leman and sail down to Vevey and to the castle at Chillon. The man and the boy did not speak much to each other. It was all right; they both understood the value of silence.

Besides, they both felt the absence of Rita on those Sundays when she was away. She warmed them both, a cold black child who had seen murder and war and a cold white man who had made murder and war. They felt damned unless she was with them.

"Encore, s'il vous plaît," Devereaux said to the woman behind the bar. It was just noon on the fifth of March.

She was a pleasant-faced Swiss with small eyes and an intent expression. She thought she had a nose that was too large but she was wrong. She thought that Monsieur Devereaux, who came to the little café nearly every day, might be a professor at the university. He was always reading.

She opened a bottle of Kronenbourg and poured it into the new cold glass. He liked chilled glasses and cold things. He had requested the chilled glass and she had been pleased to refrigerate his glasses for him.

Devereaux sighed, put down the very funny column by William Safire in the *Herald-Tribune*, and tasted the new beer. It was sweet and bitter at the same time, the way beer can be when it is very cold and very welcome.

He saw his face in the mirror behind the bar. He had been lost in newspaper words and had tried to forget about Hanley. Something had jarred him to think of Hanley again. So he had called Hanley yesterday and Hanley was gone. Gone.

He called Hanley at home. He had never been to Hanley's home but he knew all the numbers he needed to know. He had called and the telephone rang briefly and then an operator interrupted to explain, with a recorded voice, that the telephone number had been disconnected. Disconnected with no forwarding number.

Hanley was gone; where had Hanley gone?

Devereaux tasted the beer again. He stared at nothing at all and tried to picture Hanley in his mind and hear again the disjointed words of those two telephone calls, the first when he and Rita were making love, the second when she was gone.

Claudette, who was the girl behind the wide oak bar, gazed at M. Devereaux and thought she might be in love with him. Why not? Didn't he come every day to see her? Didn't he give her extravagant tips? Exactly as a lover might do. He was shy; he wanted her attention. She was so ready to please him. Dear man.

"That's just it. No November. There are no spies. I think I can tell you. I need to tell you. And did you know that your November is on his way to Moscow?"

Warning. Or threat?

Rita had sprawled in bed, in afterlove, her nakedness warm and open, her body ajar. She had stared at him as he listened to Hanley that night, listened to the mad words: Warning. Threat. It didn't matter.

And then Hanley spoke of a nutcracker and that made

no more sense and Hanley was truly mad, Devereaux had thought. Nearly two weeks before.

Now, in the *Herald-Tribune*, he saw a little essay on the editorial page, arguing that the day of the spy was passed, that electronic devices had made the work of spies irrelevant. He had smiled as he read it and then he had thought of Hanley. He had decided to call Hanley. And Hanley was gone.

Devereaux felt a peculiar chill growing inside the coldness already inside him. Rita Macklin was a million miles away. He felt the prickle on the back of his neck that signified awareness and the presence of danger. And yet, what was all around him but this dull life and the girl behind the bar with the small, secret smile?

Devereaux did not trust R Section or Hanley. It was a matter of survival. It was a wise course.

He frowned. Claudette saw the frown and frowned in sympathy, worried for the professor. She hurried along the polished oak bar to him and asked him, in French, if everything was all right.

He tried a smile. He said yes. He looked away, back to his newspaper.

So shy, Claudette thought. She blushed. She felt warm, thinking of him. It didn't matter even if he was married. It didn't matter. All right, she thought: Take me. He needs comfort and I am comfortable. I will make no demands; I earn my own way, I can do as I please. She thought of him holding her and his weight pressing down on her the length of her body, pressing her breasts and opening her legs. So close together.

Devereaux stared at the paper and only thought: There was Hanley, Mrs. Neumann, who had buried the files, and

Yackley. But had any of them told the others? Was Hanley saying that Colonel Ready convinced Moscow to come after him again? Spies were terrible at keeping secrets. Secrets were meant to be broken and exposed.

There are no spies.

Could it mean: There are no secrets?

Hanley was dull, stable, and the most predictable man in the world. Was he drawing Devereaux back into the trade with riddles and puzzles? It was childish and very much like Hanley.

Claudette decided she would surrender herself on the first night because the professor was too shy to be flirted with. He had to know he did not have to be shy. She would be the bold one.

She offered him a bowl of pretzels.

He was startled. He looked up at Claudette. She was young and fair and her eyes were empty and shining. He said no in a polite way and shut her out of mind.

But she hovered now. "Another beer?"

No. No. No.

He rose from the chairlike stool with back and arms and put down a note that was probably too much to leave as a tip.

She thanked him and tried to put meaning into her voice. She smiled at him. She had beautiful teeth.

He tried another smile on her. He used smiles like disguises. He nodded and took his papers and walked out of the café.

March was chill and damp and bright. Clouds brooded above the snowfields in the mountains. The lake at Ouchy below was choppy and bright. The day was a promise of warmth, which, after a long winter, was good enough.

It was a day to be with friends and find warm places to drink in and find laughter. Devereaux only knew the old man from Ouchy who played chess as though it were war. All the Swiss men played at war all their lives. And they only took those things seriously that were not war.

He wondered if Hanley had a new game.

He walked up the steep streets to the upper town and was lost in thought and the exertion of the climb. He walked along the Rue Mon Repos and failed to see as clearly as he was trained to see. He was so preoccupied with thoughts of Hanley that the two men in the Saab who followed him had no trouble at all.

7

DR. GODDARD

Hanley was not given clothing. He understood the technique. Everyone in intelligence knew the technique and used it. The naked prisoner is like the naked patient or the naked captive: They are all rendered defenseless by their nakedness.

Hanley sat on the vinyl side chair in the examining room. His naked bottom pressed against the vinyl. He wondered if it was cleaned with disinfectant after each use.

It was the first full day of his captivity. They had given him oatmeal with prunes for breakfast. He had wanted to gag.

And no coffee.

"Coffee isn't good for you," chirped the nun who had brought his tray.

"Where is this place? Why am I—"

"When you see the doctor," she said, smiling and flitting about the room like a nervous bird. She said "doctor" as though saying "God."

He sat on the vinyl chair and stared at the man at the empty desk. He guessed there was a tape recorder set up somewhere. On the cheerful blue wall behind the desk was a very bad print of a painting by Modigliani in which a reclining woman is represented in bright colors. Hanley did not like modern art. Hanley did not like sitting on a vinyl chair wearing a ridiculous hospital gown. He wasn't sick; he was tired. He had felt frightened and confused last night; now he felt anger.

"My name is Dr. Goddard," began the man with the salt-and-pepper beard and the guileless brown eyes. He had large hands and clasped them on top of the desk. He spoke in a voice that was made for a lecture hall. He smiled at Hanley.

"Doctor of what? And where am I? And why was I brought here?"

"This is St. Catherine's," said Dr. Goddard, still smiling. His glasses were brown and round and owlish. He seemed to have all the time in the world. "This is a hospital. Do you remember anything?"

"I remember two goons who came to my apartment and showed me some papers. I said there had to be a mistake but that I would go with them. And then one of them wanted to put me in a straitjacket, for God's sake. What is this place, a nut house?"

"Unfortunate word," said Dr. Goddard. The voice was a pipe organ played by Lawrence Welk.

"You don't have any right—"

"Mr. Hanley. I assure you we have every right. You understand this is a matter of both national security and your wellness."

Hanley blinked. "What did you say?"

"Mr. Hanley. St. Catherine's is equipped with all the best medical equipment. We intend to examine you thoroughly for physical causes of your , , , depression. But I think this will go deeper than mere physical causes."

"What are you talking about?"

"What are the causes of depression?" said Dr. Goddard as though speaking to a classful of students. "Many. A chemical imbalance is certainly involved. Perhaps some trauma that has created a subtle neurological impairment. Perhaps—"

"Who are you, Dr. Goddard? What kind of a doctor are you?"

"I'm a psychiatrist, Mr. Hanley. As you suspected." He smiled with good humor. "There. I'm not so frightening, am I?"

"I'm not afraid of you," Hanley said. "But you can't keep me in a place against my will."

Dr. Goddard said nothing.

Hanley stood up. "I want my clothes—"

"The hospital gown is appropriate when—"

"I want my goddamn clothes," Hanley said.

And Dr. Goddard did a strange thing. He took out a can of Mace from his white cotton jacket and sprayed Hanley in the eyes.

Hanley was in his fifties. It had been forty years since he had been assaulted physically. He understood the uses of assault, he understood terror. But in that moment, he was hurtled back more than forty years to when he was a child. Suddenly he was falling, his eyes stung by the liquid, the burning creeping over his face. He cried out in pain. And no one came to him.

The pain and burning lasted a long time and he thought he made a fool of himself, writhing helplessly on the floor, his senses distorted by the pain and the suffocating powerlessness. His hospital gown was opened; he realized his backside was naked to anyone who might see him. He didn't care in that moment. He wanted the pain in his eyes to end.

Dr. Goddard gave him a damp towelette. He wiped at his face.

"You're not harmed," Dr. Goddard said. His voice was Bach playing variations on the fugue.

"Why did you do that? How dare you—"

"Mr. Hanley. I am the doctor," Dr. Goddard said.

"You're a goddamn sadist. Is this a prison? Who sent you?"

"You were referred by your superior officer," said Dr. Goddard.

"What are you talking about?"

"I know all about you. I have access to your 201 file, profile chart, skills index rating, your entire dossier. I know all about you. I don't want you to see me as the enemy."

Hanley had staggered to his feet.

"Sit down," Dr. Goddard said in that voice lurching into the third Brandenburg Concerto. The notes progressed relentlessly. It was enough to drive a person crazy.

Hanley sat. His bare behind was cold on the cold vinyl seat. He shivered. He felt humiliated, as though he might be a child again, forced into some ridiculous position because of something he knew was not his fault. It had not happened to him this way since he was in the sixth grade, nearly a lifetime ago.

"We are here to help you," began the voice, sounding the theme. "You have altered your behavior severely in the last six months and your superior is concerned for your mental balance. You have become moody and distant—"

"I was tired," Hanley began.

Dr. Goddard stared at him. When the room was silent again, he resumed:

"Tiredness is a symptom of a greater problem. Your problem, in all likelihood, is not physical. It is deeper than that."

"Why?" said Hanley.

"Why what?"

"Why is it deeper than that?"

"Aberrant behavior can be a symptom of many things. It can be a cry for help," Dr. Goddard said.

Hanley shrank with chill.

Dr. Goddard continued. "Fortunately, our knowledge of the mind has made wonderful advances in the past thirty years. We now understand and can categorize behavior that would have defied categorization only a generation ago. We have a powerful range of psychological drugs—a chemotherapy—that we feel, and I think you will find we are as good as our word, can help restore you to normality and to a vigorous life again. Perhaps not as before; but to return you eventually to a useful participation..."

Eventually was such a terrible word, Hanley thought. The words went on and on. He realized he was shivering. He wanted to say he was cold, sitting in this ridiculous and humiliating hospital gown, listening to this nonsense. It was coming clear to him.

He began to cry as the doctor droned. He had found tears easy these past weeks and months. The tears released many feelings in him. The tears made him feel weak and relieved to be helpless.

Dr. Goddard stopped speaking.

He saw the tears stream down Hanley's pale, drawn cheeks.

He understood tears. They were useful as part of the "grieving" process in which the patient understands his status as a patient, understands there is something wrong with him, understands Doctor is there to help him. Dr. Goddard did not smile outwardly because he did not want to appear to mock the grieving process. Or to stop it at the moment.

8

HITTERS

Claudette was behind the bar at ten in the morning. It was too early for respectable Swiss to come in for a drink but she needed the extra hour to clean the bar. The place always smelled sour in the morning. She would open the window in the back and leave the front door open, even in cold weather, to let the place air out and remove the odor of stale tobacco and spilled beer.

The two men walked in at nine minutes after ten. Claudette was so intent on washing the glasses that she did not notice them until they sat down at the bar.

"Hello, dear," said the first one. He was large and had flat fingers on his large hands. He rested his hands on the bar. "Anyone else around here?"

Claudette stared at his lizard brown eyes for a moment and then shook her head.

The second one was thin and quite hairless. He did not have eyebrows. He looked as though he might have been ill—except his very black eyes glittered with life. His face was tanned, which was unusual enough for Claudette to notice it.

They both spoke French but with strong accents.

"No one is in back?"

"No. Not at this hour. The owner doesn't come until the lunch hour. If you want to see the owner—"

"No, that's all right. You're the one we wanted to talk to."

Claudette was bent over the sink as she spoke with them, washing glasses. Now she stopped. She straightened up and wiped her hands on a damp towel on the bar. She stared at the large man and then at the hairless man and waited.

"We want to ask you about the man who comes in here at lunch almost every day."

"We have our regular patrons—"

"Look, we mean the man who comes in here, sits right here at the bar every day. You know who we mean."

She stared at the big one as though she knew. She said nothing.

"Are you sure no one is in back?"

"Yes."

"You're all alone here, then?"

"Yes."

"I see," said the big one.

"All alone," said the hairless one. They didn't look at each other. They were staring at Claudette very hard.

Claudette was afraid of them. "What can I do for you?"

"Do for us? We told you."

"Yeah. We were talking about the American who comes in here every day. Around lunchtime."

"The one who reads the papers."

"Gets all the American papers to read."

"You know who we mean."

"You don't get that many Americans up in this neighborhood, not in winter."

She knew who they meant.

"You got a tongue, don't you, dear?"

"I'll bet she knows who we mean," said the big one. He wasn't smiling.

They were silent for a moment. The silence was like a pause planned in a symphony.

The big one said, "You see, we want to know where he lives. You know where he lives?"

"No. I don't know."

"But you know who we mean, don't you?"

"I—"

"Don't lie. I mean that. The last thing you want to do is to lie."

"Yeah," said the hairless one. "The thing is, we have to find out where he lives because we've got something to deliver to him. You know what we mean, something special for him. Only we know he drinks here but we don't know where he lives and his name isn't in the telephone book."

"No. He has an unlisted number."

"It's too bad," said the hairless one.

"Please," said Claudette. Her voice sounded very thin to her. She tried again. "Please, I don't know what you're talking about."

"Is that right?"

The big one got up then and came around the bar. He ambled like a walking bear. He was almost too large for the back way behind the bar.

"You are not permitted—" began Claudette, her Swiss sense of order horrified by this breach.

He picked up a bottle of Johnnie Walker Red Label Scotch whisky, opened it, and began to pour it into the sink. She took a step forward and the hairless one reached across the bar to grab her arm.

"You see, dear," said the big one. "We are permitted just about anything we want. So when we ask you where the American is, the one with gray hair who reads all the papers, you should tell us where he lives."

"Definitely," said the hairless one. He had small hands that held her arm like pliers.

"See what I mean? Anything we want to do."

"Anything," said the hairless one.

"Please," said Claudette. "I don't know. I honestly don't know where the professor lives—"

"Professor? Professor?"

The hairless one smiled and twisted the skin beneath his grip.

Claudette winced with pain. The bar was dark. She noticed they had closed the front door when they entered.

"I like that," said the big one. "You think he's a professor of something because he spends all his time reading? Ha. He was a professor."

"A long time ago."

"But he hasn't been in a classroom for a long time."

"And he needs a refresher course."

"He needs a review of old lessons."

"We were sent out to teach him a few things."

"It's too bad you don't know where he lives. It would make things simpler."

"Yes," said the hairless one. Her skin had a burning sensation beneath his hand. He let her go and her arm was ugly and red.

"Well, we'll go now."

She stared at both of them.

"One thing, dear. I don't think you would want to tell him we were here looking for him. I mean, this is to be a surprise. Understand?"

"Yes. We don't want you to tell him a thing."

"Because if you tell him we were here, we'll be coming back here."

"Definitely," said the hairless one.

Devereaux sat at the bar, watching Claudette move anxiously up and down the bar, serving beer and wine and schnapps while the owner pulled out plates full of steak *haché* smothered in onions and gravy, prepared in the minuscule kitchen at the rear.

The owner had not noticed the missing bottle of Scotch. He would in the afternoon, she knew, and he would question not Claudette but Monique. Monique would be innocent but Claudette felt, at that moment, too afraid to intervene in the coming storm. She hurried; she was clumsy; she broke two glasses and the owner scowled at her.

When she served the professor, she did not look at him. This was not usual.

Monsieur le professeur.

The dinner hour progressed and everyone could have seen that Claudette was upset; save that no one engaged in the hurried business of eating chopped steak and onions and potato salad in a little dark café had the time to observe Claudette's distress.

Devereaux ordered a second bottle of chilled Kronenbourg.

She pulled the green bottle out of the cooler and opened it and took him a fresh glass chilled in ice, the way he preferred it.

"Merci, Claudette," he said. He had never spoken her name before. She blushed for a moment.

Devereaux stared at her for a grave moment.

"Is there something wrong, Claudette?" he said at last. The voice was low like morning fog. It was remarkable: In six months, he had not exchanged two dozen words with her. He had never called her by her name, though she had offered it from the beginning.

She thought he was concerned. She was touched. Her fantasy of herself and her professor returned, burning to the surface. It pleased her that he was concerned and made her brave.

Devereaux was not concerned. He was observing her as he observed all his surroundings, trying to spy what was unusual. He would walk down a street and refocus his gaze automatically every few seconds: First street, then walk, then buildings, then mailbox, then lamp post, then car, then street... It was the technique learned painfully over the years. It had to do with survival. In a way, it served to slow down the sense of life rushing past. With the senses focused intently on the surroundings, the mind worked on the unconscious and semiconscious problems that were presented.

"I am a little upset, monsieur," she said.

He said nothing.

"Monsieur, it concerns you—" she blurted.

He almost smiled.

But then she spoke slowly about two men who had entered the café at nine minutes after ten in the morning and who had frightened her. She tried to remember what they said and the professor's gray eyes did not leave her face. She felt like a schoolgirl under his gaze. She told him everything; it was important to hold nothing back.

She told him the last part, about not telling Devereaux any of these things. His eyes gazed into hers as she told it, and it seemed to her that he must understand how brave she was, how uncaring for her own safety.

Devereaux wanted to know what they looked like and she told them. She had been too frightened of the large man to notice much about him. But she remembered details about the hairless man. Devereaux began to construct an image of him.

He listened to the woman's trembling voice for a long time, and when she had finished her story he took her through it again, questioning her to extract every bit of information. As she talked the instincts rose in him and made his face tingle.

He thought he had accepted the idea of impermanence but he had not; he was unprepared for what Claudette said about the two men. They were emissaries from the world he had hoped to leave behind. It was too bad: He saw Rita and the boy, Philippe, and he saw himself as though all three were framed in an old photograph kept in an album as a souvenir.

It was probably over now.

And while these melancholy feelings came in waves over his consciousness, another part of his mind was deciding where to run and how to run.

He felt as he sometimes had felt on fall mornings in the old place in the Virginia mountains, when the air was crisp and dry and the leaves in the forest on the hill crackled with the alert movement of animals. He felt aware of all things around him. It was what he had been trained for.

"It's all right, Claudette," he said at last.

"*Monsieur le professeur*, I am afraid. For you, not for me." This was true, she felt. The steadiness of his gaze and the concern she read in his eyes had warmed her.

"There is nothing to be frightened of—"

"If they come back—"

"They won't come back," Devereaux said. "If they know this place, they could watch for me easily enough. They had some other reason for saying what they said to you."

"I don't understand," she said.

"Neither do I." He tried a smile. "But it's going to be all right."

"What will you do?"

"Go away for a while, Claudette. But I'll be back."

As he stood up he saw that she knew he was lying to her in that moment, and it made him feel a peculiar emotion, one he could not place at first. Yes, he realized: It was sadness. This café, even Claudette's presence in it, had become one of his touchstones, though he had not consciously attempted to create touchstones in a foreign land. It was weakness to need such things. Was he becoming weak? Did he need the ritual of morning newspapers, this café, the old man who played chess on the pavilion outside Ouchy?

He left a ten-franc note and Claudette thought to say something else, something to draw them together. But there was nothing to say.

Devereaux was in the street, standing for a moment framed in the door of the café. The day was brilliant. The sun was high and there was a warm breath of wind from the French side of the lake. The sun glinted on the perpetual snowfields in the high reaches of the mountains.

There was no need to return to the apartment. Whatever had to be arranged could be arranged from another place. He considered the pistol sealed in plastic and strapped to the underside of the toilet tank lid. He would find another weapon. He had his passport, his bankbook.

He walked down the hillside to the Avenue de la Gare and went into the first branch of the Credit Suisse and withdrew 10,000 Swiss francs. Because he wanted the money in denominations of 100 francs, there were 100 bills and the wad was thick enough to split in two—half in his inside jacket pocket, the other half in the lower "cargo" pocket of his denim trousers.

While he made these preparations for flight, he tried to see what was unusual around him. He had lived long enough in Lausanne to find the oddities in the colorful scenes on the street.

There were old women in black coats hurrying to do their shopping and men in brown caps, smoking curved pipes, and businessmen with their coats open to the warm breeze, walking with the light step of their younger days. What did not fit this scene?

And he saw the two men sitting in the Saab down the street, watching the life surge around them.

Two men at noon on a weekday in a car bearing the license plates of Bern. This was Vaud; they were far from home. They were sitting in an expensive Swedish car in the middle of the day on a side street, waiting for someone. They had to be waiting for someone. In a rental car most likely. Businessmen from abroad.

They seemed to be parked just on the periphery of his activity.

He thought about the crude warning given Claudette in the café. It was stupid, almost self-defeating. It invited him to flee, which was what he was doing.

Why?

KGB, like the other espionage services and some terrorist organizations, passed through Switzerland easily on their way to activities in the north and—more likely—the south of Europe. But incidents of terror in Switzerland were rare enough to be nonexistent. The reason was simple: Switzerland was a compact, orderly country with a fierce military tradition and an absolutely cold-blooded approach to dealing with terror. It was not acceptable, not negotiable, and, in the long run, not worth the effort on the part of terrorists. Devereaux considered all this information in a split second, as a computer might, except that the mind worked faster when it was trained to consider information with both thought and feeling.

Devereaux crossed the broad avenue to the long, red stone train station. A white-gloved policeman held up his hand against the traffic.

Devereaux stopped at the kiosk where he usually bought the papers and chose the current copy of the *Economist*. Exactly as a potential railroad passenger might, choosing a magazine to kill the time on the train. He paid and turned around and saw the Saab parked illegally at the curb by the Continental Hotel across the way. He walked into the train station, across the concourse, to the ticket windows. He stood in line behind two schoolgirls who were talking to each other between giggles. When he reached the window, he bought the ticket for Zurich.

He stood with the ticket a moment and looked in a glass window of a confectionary shop inside the terminal. He saw the two men at the entrance of the station.

Devereaux crossed the concourse to the platforms. The train for Geneva was just pulling into the first platform. It didn't matter: They had seen him buy the ticket, they had observed him walk to the platform. They would draw the right conclusion.

He climbed aboard.

The train waited.

He went to one of the windows and watched.

The two men stepped onto the platform and they stared at the train, at the very car where Devereaux waited. They looked at each other and then looked up and down the platform. At the last moment, they started across the concrete platform toward the waiting train.

Perhaps they had miscalculated and thought he would flee by auto.

Devereaux opened the door at the end of the car and dropped from the train onto the platform as the electrified express to Geneva quickly picked up speed. A conductor at the far end of the platform frowned at Devereaux. He walked over and shook his finger and told him about the dangers of jumping from a moving train. Devereaux had broken the rules in a country of rules.

Devereaux crossed the platform slowly, watching the train swing out east of the city in the tangle of tracks. He entered the concourse and looked around. There were the usual crowds of midday travelers. The trains were swift and frequent so that all classes and ages took the trains as a matter of course. Devereaux tried to see if there was anything different he could find in this crowd around him.

There had been two men. Perhaps there were more. He was a patient watcher, falling easily back into the habits of a trade he had sought to quit more than once. The habits couldn't die—they merely became rusty through disuse.

Outside the station, the sun was still blindingly bright. The passersby were shedding themselves of heavy morning coats and scarves and soaking up the sun and the warm southern breeze. There was a cheerful feeling on the Avenue de la Gare.

He crossed the street to the abandoned Saab and opened the door. He saw the keys in the ignition. He reached in the glove compartment and took out a rental agreement between a M. Pelletier and a Swiss rental car company at the airport at Geneva. So they had flown into Geneva, picked up a car with Bern registration, and gone directly to Lausanne. They had arrived yesterday.

They had known exactly where to find him. He had eluded them. But it had been much too easy.

He felt the vague chill that he had learned to live with in the years in the old trade. He had the feeling of watching and being watched. He looked around. A policeman approached with a sour look and told him to move the car.

Devereaux started the engine. Devereaux turned left on the east side of the station, went under the viaduct and down the road that parallels the Metro to Ouchy at the bottom of the hill. It would be better to get out of the tangle of Lausanne, to find an open road and see who might be on it.

A gray Renault pulled from its parking spot in front of the McDonald's and followed the Saab down the steep hill toward Ouchy and the lakeshore.

Devereaux drove quickly enough to see if anyone kept up with him.

The gray Renault leaped ahead of a slow-moving bus and pushed between a dull limousine and a truck turning into a service drive. There was no one between Devereaux and the Renault.

They wanted him to flee.

They wanted him to leave Switzerland. They wanted to isolate him, he thought. There had to be a killing field where he could be hunted in the open. Switzerland was never a good place to trap a spy.

He turned at Ouchy and followed the line of the highway toward Vevey and Chillon. The highway rose into the hills above these coastal towns, suspended on pilings driven deep into the rocky hillside. All along the highways were disguised pillboxes, arms depots and rocks set in such a way as to cause a rockslide across the roadway at a signal. The Swiss perpetually booby-trap their country in preparation for a war that has not come in five centuries.

Devereaux pushed the Saab now, screaming through the gears, pushing the tachometer to the red line with each gear, shifting down hard, driving the engine to its limits. He was pushing 150 kilometers and the Renault was keeping pace.

The midday traffic was thin. Travelers were taking their dinner breaks. The countryside was empty and full of peace. The road was rising into the hills above the lake. Down on the lake, the ferry boats plowed through the waters.

Devereaux thought there might be two men in the Renault but the light was so brilliant that it made a mirror of the windshield behind him.

The light blinded both drivers. He thought of what he would do then.

He had no weapon but the car and his own knowledge of the roads around the lake.

There was a small road that tumbled down the mountain from the main highway toward Chillon. The road was made for slower transport in a slower age. He tried to remember exactly what he knew of the road. And then he remembered.

If they wanted him to flee, they would expect him to be running as fast as he could.

The Saab growled and whined as he pulled off the main road and onto the smaller road down the mountain. He pushed the gears down, taming the engine, feeling the tires catch at the asphalt and hold it despite the sway of centrifugal force. He pushed into a slow slide around a long and lazy curve and then pushed the car into a screaming acceleration down a short stretch of straight ground. He glanced behind him once in the rear-view mirror and saw the Renault. Was it ten seconds behind? Was there enough time?

The Saab whined through a second, sharp turn around a boulder and Devereaux slammed the brakes with brutal force, so that the rear end of the car bucked and the tires squealed as the car lurched sideways toward the edge of a cliff at the margin of the road. The car nearly turned around. Below was a farmer's field with the earth waiting for a plow.

Devereaux was out of the car in a moment and across the road to the rocks.

Two seconds later, the Renault surged around the blind turn and slammed into the left side and rear end of the Saab.

There had been two men.

One hurtled through the windshield, over the Saab, and over the cliff to the broken field below.

The second hit his head hard against the crumpled steering post.

The Saab and Renault ground into each other in slow motion. There was no fire.

Bits of metal exploded against the rocks around Devereaux where he crouched in a ditch. Below the road was the old castle sitting in the waters of Lac Leman. It was the place where Byron had come and meditated on the prisoner held there twelve years and written a poem. It was peaceful and of another world.

Devereaux ran to the door of the Renault. The driver was unconscious or dead. He could not open the crumpled door. The window was broken. Devereaux used his elbow to break more glass, to get a way into the car. Devereaux reached through the window and felt into the pocket of the driver. He pulled out the pistol. It was an ordinary Walther PPK with a short barrel and six hollow-point bullets seated in the clip. He shoved the pistol in his pocket.

The wallet was inside the vest pocket.

He opened the wallet and found a sheaf of French banknotes and a photograph of a young man and a young woman and an American Express card made out to Jonathan DeVole.

And a second card.

Devereaux stared at the second card.

It was plastic, cut hard and brittle exactly like an ordinary credit card.

Except it was gray. Without numbers or letters on it. The card was perfectly smooth and unmarked.

Devereaux saw that his hand was closing over the card

as though to swallow it and make it disappear. It was as though his hand were separate from his body.

Devereaux knew the card.

It was familiar to him when he had worked for the R Section in a life he had abandoned.

The card was accepted at 120 machines located throughout the world, identifying the cardholder as a member of the operations division of R Section, a very secret intelligence agency of the United States.

Hanley's division.

9

ALEXA BENEATH THE STARS

Alexa waited until dark to enter the apartment building. It was small and there was a concierge but Alexa had taken care of that—the concierge was distracted from her apartment on the ground floor by a boy who threw a brick through one of the ground-floor windows and then ran down the Rue de la Concorde Suisse. It was not so difficult to find vandals, even in Lausanne, if they were well paid.

She climbed to the third floor and went to the apartment at the end of the hall. She had waited outside the building all day, sitting in the Volkswagen at the end of the block, watching for any sign of life at all.

The information had come with unexpected precision and it was timely.

The agent named November—the second moon of November—had been observed twenty-four hours previously in this apartment, in this building. It had been determined by the resident extra at Geneva that he had been living there for nearly two years.

Why was everything so precise, so exact? And yet,

Alexa had a strange feeling that this was all too easy. What was it about, exactly?

She wore a black sweater that had a high collar; she wore black cotton trousers and black running shoes. Her jacket was a variation of a sailor's pea coat. Her long black hair was tied up. She wore no makeup at all and her pale features were small and frail.

The lock was not so simple but she found the way in after a few moments with a pick and tumbler setter which electronically felt for the tumblers and tripped them.

The apartment was dark as it had been all day. It was still, save for the ticking of an electronic clock on the wall of the kitchen. The clock was quartz, the ticking was added to fake the sound of a real clock.

She went into all the rooms. She opened the closets. They did not have many clothes, the agent and his mistress.

There were no photographs. There was a sense of impermanence to the apartment.

She saw that the Panasonic answering machine was on but that there had been no calls. The red call button was not blinking.

She found a chair near the window where she could watch in the shadows down the length of the Rue de la Concorde Suisse.

He did not own a car but rented them often from the Avis garage next to the Lausanne train station.

He had not rented a car in a week. He was usually back in the apartment by eight. The mistress was gone, the resident extra in Geneva had no information on her. But he had so much other information that it amazed Alexa.

Alexa frowned in the darkness. This was not usual. She had spent two days in Zurich waiting for contact.

She had not expected to be given much information   but when the contact was made she had received a cornucopia of detail. If they knew so much about this man, why had they not taken care of the matter before this, before the bungled business on the *Finlandia*?

Alexa removed the Uzi from her purse. It was made in France, fitted with a silencer, and it had eighteen shots. It was sufficient to tear a living man's body in half.

The final arrangements were her own. It was a form of self-protection. After all, if she were to survive, it must be on her own terms. KGB ran her on a very loose leash; it was necessary to the business at hand.

The quartz clock in the kitchen ticked with a false sound. The bright day had turned to clear night. There was a full moon and she could see the street clearly.

When she had been a child, living in the flats along the Lenin Prospekt in Moscow with her mother, her brother, and her youngest sister—her father had been a colonel in the Soviet army and had spent long periods in command of troops on the Sino-Soviet border seven thousand miles to the east—she had thought once to count all the stars and end the mystery about the endless number of stars in the heavens. She was nine or ten and had a very precise mind and nature, however naïve. She reasoned with her mother this way:

The stars we see cannot be infinite because the scope of heaven we see is not infinite. So it is possible to count all the stars you can see from Moscow.

Her mother, who was intelligent and who had been beautiful when she was young, said it was impossible because the sky changed each night as the earth revolved around the sun.

Alexa had said it was still possible. On one night, a determined person in Moscow (such as herself) could count all the stars visible from an apartment on the Lenin Prospekt. It could be done in winter, on a clear, cold night, when the night stretched from the middle of the afternoon to the middle of the next morning.

Her mother had seemed amused and would not argue with her. She was a child.

Alexa thought of a child growing inside her body. It would be a splendid idea. But not now. Not for a while yet. The child would be magnificent. It would be a boy.

She had waited until winter to count the stars and when winter came she was older and wiser and she knew it was foolish to want to limit the number of stars by counting them. It was better to ignore them. Or accept the word of the scientists who did such things.

Still.

What if she had counted all the stars on a clear winter's night in Moscow, from horizon to horizon? What would the number have been, all the stars seen with the naked eye? Would it have been possible at all?

She saw both men at the same time.

They approached from opposite corners, where the Rue de la Concorde Suisse ends in a terraced wall above the streets below that lead to the Cathedral.

They were on foot and there could be no car behind them because the walkway along the wall was a mere pedestrian path.

She watched them approach the building from opposite sides of the street.

She knew they were coming to this place and she felt trapped. Why had she been trapped?

For the first time, she felt a sense of guilt. Was there something in the past, something she had done or said that would have forced her Committee to list her for a "wet contract"? A contract to be carried out as far away from Moscow Center as possible?

But she had made no mistake. The careful child who wanted to count all the stars above Moscow had made no mistake. What had Alexei said in Helsinki? The mistakes had to be blamed on someone.

She rose from the chair and looked down at the two men on opposite sides of the street. They were staring up at the darkened window where Alexa stood. They glanced at each other and she thought one of them shrugged.

They entered the building, one at a time.

The street was nearly fifty feet below. There was a balcony outside the window. At the end of the hall, there was a fire escape. She hesitated. She felt terribly confused.

When she decided, it was too late.

She went to the door and reached for the handle and heard steps in the hall.

She waited at the door, the length of the Uzi pistol extended away from her body.

There were no voices, only steps in the hall. Then one of them knocked on the door.

The three waited, two outside, Alexa inside.

The dark made all sounds more intense. The clock in the kitchen seemed to reverberate with sound.

They had trouble with the lock, just as she had. They opened the door cautiously.

Alexa fired through the door. The Uzi thumped and bucked in her hand. The door splintered and she heard them cry in pain and surprise. She expected them to push into the room. Instead, the second one retreated back into the hall.

That would be messy.

She sprayed six shots into the hall, firing from right to left as she filled the frame of the door, straddling the man on the floor dying between her legs.

The flash of her pistol was met with the *whump* of another pistol, fitted with a silencer.

They've killed the concierge, she thought dreamily in that moment of action. It was so messy and they didn't care, as though they wanted this to be done quickly or not at all. She thought they must be in a hurry and that puzzled her. All these thoughts crammed the moment needed to spray the darkened hallway with death from the Uzi.

The second one fell heavily and then she realized the first one was alive because he stirred against her feet. She lowered the pistol to finish him off—and stopped.

She knelt and turned him over.

The bullet had grazed his head, he was bleeding heavily, he might even live. His eyes were open wide but he did not seem to be conscious.

She reached into his pocket and found money. She pushed the bills into her own pocket. She stared at him in the moonlight and saw a man completely bald. He didn't even have eyebrows. She knelt and cradled his head and spoke to him harshly in the voice of the Moscow agent, the voice of death that is without sex or promise—only a threat:

"Why do you come to kill me?"

But the hairless one only stared wildly at her, frightened into unconsciousness or mere inability to speak.

She went through his pockets, all of them, turning over his body roughly to go through his pants. Nothing at all.

She went to the second one in the hall. One of the shots had caught him full in the face and now there was no face left. Brains were splattered against the wall behind the body.

Without distaste, she knelt again and pushed her hands patiently through his clothing.

There was a wallet at least.

She opened the wallet and saw the bills.

There was nothing else.

Two contractors, she thought. Not even someone from Moscow Center but contractors hired on the broad assassins' market in Europe. They might even be Swiss.

But Switzerland was a dangerous country to act so boldly in. They had not been careful at all. They had come into a peaceful neighborhood in the old city and they had surely killed the concierge to gain access to this apartment.

It occurred to Alexa then they had not come to kill her at all. But to kill the same man she had been sent to kill. She felt anxious. She smelled the beginning of death in the hall. It was the warm and sweet smell of the slaughterhouse and killing ground.

She stepped over the body in the hall and went back into the apartment. She looked around her, took her purse from the chair and glanced down again at Rue de la Concorde Suisse. The lights of Lausanne, low and few, spread down the hill. The sky was full of stars, too many to count because one no longer could believe in counting stars.

10

BREACH OF SECURITY

The Assistant National Security Adviser was the less formal contact between the executive branch and the various intelligence agencies that operated under the umbrella of the Director of Central Intelligence. These included R Section.

Yackley had not been kept waiting. The assistant adviser was not a rude man. His name was Weinstein and he was more intelligent than most of the people he had to deal with.

His office on the sixth floor of the Executive Office Building—the ornate hunk of Victorian architecture that squats between Seventeenth Avenue and West Executive Place, just off the White House lawn—was the office of a transient. There were no photographs on the rather plain government-issue metal desk; there was not the requisite couch or even two upholstered chairs set off to the side for informal tête-à-têtes. Everything in the office seemed careless and temporary. There were cardboard boxes and a battered Selectric II typewriter on a rickety metal typing stand. The assistant adviser might have been his own aide-de-camp. He projected a sense of energy, of wearing shirts two days in a row, and of being a bachelor who probably did not eat very well. He wore horn-rimmed glasses that made his thin face seem thinner. He was forty-one years old and looked thirty.

"Hi, Frank," he said, as his secretary led Yackley into the office. "Get you something? Coke or coffee or something?"

"No thanks, Perry," Yackley said. He felt uncomfortable with the informality yet thrilled by the intimacy. Everyone did. The administration projected a sense of order, tuxedos and gray business suits. Perry Weinstein might have been a holdover from the Carter administration. Save that his accent was West Coast and his politics were the kind satisfying to readers of *National Review.*

Yackley sat down in one of two side chairs pulled up to Perry Weinstein's desk.

"We have a problem," he began in that way of his that indicated a long recitation of the facts. Yackley was a careful man who carefully screened his own words before uttering them.

"I know. How is Hanley?"

"It's too early. He's still being tested—"

"It's a shame. The best sort of bureaucrat—no strong partisan stance, devotion to duty beyond and above. I think I met him the first time when I moved in. Two years ago. A strong 201 file—"

"You read his 201?" Yackley seemed amazed. It was such a pedestrian thing to do. There must have been 150 bureaucrats at Hanley's level in the intelligence establishment, counting all the agencies.

Weinstein nodded. There was no color in his face. His eyes were light blue. Everything about him spoke of innocence, of straightforwardness. Naturally, everyone was suspicious of that.

"I've read everyone's," Weinstein admitted with a smile and a blush. "Two years. It doesn't seem that long. I'm still not moved in."

Yackley said nothing to that.

"Well, what's it about?"

"You saw the transcripts I sent over. When Hanley tried to make contact with this former agent—"

"Sleeper named November," said Weinstein. Perfect memory. Mind like a steel trap. Never misses a trick. Every cliché in the large book kept in Washington applied to Weinstein. And Yackley, a master of clichés, was just the man to apply them.

"November's come awake again," said Yackley. He spoke the words with care and precision. He said, "There were two incidents in two days. We sent two agents—contractors—to make contact with Devereaux, to see what his game was. I indicated in my memo that I was disturbed about Hanley. Lest there was a breach of security. I'm afraid we have troubles—"

Weinstein waited. There was no judgment on his face. He might have been waiting for a bus.

"Devereaux apparently killed both men. On a mountain road outside of Lausanne. The details are incomplete and we have a stationmaster from Zurich down there—"

"It would seem better to have sent someone from Geneva or even France. I suppose a German speaker will seem odd in Lausanne."

Perry Weinstein said this softly and quickly, also without judgment. But Yackley blushed. "He was the easiest man—"

"It doesn't matter," Weinstein said. His voice said that it did.

"Then there were two more men killed. This time in Devereaux's apartment in Lausanne."

"And who were they?"

"We don't have the faintest idea. Except that it's obvious that Devereaux is on some sort of rampage. I mean, we sent two agents to make inquiries—and they're killed and—"

"How killed?"

"He arranged an auto accident. I don't have details. He was in a car on a road, apparently the car driven by our two chasers was—"

"This seems botched, doesn't it, Frank?"

Yackley felt acute embarrassment. There was silence. Weinstein stood behind his desk, his hand fiddling with some papers. The desk was littered with papers, some of them secret. Behind Yackley was the window that opened to a view of the White House. The White House occupied a bucolic space in the middle of crowded Washington with its littered streets full of hurrying office workers and the shuddering roars of planes bombarding the suburbs from National Airport. Life and noise and layers of society pretending other layers did not exist—and in the middle of it all, the quaint White House with the porticos and plain windows and the gentle lawn where the children gathered to roll Easter eggs with the President. Only the ugly concrete bunkers at the edges of the lawns reminded you of the absurd importance of it all.

"Yes. I was concerned from the beginning, I was in a hurry to see if there had been a breach. I think there has been—"

"How? Your tapes don't show anything."

"Hanley had other ways to reach Devereaux—"

"Why Devereaux? I mean, what is the importance of this agent except that he doesn't exist anymore?" Weinstein softened all the hard words. You might have missed them if you weren't listening closely.

"He killed two men. Chasers from Section."

"Oh, yes, the chasers," Weinstein said. "What was it the chasers were going to do when they contacted Devereaux?"

Yackley winced. "I didn't send them. Hanley—"

Weinstein ignored that. "Wasn't this a bit drastic? Why not send down your stationmaster from Zurich?"

"Hanley must have ordered the chasers. Before he... went away. It was done without my knowledge. But they existed, they were sent from Section. Hanley must have—"

Weinstein seemed to consider this, fixing his pale eyes on a spot somewhere above Yackley's head. "Hanley," he said. "Hanley is very ill, I think you said?"

Yackley cleared his throat. "He is being tested," he said. "It's not possible to discuss the thing with him now... At least I don't know if we..."

Weinstein's eyes focused full on Yackley's face then. "I see," he said.

Yackley seemed confused and reached for a metaphor to help him: "I would have preferred to let sleeping agents lie; I wouldn't want to disturb the fabric."

The mixed metaphor amused Weinstein. He let the trace of a smile float across his pale, soft features. He pushed the horn-rimmed glasses up his long nose until they reached the bridge.

"Well, what about Devereaux? Where is he? After his murderous rampage?"

Yackley looked up sharply. Was Weinstein mocking him?

He wanted to use just the right words. He thought he found them: "We don't know."

"I see."

Struggled on: "As far as I can tell, from signal section, the Swiss are puzzled as well. And they've got a lot more men looking for him."

"Devereaux makes trouble, doesn't he?"

"Yes."

"Disturbed," Weinstein said.

"Crazy," Yackley said.

"Outside the rules."

"Not a team player."

Weinstein blinked. "This isn't polo, Frank."

"I meant—"

"Hanley tells him about Nutcracker. What about Nutcracker, Frank? You said it was important. What is in that old man's mind?"

"We're trying to find out—"

"And why did he say to Devereaux 'There are no spies'? Tell me that, Frank."

"I...I." But there were things Frank Yackley did not know. Or did not seem to know.

"Code? Was he making a joke out of it? Like the graffiti in your washrooms over at D.A.?"

Yackley was amazed that Weinstein knew about the oars on the walls. He had had the walls scrubbed clean in two days. Weinstein really was on top of things.

"I wish you had come to me earlier," Weinstein said.

"Before all this mess with Hanley. When you first had suspicions about Hanley."

That was a warning, Yackley thought. "I don't see what else I could have done. It was so unusual. Nutcracker was such a strange idea."

"No one denies that," Weinstein said. He turned from Yackley to the window and clasped his hands behind his back. The White House below was bright under a bright March sky. Washington was warm with the approach of spring. The coming season seemed to move visibly from day to day. The blossoms would be blooming soon on the Japanese cherry trees that surrounded the tidal basin south of the White House.

"Why has Devereaux gone crazy?" Perry Weinstein said in a soft voice, still facing the window.

"I don't know."

"Hanley. And Devereaux."

"Hanley isn't crazy. I think he's been under a strain, I think—"

"You think security may have been breached—"

"I think it is my duty—"

"Yes, of course." Perry Weinstein turned around and faced Yackley, who fidgeted in the small side chair. "So what do we do about our long-sleeping agent?"

"That's what I want to know."

"You want a sanction, is that it?"

"I...I don't know. I really don't know," Yackley said, dancing away from the word.

"There is no sanction," Weinstein said. "The term does not exist. It cannot be authorized. It isn't in law or in case studies. It is illegal to sanction anyone, let alone a former employee of the government. It is impossible to authorize a sanction." The words were delivered without tone, softly, as though a child in first grade, without understanding, were reciting the Pledge of Allegiance.

Yackley waited.

"What do you suppose he will do?"

"Go to the Opposition," Yackley said. "He has committed himself. He killed our chasers."

"You really think so?"

"I think so. It is my best guesstimate," Yackley said. "I have asked Mrs. Neumann for the full file, 201 and appendages. Here it is." He handed the file in the folder to Weinstein but Weinstein did not take it. "Put it on the desk," Weinstein said, staring at Yackley with curious eyes.

Yackley let the file drop onto the papers already littering the desk.

"You want a judgment." Weinstein did not say it as a question.

"Yes."

"All right."

"The sooner the better."

"I understand."

"It's important...that—"

"That it be handled inside the Section, you mean? Not by NSA? Not by CIA?" Weinstein's voice, for the first time, took a tone that might be considered mocking. "Yes, I figured out why you wanted to see me. The buck stops here. It was the only true thing Harry Truman ever said. And then I doubt he said it in the first place." Perry Weinstein smiled. He took Yackley's hand though it had not been extended. "I'll get back to you by morning," he said. His eyes were cloudy now.

11

HANLEY'S GAME

It was March 11. Hanley had been held for a week and a half. He had learned to adjust to life at St. Catherine's.

Sister Mary Domitilla thought his progress was absolutely wonderful. She began to include Mr. Hanley in her prayers and in her sacrifices, including the sacrifice that involved the pain of cutting her nails severely almost every night. Her fingers were always raw and she refused to put salve on them.

Spring was not ready to come to the valley. There had been snow the previous morning and the valley was enveloped in whiteness from the streets of the old town all the way up the hill to the St. Catherine's grounds. The four-wheel-drive vehicles marched through the hilly streets and people with ordinary cars did the best they could. They were all accustomed to hills and slick streets and the sense of isolation in endless winter.

Hanley was given clothing as a gift for good behavior on his sixth day. The clothing consisted of blue denims and a blue shirt marked with his name above the left pocket. He looked like a prisoner.

They ate in their own ward at night but there was a time, between three and five, when they went to the enclosure between the two fences for exercise. They could run along the enclosure or they could just stand around and breathe the clear, damp air of the valley. Hanley chose to run. Dr. Goddard said he was pleased because his response to the situation was "appropriate."

The truth was, Goddard was puzzled.

The dose of HL-4 prescribed for Hanley from the first day was enough to render him harmless, perfectly docile, drowsy and enfeebled. Hanley was certainly more compliant than he had been—but why should he show such extraordinary energy in the afternoons in the yard between the electrified fence and the inner fence?

The electricity was never shut off for these afternoon excursions but the killing voltage was turned down. Now and again, one of the patients would make a bolt for the fence and touch it and be knocked down by the force of the electrical charge.

Hanley had been given a battery of examinations that showed he was in reasonable health for a man of his age. Dr. Goddard, in his second interview, said the absence of any physical cause of Hanley's illness proved Dr. Goddard's thesis that Hanley suffered from depression. The depression was induced by a chemical imbalance, Dr. Goddard said, as well as a "cross-wired burnout" in the brain.

Hanley had blinked at that.

"The brain is like a computer," Goddard said. "The information it can process is controlled by the raw data fed to it. But computers can go haywire. That's why computer owners have service contracts. That's why you have government health insurance—it's your service contract, in a sense."

Hanley was given pills twice a day, at the morning and evening meals. He and the other patients stood in line at the nurse's station outside the mess hall and docilely received the pills prescribed by Dr. Goddard. These were issued by the nurse on duty. In the morning, it was Sister Duncan, a simple soul of pressed habit and acne-infested features who could not be more than twenty, Hanley thought. In the evening, it was Nurse Cox, a formidable beast in a nurse's white pants suit. The difference in their techniques helped Hanley's game.

Both issued the pill and waited for the patient to swallow it.

There was a technique of slipping the pill under one's tongue and throwing the paper cup of water back on the tongue and making a swallowing noise. The nurse then was to examine the mouth, to see that the pill had been actually swallowed. The patient opened wide and made an "ah" sound and then lifted his tongue, first on one side and then the other, to show that the pill was not being concealed.

Fortunately, Sister Duncan hated to look into people's mouths. She was still a nurse in training and she thought there might be matters of human anatomy she might be able to avoid in the future: Men's sex organs, blood, and bedpans.

Hanley could not fool Nurse Cox. He didn't even try.

And so, during the days, his strength increased and the nausea and sense of profound depression only returned at night, when the evening pill took effect. He slept badly because of the pill; he would awake at three in the morning, sweating, shivering, wondering where he was.

He knew he would never ask Dr. Goddard about the pills he was forced to take. Dr. Goddard did not invite questions because he had all the answers. Dr. Goddard, Hanley thought, knew exactly what the pills were doing, to Hanley and to the other patients.

They were a sad lot.

Kaplan had been the third-ranking officer inside the Internal Revenue Service until it was revealed he was the self-ordained founder of the Church of Tax Rebellion, a nonprofit enterprise in Falls Church, Virginia. Kaplan had not paid income tax for fifteen years—and somehow this fact had escaped the computers which constantly cross-checked the tax forms for those in IRS to make certain the collectors were collecting from themselves as well. Poor Kaplan: If it had been a simple matter of fraud, it would not have been so bad. But his scheme was perfectly legal, according to at least six experts in the department. There was the matter of freedom of religion, even for IRS employees. It was important to cure Kaplan of his delusion that the Lord had not meant that one should render to Caesar anything more substantial than a Bronx cheer.

Kaplan, Hanley thought, was crazy. And then he learned that Kaplan had been in the place for two years. He had disintegrated in mind and body in that time. He scarcely weighed more than a hundred pounds. He spent his days reciting scriptural verses and summarized rulings from Tax Court.

Hanley thought he would not last as long as Kaplan.

There were no women, save the nuns and Nurse Cox, in Ward Seven. Hanley had inquired about that and been told that women were treated at St. Trinian's in Ohio.

There's a network of these places, Hanley thought with horror then. And he had been unaware of them.

It was the second Sunday of his incarceration. The model patients from Ward Seven were taken to the chapel for the "Patients' Mass" at nine in the morning. The chapel was segregated at this mass and no outsiders were allowed. There were no services of other denominations. Kaplan conducted his own services in his room inside Ward Seven but he had only three converts who joined him for the ceremonies involved. He tore up symbolic 1040 forms (actually, since he was not permitted forms, sheets of writing paper with "1040" inscribed on them) and distributed them to the members. They ate them.

On Saturdays and Sundays, Sister Duncan handled the administration of the morning and evening pills. Hanley, by Sunday morning, began to feel much better. The poison of the pills was having less effect on his body.

It was cool and damp and the clouds clung low in the valley. At two in the afternoon, the patients—except those locked in their rooms for various infractions of the rules of St. Catherine's—were permitted visitors.

Hanley was surprised to see them.

There were Leo and Lydia Neumann, emerging from a large, dirt-streaked gray Oldsmobile, crossing the gravel path that crunched beneath their feet.

He felt so grateful that he realized he might weep. He could not weep. It was more than a sign of weakness now; it was a sign of craziness.

On Sunday afternoon, they were allowed to walk on the grounds beyond the double fence. On Sunday, a special effort was made by staff and patients to show the normality of the surroundings and the institution.

Hanley led them down the path through a grove of elms. Buds decorated the thin branches of the elms. It would be spring, even if there was snow on the valley floor.

Leo Neumann was not in government service. He was a mechanical engineer and he cut his wife's hair, which is why it was short and spiky and looked terrible. Leo Neumann was a man unaware of his faults; everything he did was a matter of love or self-respect. Cutting his wife's hair every three weeks was love and Lydia Neumann understood that and accepted it. Leo Neumann knew what his wife did and never said a word about it. They couldn't talk about their jobs in any case: Lydia did not understand engineering and Leo was horrified by computers.

The gravel path circled back, almost to the double fences, and they did not speak beyond greetings. At the fences, Hanley paused and gazed at the path between the fences where he was confined with the others in Ward Seven on their daily outings during the week.

"You seem a lot better," said Lydia Neumann.

Hanley turned and looked at her. "Do I?"

"Your old self," said Leo Neumann. He had met Hanley only once.

"I was wrong," Lydia said. She stared at Hanley with the gaze of a mother examining a sick child. "I argued against sending you here."

"You were not wrong," Hanley said. He looked at Leo. "Can I speak to you for a moment, Mrs. Neumann?"

Mrs. Neumann and Hanley left Leo. They strolled a little farther along the double fence, looking in at the path between the fences. When he thought they were alone, Hanley said:

"I was depressed. It began last summer, during all the spy exchanges. I started to examine them. I used computers to set up scenarios."

"I know," she said.

"Of course you know. But not the results. Not the results. The computer logic—I think I've learned it well enough to understand that the logic is not really logic but a way out of a puzzle once the puzzle is described."

"Something like that," Lydia Neumann said. "It has as much morality as you give to the puzzle."

"Morality was not a factor," Hanley said. He stared at the double fences. "We're confined there, between the fences, during the week. The outer fence is electrified. When the juice is turned down, they let the dogs run between the fences at night. Three Dobermans."

Lydia Neumann said nothing. Her face was white. Hanley saw her hand was clenched. She stared at the path between the fences.

"They're killing me," Hanley said. Quietly.

"No—"

"The pills come morning and night. On Saturday, I get rid of the pills. I feel much better today. Tomorrow, it's back to the pills. This is called HL-4. Can you find out what HL-4 is?"

And he handed her one of the morning pills, wrapped in Kleenex. She stared at it in her hand and then slipped it into her pocket.

"I have to get out of here," Hanley said. "The first day here, the psychiatrist in charge, Dr. Goddard, he sprayed me with Mace when I asked for my clothes—"

"You were kept naked?"

"In one of those hospital gowns."

"This is horrible," Lydia Neumann said.

"Most of these places are, I think now," Hanley said. His voice was very soft. "I called Devereaux. Twice, I think, when I was ill—"

"But you were ill, you really were ill—"

"I must have been. It seems like a long time ago. Like thinking of yourself as a child. I really must have been ill."

"You called him. I thought that's who it was. When Yackley had the conference. On what to do with you—"

"And you stuck up for me." Hanley's eyes were wet. "Don't mistake my tears, Mrs. Neumann. I'm not crazy. I'm really not crazy. I feel so broken down. Tears are the last refuge of the weak—"

"Cut it out, man," Lydia Neumann said. "I don't think you're crazy. You were sick. You called Devereaux—"

"Mrs. Neumann. I need an outside contractor. I wanted Devereaux to...come back into the trade for a while. I have to find out something—"

"What?"

"The computer analyzed the spy transactions of last summer. Before the summit. First there were two men from the West German intelligence agency who defected East. Then the Brits picked up the mole in Copenhagen and revealed he had been turned for three years. Then CIA picked up that Soviet in Rome. And then he defects back to the Soviet embassy in D.C. There was also the Chinese agent in Seoul and the two ROKs uncovered in Peking. Trumpets and flourishes. So I went through our own network. Who belongs to us and who, on our side, belongs to them? And how do we know which is which?"

Lydia Neumann blinked. Hanley seemed so intense. He was staring at the path between the two fences. Hanley's face was pale and his eyes were dull. He seemed very tired.

"I wondered if there were any spies at all," he said.

"What are you talking about?"

"We go into budget crunch and the people at NSA can show figures—what they are based on, I don't know— they can show figures that show eighty-five to ninety percent of all intelligence is done by machine. Satellites, computers, bugs. Raw data. The listening post at Cheltenham, at Taipei. The goddamn space shuttle overflies the Soviet Union and Eastern Bloc on every second mission. It all comes down to coming down to the mountain. I was convinced of it."

Tears again. Mrs. Neumann looked away while Hanley found a handkerchief and used it.

"Yackley was on me day and night. Cutbacks in stationmasters, networks...my God, he thought it was all just so much meat cut off the bone. It wasn't that. And then there was Nutcracker—"

He stopped, frightened.

"What are you talking about?"

"Nothing. Nothing at all. Forget that. It was over long ago." Frightened. He gazed at Mrs. Neumann. "I played with the computer and there were all these coincidences in which we got their spies to defect to us and our spies defected at the same time, almost as part of a game. Musical chairs. But aren't there real spies?"

She said, "You should know that."

"But Yackley doesn't believe in them."

"Yackley is a fool," she said.

"Yackley does not believe in spies. He says there are no spies any more than there are elves or leprechauns. There are only intelligence agents on each side analyzing computer materials, making value judgments..."

"Hanley, get hold of yourself."

He was crying again.

"Pawns. He said they are pawns. The game moves in feints and little gestures. I said he was wrong. I would prove it. I could have proved it—"

"Proved what?"

He looked through his tears at her. She wanted to understand, he thought.

And he knew he didn't trust her at all.

"They know our secrets, the Opposition," he said. "We know their secrets. That's all it is, two sides equal, starting from scratch just to stay even. But what if they had advantages over us that we didn't have?"

"What are you talking about?"

Hanley looked puzzled. He put his handkerchief away. "I called November, I wanted him to understand. At least, he said he was outside the game. Maybe everyone was in it together. Even you?"

Mrs. Neumann bit her lip.

"I have to get out of here," Hanley said. He looked at the path between the fences. "Dr. Goddard keeps saying 'eventually' as though he knew it was never going to happen. Eventually can mean when I die. I have to get out of here."

"What do you want me to do?"

He stared at her. "Whatever you do, don't pray for me. I have a nun here. She prays for me. It is sufficient. I couldn't stand any more prayers."

"Hanley—"

"Get me out of here," Hanley said in a low and terrible

voice. "I need to get away, get away from the drugs and routine. I have to think about—" He almost said something and stopped. "I have to think."

"I'll talk to the New Man, to Yackley—"

"No, Mrs. Neumann." Very cold, very much like the old Hanley who had not been ill. "You will not talk to that man. I've talked to you too much. Do you want my secrets? Try my test: Do not talk to Yackley. You are going to have to help me get out of here."

"I can't."

"November," he said.

She shrank from his grasp and the name. "He's buried, dead in files."

"Asleep," Hanley said.

"Buried," she said.

"Wake him." His eyes glittered. "But you're afraid, aren't you? You don't want him to wake up, do you? My God, is it all true?"

"Is what true?"

But he had turned. He began to run back toward the ward. She started after him. She stopped, listened to his footsteps. Poor frightened man, she thought.

Perhaps the horrible best thing to do for Hanley was to keep him here.

Right between the fences.

12

MOSCOW IS WAITING

Not all of the intelligence operations of KGB are head-quartered in the dreary building on Dhzerzhinski Square, which the other intelligence services call Moscow Center. The Committee for External Observation and Resolution, for example, is located in a long and window-less building two miles east of the square.

The man who was called Gorki (by the same computer that named Alexa) sat in his office at the end of a long hall. There was a reception area at the end of the hall and three closed doors. One of the doors led to Gorki; a sec-ond led to a supply room; the room beyond the third door was not spoken of by anyone.

Gorki's office was wrapped in darkness made more acute by the fluorescent lamp on his desk. Everything in the office had been chosen as a prop, save for the giant General Electric air conditioner built into the wall. The building was something of an embarrassment. It had taken too long to construct, it was gloomy (even by Russian standards), and the marble corridors had been stripped at last because the great slabs of marble kept falling off the walls. A party undersecretary had been injured shortly after the building opened by a piece of marble that separated from the wall. The stripped marble was now used as flooring in the various dachas of high Party officials around Moscow.

Gorki's office was decorated with the portraits of three men: Lenin, Felix Dhzerzhinski, the founder of the secret police, and Gorbachev. He had no other ornaments. He was a spare man with Eurasian features and small, quick eyes that seemed to glitter in the light of the single lamp in the room. His skin was parchment and it was yellow with age and liver disease.

The man across from him was an agent called Alexei, a man of little consequence from the Helsinki station.

Alexei was sweating profusely though the office was very cool in the way a tomb is cool.

Gorki did not smile or speak; he sat very still for a long time. He took a file folder and dropped it on the desk and indicated with a nod of his head that Alexei was to retrieve it. The desk was very wide and Alexei, sitting in an overstuffed chair in the cramped room in front of the large desk, had to rise awkwardly and reach across the desk for the file folder. When he sat down heavily, he was sweating all the more. He had to squint to see the photographs.

"She killed these men," Gorki began.

"I don't understand. I don't understand any of this," said Alexei. He really didn't understand. He stared at the faces. There were four photographs. They were grouped in twos by paper clips. The first man was shown as he appeared for his official photograph (updated each year— the Russians have great faith in the power of photographs to identify people). The second had a man with his face blown away.

"It's the same man?" said Alexei.

"Of course."

The second grouping featured a hairless man staring at a camera. The "after" picture showed him on a slab in a morgue, his eyes open, a large wound on the side of his head.

"She killed them? Alexa?"

"Alexa. She was informed at Zurich they would accompany her on her . . . assignment. The contract on this second November. November." Gorki closed his eyes a moment. When he opened them again, they were liquid and on fire. "Will no one get rid of November for me? Does he subvert every agent? Does he have nine lives?"

Alexei said nothing. The questions were not to be answered.

"Alexa was our most formidable agent in her specialty. What has happened to her? She goes to Lausanne and she betrays us. Why?"

"How were they killed?"

"She had gone to the apartment of the agent. The American we had told her was the second November—"

"The blue moon," Alexei said.

Gorki blinked. "I beg your pardon?"

"I was—" Alexei blushed. "It was nothing, Director."

Gorki resumed in the same sandpaper voice. "I want to question you as I will question our stationmaster in Zurich. I want to be absolutely certain that Alexa understood the contract and what was expected of her. The two agents she murdered in that apartment—I say 'murdered' because it was nothing more than that—I want to know exactly how this came about. There was an old woman also killed. The police in Switzerland are not very happy. The missions in Geneva and Zurich have been shut down in part until the matter is over—"

"How do you know she killed them? It might have been this November."

"The police are looking for this woman. There was a child she hired to distract the concierge, to gain entry to the apartment in the first place. It appears she ambushed Yuri and Vladimir—the agents, I can use their names now, they are dead. November is gone, Alexa is gone. What does that suggest to you?"

"Comrade Director," Alexei began. "I don't know what to make of it. I told her to go to Zurich. To wait for her instructions. You have talked to our Zurich stationmaster—"

"Not yet. He is sent for. He filed a long dispatch and he is flying into Moscow this afternoon from Zurich." Gorki projected a sense of self-pity: Alexei knew this would be marked against him; something like this had to have blame affixed. It was nearly a repeat of what had happened to the agent Denisov who had been sent into the United States once, to Florida, who had been turned by November and induced to defect... And now Alexa. "I cannot emphasize too strongly the displeasure felt by the Committee—"

"My deepest sympathies, Comrade," said Alexei, who understood that the focus of scrutiny was on Gorki and that Gorki wished to shift it to another. But not Alexei. Alexei had been in Helsinki. Alexei knew nothing. Alexei was quite certain he could not be blamed.

Gorki had spent the morning with the Secretary of

the Fourth Directorate. It had not been a good morning.
A new administration in the Soviet Union was cleaning
house in all areas, including the area called Committee for State Security. There were, nominally, 300,000
agents who qualified to call themselves KGB. But some
were nothing more than timekeepers in factories that consistently fell below quota or where the level of theft was
unusually high. Simple policemen and nothing more. The
business of intelligence-gathering and disinformation dis-
semination and the business of agents like Alexa—they
were handled by a select group, carefully screened, given
long profile tests and psychological examinations. How
could Alexa have gone crazy?

It was the perpetual question of the Secretary of the
Fourth Directorate, who had pounded his desk again
and again, until the little toy railroad engine on the desk
danced to the edge and fell off and broke. It did not
improve the Secretary's humor. There were breakdowns
in security at every level. Just this winter, the second
man in the San Francisco station in the United States had
been seduced into defection by a homosexual CIA agent.
A homosexual! the Secretary had stormed. Why did our
profiles not screen out the homosexuals?

Gorki could not explain that the homosexual agent
had been sent to San Francisco in the first place to seduce
other homosexuals in positions of power inside Silicon
Valley. The world of spies, Gorki thought, was a mirror
constantly reflecting different images—but always the
mirror image of itself.

What was real? The mirror or the thing beyond the
mirror?

Alexa was an embarrassment particularly because

November had been presumed dead once and then presumed to be another man—a man named Ready who was still unidentified in the morgue in Helsinki. Was it so simple to fool a bureaucracy? the Secretary had asked with sarcasm as he put the pieces of the broken toy train into his center drawer.

Gorki had no answer that would satisfy either of them. He interrupted his thoughts to speak: "You and Alexa worked together. A long time ago."

"Yes, Comrade Director," said Alexei. "I reminded her of this when I saw her in Helsinki. I can assure you, the meeting was brief. I had many matters—"

"You were reprimanded—"

"I can assure you, we met in the open, in the lobby of the Presidentti Hotel. I told her the assignment as I knew it and she caught the afternoon plane to Zurich." He reached into his pocket for a notebook. "Flight 21, Finnair to Zurich, it left at 14:22 hours—"

"Yes," said Gorki. "We know." He sounded disappointed. He sounded tired. Where would he be able to begin?

The red light on the telephone console flashed on.

He picked up the receiver and said nothing.

He replaced it without a word. He looked across at Alexei.

"Go back to the hotel, Alexei. We'll send for you—"

"Comrade Director—"

Gorki looked at him sharply.

Alexei blushed, struggled to rise, and squeezed out of the chair. He went to the door in the dark room and looked back for a moment. If only there was something he could say.

But he opened the door in silence, stepped outside and closed it. The secretary in the bare, depressing foyer with its linoleum floor and blank white walls stared at him. Alexei saw that a light on her telephone console was flashing. There was a call waiting for Gorki and he wished to take it alone; it was probably from the Zurich stationmaster, kept in another anteroom, waiting to tell Gorki that the problem of Alexa had been the fault of the man in Helsinki, that he must have fouled the message in some way. Alexei felt very sorry for himself as he crossed the bare reception room with its straight wooden chairs lined along one wall. He said something to the secretary, apologized, took his coat from the rack, and opened the door that led to the hall.

Gorki picked up the telephone again.

He heard the voice of his secretary. She said the call was waiting on the third line, the one protected from listening devices by the expedient of a black box that emitted radio signals to jam the line. It was not as efficient and marvelous as the electronic scrambler system used by the Americans but it worked well enough. He dialed to line three and waited.

The line crackled and then was silent. Then he spoke in a whisper: "Moscow is waiting."

They were the usual code words.

The voice at the other end of the line finished the obligatory salutation: "Everything must go ahead."

So. The code was complete.

Gorki realized he felt immense dread in that moment. He gripped the receiver tightly.

He knew the voice on the line. There was no mistake.

It was Alexa.

13

CAPTAIN BOLL

Devereaux walked into the apartment building on the Rue de la Concorde Suisse. It was a bright morning, three days of hiding after the incident on the road to Chillon. He had taken the time of retreat to try to think his way through all that had happened. Twice he had visited Philippe in the school the boy attended. Philippe had understood about everything Devereaux told him. To see the understanding in Philippe's clear blue eyes—which were set hot and shining in that brown face—was to see a clear reflection of his own thoughts.

He did not try to telephone Rita Macklin in the troubled Philippines. There was no way to explain to her what he would do next.

They had had a conversation once upon a time and it had never reached a resolution.

In the conversation, Rita said, "Would you try to go back? Into the old trade?"

In the conversation—which they both believed they had never actually taken part in—Devereaux replied, "I would never go back. That's what we went through all that for. That's why we can be together."

Rita said, "But if you had to go back. To survive?"

"I wouldn't do it. But if I had to go back, to survive, what would it do to us? I mean, what would you do then?" Because they both knew the linchpin that held them together was that he was quit of the old trade.

It was a conversation that always stopped at that point—if it ever took place in reality or only in their separate thoughts. It had to stop there. Neither of them wanted to know the end of the conversation.

Devereaux turned in at the gate and crossed the walk lined with tulips to the door. He expected what he found there.

He opened the door to the lobby and the large policeman in bulky blue seemed to have been studying him through the glass. The Swiss are not subtle about their weapons. The policeman had already produced an automatic weapon—it looked to Devereaux like a variation on the Uzi—and had it pointed at Devereaux when he entered the lobby. The policeman had some words and Devereaux gave him some others.

The journey to the police station was framed in silence. Devereaux had made all the necessary calls abroad from the hotel in Lugano, during the three days of his hiding.

The police station of Lausanne smelled exactly like all the other police stations in the world. There was sweat, a certain musty sense of hopelessness, and the smell of despair that is mated with the sounds of iron doors closing shut very hard.

Captain Boll was on the second floor and his room was

spare. The window faced south, toward the lake, and you could even see the lake through the trees. The trees were gaining foliage quickly in the warm sun and thickening above the red rooftops on the terraces below.

Captain Boll was even bulkier than the policeman who had been waiting in the apartment building. He did not wear a uniform and he seemed put out. His eyes were small, not particularly shrewd, and his brows beetled together above a long, wide nose that betrayed some liking for Swiss wines.

Boll indicated a hard chair in the middle of the room—directly in front of the large, bare desk. Devereaux sat down and waited. His face was wreathed in wrinkles and calm. His eyes were steady and cool. He felt ready—which was not the same as feeling in charge. To do something was to exist. He had begun the process.

Boll said his name and Devereaux waited.

"This is about murder. Three people killed in your building. Two of them outside your apartment."

Devereaux said nothing. Words were not really expected, he thought. Captain Boll had something to say.

But Boll surprised him by waiting as well, his hands flat and placid as rowboats on the desktop.

"I was in Lugano," Devereaux began. "Three days. Visiting my son."

"I know that," Captain Boll said, surprising him for a second time. "It was convenient to be in Lugano, wasn't it?"

"I don't know what you're talking about."

"The policeman said you didn't seem surprised to be arrested."

"I am rarely surprised. Or perhaps my innocence reassures me," Devereaux said.

"You aren't accused of anything."

"Of course I am," he said.

Silence again. There was a wonderful warm breeze from the south that brought smells of the lake and the trees through the window. The bare room warmed with the sun. The two men waited. The silence was complete.

Captain Boll sighed. He got up and went to the window and looked down at the housetops. "I should be sailing today. It's early but it is running good and no one is in the lake," Captain Boll said. His voice was surprisingly soft, Devereaux thought. Devereaux was on guard now because the soft voice did not seem to fit the big man or the situation they were talking about.

"You are an American agent." Boll turned as he said it.

"Was," Devereaux began.

"Peterson," said Captain Boll.

"That's one of the names," Devereaux said, giving ground a little the way a fisherman feeds the line after the hook goes in.

"How did this killing concern you?"

"I don't know."

"But it did concern you?"

"It must have," Devereaux said. "There would be too much coincidence to suppose it didn't."

"You are retired. From your . . . profession?"

"Yes."

"You are much too young."

"I am much too tired to continue."

Boll smiled. The smile might have meant anything.

"The same with me. But I have not grown rich enough yet to sail every day."

"I was in Lugano," Devereaux said.

"Yes. And the woman at the brasserie, Claudette Long-temps, she said two men came for you the day before. They questioned her and threatened her. Very nasty people. They were killed. But you were in Lugano. So. Did you have someone kill them?"

"No," Devereaux said.

"A woman, perhaps?"

For the moment, puzzlement crossed Devereaux's face. That made Boll frown. Was he such a good actor?

"A woman, M. Devereaux?" said Captain Boll.

"I don't understand." The words came out simply, like the truth.

"A half hour before this horrible thing, a woman—a woman who was noticed with great interest by so many men in the area that their descriptions make me believe she is quite beautiful—hired one of our young thugs in Lausanne to break the window of the lobby of the building in the Rue de la Concorde Suisse. The woman wanted to draw the concierge from the lobby briefly enough to pass into the building. To go to your rooms, M. Devereaux."

"What description?"

"It is not your wife, M. Devereaux. We have had a good long time to check on everything. Your wife is a journalist?"

"Yes. She is not my wife," he added, automatically trying to separate Rita from this though he knew that was not possible.

"She is in Manila. She booked Swissair. She left a wide trail."

Devereaux twisted in the chair. He realized it was designed in such a way that it would never be comfortable, like one of those modern stools attempted from time to time by famous architects which never work out.

"Rita is a journalist, nothing more. I came to Switzerland to live, to be on the edge of things and not in them anymore."

"Do you think I'm a policeman, monsieur? I am something more than that. The Swiss are prepared for nearly everything, monsieur. That is our nature. That is why nearly nothing ever happens. And then something like this. Do you have an idea of what has happened?"

Devereaux waited for a long moment to pass between them. He spoke in a monotone. He knew the tone of voice that would satisfy both of them.

"The woman, whoever the woman was, went to the apartment to kill me. The two men, whoever the men were, went to the apartment for the same purpose. Apparently, neither of them was aware of the other."

"And the woman killed all three—"

"No. Not the concierge. She wouldn't have hired whoever she hired to lure the concierge out of the building just to end up killing her."

"Yes," said Captain Boll. "What I thought as well." And he started at Devereaux for a long time. "They want to kill you."

"It would seem so," Devereaux said.

"Are you so cool to face death?"

"I did not invite it," Devereaux said.

"What will you do?"

"Not impose on the hospitality of the Swiss in this matter. I am going back."

"Is this so?"

"Yes."

"Then why come back here to face me?"

"Because it had to be done this way."

Boll was perplexed. He crossed again to the window and looked down enviously at the long finger of the lake that stretched to the mountains.

"When it's done, I'll tell you," Devereaux said.

"And if I kept you here?"

"For what reason?" Devereaux said.

"We found a pistol taped in the toilet in the apartment. Is it your pistol?"

"No," Devereaux said. "It was planted there."

Boll turned. "You lie to me."

"Perhaps."

"This is not some joke. You should not have involved an innocent person. Like Claudette Longtemps. She was very shaken, I can tell you, to identify those two men in the morgue. She thought they had killed you. I had to assure her that you were alive. You live with one woman and you have a black child—God knows where you got him—and you have this young girl from the countryside who is so much in love with you. I tell you, you disgust me."

Devereaux waited.

"Damn you, man," Boll said and came around the desk and struck Devereaux very hard on the face. When he drew back his hand, there was blood at the corner of Devereaux's lips. The blood trickled down, dropped on the dark fabric of the corduroy jacket. Devereaux did not move. He looked at Boll. His eyes were mild and waiting, as though Boll had to finish some private game he was involved in.

"I could lock you up a good long time."

"That's one way to do it," Devereaux said. Now the voice was flat, without any tone at all. The gray eyes were steady.

"That would suit you?"

"I can take it, if that's what you mean. If I were in your

prison, it would be up to you to keep me safe. You believe the woman came to kill me. You didn't get her, so she will try again. Or others will try again. If you want to make this a Swiss matter, then I'll oblige you by going to prison."

Boll thought about that.

There were birds in the trees and both men could hear them clearly.

"And if I expel you—"

"On what grounds?"

"I can find grounds."

"I have an attorney retained in Geneva. There are laws in Switzerland."

"You are a guest of the country and you abuse the country's hospitality."

"It was not me, Herr Boll," said Devereaux. "I will leave the country. I'll resolve this—this is an American matter. In a little while, when it's resolved, then you'll know what happened."

"Are you so sure you won't be killed?" Boll smiled.

"Not at all." Devereaux waited. "If that happens, then it's resolved. If I'm not killed, it's resolved. But it has to be finished. You choose where it will be finished—in Switzerland or not here."

"And your son? Or whatever he is, the black child?"

"He's in school. The lawyer has his trust. If things happen...then he's taken care of. He's fourteen. He understands."

"And Rita Macklin? Will you arrange for her as well?"

But Devereaux had run out of words. The conversation with Rita—the one in mind—always ended at this point. He had broken free twice; twice he had been dragged back.

He didn't know. Any more than Boll.

14

AMONG THE INSANE

Hanley was falling into himself. He had been in Ward Seven for three weeks and each day grew more indistinct in mind and memory. Was today Wednesday or was it the day before? Was it spring? Was it this year or last?

In lucid moments, he knew that it was the medicine. There were pills in the morning and at night and there were pills as part of therapy and there were pills to ease the pain and to encourage sleep and to end anxiety and to modify behavior. He felt drugged all the time and yet the dependency was restful to him. He needed it.

Hanley began to speak to himself for company. He knew they didn't care. They were very tolerant of the gentle patients and he was a gentle patient. He was learning all the lessons they wanted him to learn.

He sat at the window in his room and looked through the bars and watched the inmates walk to and fro in the exercise area. They were insane, he knew; at least, most of them. He was not so certain about Mr. Carpenter, who had been in the place for six months and who said he had

been an assistant security chief at NASA and that he had
been placed in St. Catherine's after he had made certain
allegations about the safety of the shuttle program. Like
Hanley, he had been a bachelor. The place was full of
bachelors, divorced men, and homosexual men. That was
an oddity, Hanley thought in lucid moments. Hanley knew
that he had few lucid moments now. It was why he sat at
the window and spoke to himself; he thought the sound of
his own voice might keep some sanity in the broken bowl
of his mind.

He felt an almost physical sense of losing control. He
felt spastic at times, as though his limbs might begin to
work or shiver without his instructions. He finally mentioned this phenomenon to Sister Duncan, who relayed
the information to Dr. Goddard, who talked to Hanley
in a chummy way and changed Hanley's daily dosage of
drugs. The condition worsened.

Hanley said aloud, "It feels as if my body has become
very small and the world has become very large. Not as
though I am a child but that I am much much smaller. As
though I am shrinking. Is that why they call psychologists
shrinks?"

He smiled at that. A smile was not such a rare thing
anymore. Much in the world amused him; at least, the
part of the world that did not frighten him.

He thought of Washington, D.C., and it seemed to him
a long time ago. Not so much a place but a memory of
something that had once been an important experience
to him.

It was absurd now, in his present state, to believe he
had been a director of espionage. Espionage was such a
ludicrous idea. Look around: What would a spy have to

do with a place like this? That world must be as insane as this one, he thought with great satisfaction.

He had bananas and corn flakes for breakfast. The taste of the food lingered in memory. When he had been a child, he had eaten cold cereal and fruit for breakfast.

Tears came to his eyes. He thought of the child he had been. He thought of that often now in the dim days of faltering images. The child he had been was gangly, alone on a farm with elderly parents, a watcher who was slow to speak. When he was a child, he would awaken each morning to go to the window in hopes there was some change in the endless, flat Nebraska landscape. The only change was weather. There was snow and blistering summer heat and, in the fall, a brief and beautiful time of color that was melancholy even to an eleven-year-old boy. He wept and watched out the window. The day was warm and bright, almost sultry. The spring came like a woman waiting for sex. There was a perfume that haunted the world. The day was lascivious, almost wanton. Hanley thought of a woman—once, a woman in memory—and open legs on a narrow bed, a woman with the smell of sex on her lips.

Hanley realized he was aroused again. Sometimes, now, he was aroused five or six times a day. The experience was not pleasant finally because the arousal—and his masturbation—had eventually chafed his penis. He had not masturbated since he was a child. Arousal was pain. He thought he should tell someone but there was only Sister Duncan, who would blush, and Dr. Goddard, who would give him more medicine.

Am I sick? he thought. He watched Carpenter walk around and around the yard with large, angry strides. How did Carpenter resist?

Resist, he thought, turning the word over and over in mind until it almost tumbled out of mind.

He blinked.

He was still aroused and he could smell the perfume of spring all around him. He touched himself and felt pain. Pain and pleasure; arousal and sleepiness; memory and failing images all around. He blinked his eyes. They were wet.

"Mr. Hanley."

He removed his hand, turned, saw Sister Mary Domitilla, a large nun shaped like a cookie. She was smiling and sweet-faced and it frightened Hanley because he did not think she was a sweet woman. He blinked and the wetness was almost gone. He said nothing.

"How are you today, Mr. Hanley?"

"I'm fine," he said. His voice was low and flat and not accustomed to being used. "I'm fine today. I'm better today, feeling better."

If you did not feel better, they gave you medicine to help you to feel better.

They were going to give Carpenter electroshock treatments in a week. Of course, they didn't say that but everyone knew that was what Mr. Carpenter's condition indicated. He was on the schedule to report to Room 9 for "therapy" sessions next week. No one spoke of Room 9 because the people who came out of Room 9 were altered. They did not seem to be the same person.

"Mr. Hanley? Mr. Hanley? Are you with us today, Mr. Hanley?"

"Oh. Yes. Yes I am." He got up from the straight chair by the window. He smiled at Sister Mary Domitilla. They all wanted you to smile; it was the first rule of Ward Seven. Smile and the world smiles with you.

"You have a visitor, Mr. Hanley," said Sister Domitilla in the manner of one giving a child an unearned treat. "I want to be certain that you're up to seeing him."

"Who am I seeing?" Hanley said.. "Yes, yes. I'm up to seeing him." He felt a nervous shiver of anticipation.

"You'll see soon enough," said Sister Domitilla. "Come with me."

He followed her out of the room. Her dark habit flowed down the hallway, accompanied by the clattering of the large rosary she wore at her belt. She was not as tall as Hanley and she was fat. She spoke in a musical voice in a way that most women have not spoken for years. Her voice had the notes of a toy xylophone.

Hanley shuffled behind. He wore bedroom slippers most of the time. They seemed more comfortable than shoes. What was the point of shoes? Or wearing trousers? He wore his pajamas and the hospital robe—it was gray and carried the insignia *St. Catherine's* above a small cross—and he hadn't brushed his hair for days. His hair was turning white, what was left of it.

"In there," said Sister Domitilla. She stopped by an unmarked door. She nodded to the door. Hanley opened the door.

He blinked.

The man who sat on the edge of the table in the small, windowless room was lean and edgy and wore glasses. Hanley felt certain he knew him but he could not place him for a moment. The puzzlement crossed his features and made him frown.

"Perry Weinstein," the man said, to jog memory. "You remember me?"

"Perry Weinstein," Hanley repeated. "You're the Assistant

National Security Adviser." There, it clicked into place just like that.

"Yes," Perry said. He paused and studied Hanley's face. "You all right?"

"Yes. I'm fine." And Hanley smiled the smile they all expected.

"Are you sure?"

"Yes," said Hanley.

"I'd like to talk to you," Perry said.

"Yes. Yes, let's talk."

"Could we go outside? Take a walk?"

"Yes. If you want."

"Do you want to dress?"

"I am dressed."

"I mean... well, it doesn't matter."

"No, not at all. I'm fine, I tell you."

"Is something wrong?"

"No, not at all."

They walked out of the room, down the hall, out into the yard. Into the open front yard, not the yard behind the building where the others walked. Dr. Goddard glanced out his window at them and frowned. It wasn't a good thing, to see Dr. Goddard frown. Dr. Goddard only frowned when he had a problem.

The air assaulted Hanley. He shivered and Perry Weinstein said: "Are you cold?"

"No, not at all. I'm fine." Could he explain that the air was a woman's perfume and the smell of trees and buds growing on bare branches and the smell of the earth itself aroused him? He could bury his face in the earth and lick it. He thought of that and he was embarrassed again and fastened his robe tightly around him. He walked painfully along.

Perry Weinstein said nothing for a long time. They walked down the gravel drive toward the other buildings. Toward the gate. Hanley saw the gate and thought about it. Beyond the gate was the valley and beyond the valley was the world.

"There are no spies," Perry Weinstein said. He said it in an offhand voice, as though saying it was a fine day.

Hanley blinked and said nothing. They stopped walking. Perry pointed to a green bench and said, "Let's sit down."

They sat down. Hanley folded his hands over his crotch to hide his erection from the other man. He felt foolish and embarrassed. He blushed and stared at the gravel and then, once, looked up and saw the gate down the path.

"Why did you say that?"

"Why did I say what?"

" 'There are no spies.' "

"Did I say that?"

"You said it in a telephone conversation. Do you remember?"

"My memory . . . is failing. I remember events of thirty or forty or fifty years ago quite clearly but I forget so much. I think I might be going blind. Not outside but inside."

"Are you on medication?"

"Don't you know?" Hanley said in a quick, sly voice.

"I don't know. I came up here to see you."

"What day is today?"

"Tuesday."

"There are no visitors on Tuesday. Visitors come on Sunday after the last mass."

"What do they do to you here, Hanley?"

"What do you mean?"

"What do they do to you here?"

"Don't you know?"

"I don't know."

"You should know." And there was a sudden and unexplainable sob in his voice. "Yackley sent me here. You should know."

Perry Weinstein studied the older man through his horn-rimmed glasses. His eyes were mild and quick. He slowly rubbed the bridge of his nose, back and forth.

"There are no spies," Perry Weinstein said.

"Yes. That's true. And all of what we do means nothing. It is pointless, fruitless, hopeless. The Section means nothing. We are to spy upon the spies. Well, there are no spies, are there?" And Hanley smiled and was crying.

"Of course there are spies," Weinstein said. His voice was cold.

"You don't know?"

"Know what?"

"Perhaps you don't have a need-to-know."

"Cut that bullshit, Hanley." Weinstein came close to his face. "Why is November in Moscow?"

"Is he in Moscow?"

"You said he was—"

"I wanted to warn him," Hanley began quickly.

"Warn who?"

"November." Hanley waited. "November was in Denmark, he was going to Moscow, he had put out feelers to Moscow Center. He wanted to go over. I had to tell November—"

"The real November," Weinstein said.

"Of course. He was sleeping. I had to tell him to come

awake. The words were all wrong. I realize that. I wanted to tell him that none of it mattered, there were no spies in any case—"

"That's crazy talk," Perry Weinstein said. "Why are you talking crazy?"

"Burke in Romania. They had him on a string for three years and pulled him in and traded him for Rostenkowski who we had. We had Rostenkowski in Paris for four years. Three for four." Hanley smiled.

"Are you crazy, then?"

"No, I'm not crazy. It is difficult to explain," Hanley said. "I was tired, it was the shock of it all, I suppose. I wasn't crazy. Every day I went to the same bar on Fourteenth Street and they closed it down. So I had to find a new place. I started to eat in the cafeteria. Can you imagine doing that? The food was awful."

"It has to be awful up to GS 13; then it improves," Weinstein said. And he smiled at Hanley.

Hanley realized he was smiling back. A tight and typical Hanley smile, the smile of the bureaucrat who does not wish to be amused about jokes concerning the bureaucracy. The smile that Hanley had not smiled in Ward Seven in the three weeks he had been there; or three months; or three years. Eventually.

The smiles faded.

"Tell me about the two Novembers," Perry Weinstein said.

Hanley shrugged in his robe, as though to recede into it. The air was still and very cold for the time of year. When he spoke, his breath was puffed.

"Do you have a need-to-know?"

Perry Weinstein nodded. His face was grave.

Hanley thought about it for a long time. The spring seemed too sultry to him; he did not realize it was cold. The spring caressed him. The woman of the season blew into his ear and licked inside his ear and it made him shiver; another person would have thought it was cold. He could smell perfume and the peculiar touch of a woman's fingers running up and down his arm. The woman in the season put her wet tongue into his ear and he shivered because she promised so many pleasures to him.

Hanley blinked. The reverie disappeared. The tongue and woman and smell were gone. He stared at Weinstein. "What did you say?"

"Tell me about November. Tell me what is wrong with Section," Weinstein said.

"Wrong with Section," Hanley said.

Weinstein waited. He was a listener.

"I have thought, for a long time, that someone inside Section does not mean us well. Does not mean well to Section."

"Tell me," Weinstein said.

"Nutcracker was taken from me. My nutcracker is gone," he said. "I was given it and it was mine. My sister took it."

"What about Section?"

"I see teeth and that face that will kill you to see you. It was my nutcracker," Hanley said. He began to cry.

"I can get your nutcracker back to you," Perry Weinstein said.

"No. You're telling me that but you can't. It was lost a long time ago."

"Tell me about the Section. Tell me what's wrong with Section."

"Is it safe to tell you?"

Weinstein waited.

"I tried to tell November. He wouldn't listen to me. I think he knows, though."

"Knows what?"

"That there is something wrong. With Section." Hanley felt the cold around him, pressing on his pale skin. "I need to tell someone."

"Tell me," said Perry Weinstein.

And Hanley began then, in a slow voice, to tell him everything he could remember.

15

Assignment

The cities of the Eastern Bloc are dark at night. There is light but just enough. In the center of old Prague was a red star, illuminated at night, revolving slowly around and around. From the top story of the restaurant in the Intercontinental Hotel—the only modern hotel in Prague—the Soviet visitors and their women of the evening could view the red star revolving above the old church spires. Even above the spires of the old cathedral on the hill.

The restaurant was expensive and glittering. The wines served were from Hungary and Romania and were not very good. The cuisine was French with a heavy touch. Everything about the restaurant was a parody of poshness because parody is the only thing possible in such a society.

Alexa thought it was crude. She honestly loved Paris, for example, and all its excesses; she loved Moscow out of an inborn love for the ancient city that seemed part of her roots; but she saw the rest of the world for what it was. And Prague was a sad old city, neglected too long and full of sorrows buried in the ancient stones.

Perhaps Gorki would have understood. Gorki was a

complex man and she was his protégée in the Resolutions Committee. She would have explained her feelings to him on any night but this one. She was too nervous.

He had seduced her in the beginning, as she expected, but had never treated her as his mistress or even his property. Gorki was a detached man who sampled pleasures, never gorged on them.

She thought Gorki had sent men to have her killed. She wanted to understand why. He had seemed surprised to hear her voice when she telephoned.

Prague was a short plane ride from Moscow and from Zurich. They had agreed to meet there because Gorki did not want her to return to Moscow. Not yet.

Gorki put down his glass of brandy—French, not the Hungarian version offered on the menu—and looked across the white tablecloth. Her eyes had never left his face. He was a small man with the delicate manners of the Oriental Soviet. No one who worked for him knew his past and no one wanted to speak too much about it.

He stared at Alexa until she looked away, out the wall of windows.

"All organizations have their duplications," Gorki said in a quiet voice as though summarizing some lesson. "I have wanted this American agent dead for a long time. The two men you killed—by mistake, dear Alexa—were backup to you and the unfortunate agent in Helsinki failed to explain that to you."

"Why?" she said.

"Alexei claims no knowledge of the two men but the truth is quite different." He spoke Russian with patient clarity, as though each word had been painfully learned and was reluctantly released in speech.

"I could have been killed," she said.

"It was such a waste—"

"I still don't understand—"

"Nor I," interrupted Gorki. "But I understand this: November is still alive and that is not acceptable."

"So I go back to Lausanne," she began. She had eaten very little. She wore a dark dress with long sleeves that framed her pale features and made her skin seem more like porcelain. She watched Gorki as though she felt she had to be certain that he was telling her the truth; it was the first time she had felt suspicious.

"No. He has left Lausanne."

"What happened?"

"He left Lausanne. He left the country after four days. He talked to Swiss police. He went to London, we think. Today or tomorrow he flies to New York on the Concorde. We think. We have this information—"

"What are you going to do?" Alexa said. Her words were soft, but she stared at him very hard.

"You," said Gorki. His lynx eyes glittered at the table. The wine steward came and Gorki waved him away.

"You have watched him so closely, then why—"

"Because this is a delicate matter," Gorki began.

She saw that he was lying to her. Why was he lying? What part of what he said was a lie and what was the truth?

She felt the same coldness she had felt the first day in Zurich, after the killings, when she tried to decide what to do next. Her first thought had been to contact Moscow but she had elected to do nothing at first. The newspapers were full of information about the killings. She could not understand who the men had been. Even now. She did not

believe Gorki at all; she had flown to Prague as though
flying to a rendezvous with her own death.

"Who is November?"

"He was our mole in the R Section," began Gorki.

She waited, her disbelief suspended. Her long fingers
held the edge of the white tablecloth as though holding on
to reality.

"It is very complex. Seemingly, over the years, he had
performed a number of actions against our interest but
that was to be expected. He had to be useful. To them and
to us. However, most importantly, we began to suspect
two years ago that he had changed allegiances—that he
had been found out and that he was being used now by R
Section to feed us disinformation that we would believe,
because we would believe him to be our man. Much as the
British did with the German spy network in Britain in the
Patriotic War."

She nodded; she knew the reference to World War II
when British intelligence managed to triple every German
agent in Britain, creating an entirely traitorous network
of German spies working for the British and still feeding
their German controls information.

"The important matter now is that he has to be dealt
with. It was to be done in Switzerland, before he had any
warning. Unfortunately, he has been warned now by the
killings and by R Section itself. His cover is blown as far
as we're concerned."

She waited and the cold feeling grew in her. Gorki spoke
in a sharp whisper, the words glittered, he was constructing
a story that seemed entirely plausible. And yet Alexa knew
it was a lie, it had to be a lie from the beginning. And if it
was a lie, then it meant Gorki wanted to eliminate her.

He wanted to kill her.

The thought fastened to her like a leech. She felt the blood draining from her face. She went very rigid and pale and cold in that moment. *He wanted to kill her.*

"You have had the training of an illegal agent and that is what you will become again," Gorki said, staring at his cognac. It seemed he did not want to look at her. "In the packet is identification. A French passport, papers, driver's license...all the paperwork. It seems better to travel to Montreal from Paris first and then shuttle to Washington. The Canadian entry is much easier."

"But our own people...in Washington—"

"This is not a matter for them. It is too delicate for more usual channels—"

She felt the words like blows; they were all lies. Gorki was isolating her and there was nothing she could do about it.

He had sent the killers in Lausanne not to kill the American but to kill her.

A rush of guilt overwhelmed her. It must be some flaw in her that exacted this punishment; some failure.

She was a woman of great beauty and cunning. In that shaken moment, she fell back on her resources.

She reached her hand across the white linen and touched the parchment fingers.

Gorki looked at her for a moment, as though he could not understand the gesture. He looked into Alexa's glittering eyes. Eyes that could not be disguised, he thought. Eyes that will always give her away.

Gorki smiled at her as though she might have been a child.

"My dear Alexa," Gorki said, removing his hand. "I

fly back to Moscow in an hour. There is so little time. Believe me—" He spoke in a soft voice and then interrupted himself with silence. His eyes spoke regret. He smiled. "Perhaps—" Again, silence intervened. He rose and she saw he had left a packet on the table. Instructions and identification and money—the usual precautions.

But Alexa felt failure. Acute and cold. He was instructing her to follow a trail of lies to her own death. What was her failure?

And what was her alternative?

She shuddered. She looked up. Gorki was already threading his way through the tables, past the Party officials and their girlfriends, his thin frame silhouetted against the black window that looked out on blackened Prague. And the great red star turning slowly, slowly, above the church spires and the steeples.

16

AMONG FRIENDS,
AMONG ENEMIES

For a long time, the bulky man in dark cashmere coat and homburg hat walked along the seawall that jutted out into the Channel in Dover.

Dover was having a British spring with drab days and the threat of rain in the air. The Channel was choppy and gray, the way it always seemed to be. The great gulls groaned madly above the waves crashing into the seawall and the chimney pots of the town boiled up with curls of smoke. It was a day for hot tea and cold sandwiches and the huddled conversations of the public house. It was a day for dampness, wet wools, and the red noses that come with sniffles and deep spring colds.

The bulky man in dark had his hands folded behind his back as he patrolled the seawall and felt a touch of spray now and again on his ruddy face. His eyes were mild as a saint's behind rimless glasses. He looked like a man of great kindnesses. He might have been one of those millionaires who gives all to the poor. In the case of Dmitri Ilyich Denisov, all those assumptions about him would have been wrong.

Once he had been an agent from Moscow; then, again, he had been made a reluctant defector to America. He was certainly a killer; he was certainly ruthless; he certainly broke laws as part of his new trade in the world of supplying those things to the world that the world wants but does not want to allow to be traded.

Denisov had once battled a nemesis named November, an American agent who had embarrassed him, nearly killed him, used him twice, and who had also given him a complete set of Gilbert and Sullivan recordings to while away his days in American exile. Gilbert and Sullivan was the only thing that had kept Denisov's sanity in those terrible first days when the American questioned him over and over and he felt the deep sense of loss: He would never be in Russia again, nor walk Moscow streets, nor smell the home smells, nor sleep with his wife, nor hear his son and sister argue for the privilege of the morning bathroom. They were things he thought he would never miss and then, on a beach in Florida, an agent named November had arranged to deprive him of everything that defined his life.

It had happened a long time ago.

Now, out of the grayness, came the hideous roar of the beast that crosses the Channel. The hovercraft was in the waters, propellers turning and the whoosh of air pounding the waters flat beneath it, the hull like a rubber inner tube inflated and absurd. The roaring of the beast grew and the hovercraft seemed to lumber sideways toward the landing apron.

"Time," Denisov said aloud, in Russian. He had a pistol, as always, and he felt for it in the pocket of his large overcoat. He turned and walked back along the seawall and down the road to the terminal where the hovercraft would crawl ashore, resembling some link in the chain of being turning from sea monster to creature of the land.

The hovercraft was late, delayed on the French side as usual. Now they were going to build a railroad tunnel between France and England and the day of the ferries would soon be over. Denisov thought he would not miss it. He hated the hovercraft and detested the slow ferries with their cafeterias full of dreadful English food. He made the crossing twenty times a year. He could afford to fly, naturally, but there were reasons to take the land-and-sea route.

He saw the other man enter the green customs line marked *Nothing to Declare*. The man had only a small suitcase and he was stopped and told to open it. He did so. Denisov watched this and smiled. They never could find a thing. It was the first thing you learned, no matter what side you were on. If clumsy assassins like the Palestinians could do it, how much better the professionals could be.

Like us, Denisov thought with something like affection. Of course, he would just as gladly have killed the other man if it had been to his advantage.

At the moment, he was curious.

Devereaux crossed into the glittering and cheaply modern terminal which was typical of so many bad buildings put up by the British in the 1960s and 1970s.

He fell in beside Denisov without a word and then passed him as though they were strangers. Everyone is careful in the trade. Was Denisov watched? Devereaux became a second set of eyes behind his back, to see who the watchers might be.

Denisov waited in the terminal, puzzled, looking for a face of a friend.

Disappointed, Denisov turned and walked out in the gray day full of spray and the cry of sea gulls. Devereaux was nowhere to be seen. Devereaux had gone around the building, waiting for Denisov's retreat.

The other passengers pushed to get on buses that would deliver them to the train station in Dover and the tedious ride up the tracks to London. The pushers were French, of course; the English can tell the rude continentals from their own people.

The green buses belched black smoke and rattled away from the curbing.

Denisov was halfway up the road to the public house with the sign of the flying fish.

No one behind; no one before. No unaccounted plain cars full of intent men who seem to be waiting for someone. No careless men in trench coats pretending to light cigarettes into the face of the channel winds.

And Devereaux followed. They both knew the way to play this particular game.

Denisov sat in a corner of the dark, dirty, and quite somber public house with a pint of Bass ale before him and a copy of the *Wall Street Journal*'s European edition. There was a little time to kill before Devereaux joined him. He was a large, lethargic man, accustomed to waiting.

His eyes followed the lists of the stocks, up and down, searching for the acronyms of his holdings.

Devereaux sat down with a large glass of vodka,

chilled with ice. The English had grown more relaxed about ice in the last few years; they had given it away in public houses with less reluctance and less sense that they were surrendering the Crown Jewels.

Denisov did not look up from the paper. "You seem unchanged by the years," he said in the voice that still contained a stubborn, thick accent. He spoke English very well because he loved the language (which is why he had loved the merry cynicism of Gilbert); but accent cannot always be lost, perhaps as a reminder to the speaker that he is still a stranger in a strange world.

"It's old home week talk now?" Devereaux said.

Denisov sighed. Tribune stock—listed Trbn—was up 1½. He folded the paper shut. "You have no time for sentiment. For cheers? For *l'chaim*?" Denisov smiled, lifted his glass, nodded, and sipped.

Devereaux watched him. He was the careful agent now, not the careless man who had wandered through his days in Lausanne. He had been so careless because he had believed in his own myth, that he could shake the traces of the old trade.

He thought now all the time about that unfinished (perhaps unspoken) conversation he would have with Rita Macklin someday, if he survived this time.

"You are too serious," Denisov said. "Lighten yourself."

"Lighten up," Devereaux corrected.

"Yes," Denisov said. "Your message was insistent."

"I would not have interfered with your life unless I had to," Devereaux said. Denisov did not understand that this was going to be a serious matter after all.

"Of course." He said it with irony. "I thought you wanted my company."

"Two men are killed in Lausanne. The day before they are killed, they go to a place—a brasserie—and they terrorize a young Swiss girl with a stupid dialogue about how they are looking for me."

"I see. The girl—is she pretty?"

"She's young, which is better," Devereaux said.

Denisov stared at him without expression for a moment and then put a smile on his face. On purpose. He was an amiable bear, like the trained bear in the Soviet circus; and yet, a bear is a bear, with teeth and claws and strength and the instincts to kill when killing is necessary.

"So. These men." Denisov stared at his beer. "Do you owe them money? Perhaps they are brothers of the young girl and they wish her to stop seeing you. I think that you must be careful about who you go to bed with when you are in a foreign country." He smiled. "There are different customs."

"Yes. You'd know about that. The widow in California."

"I have so much to thank you for," Denisov said. The edge was bared. It was steel and cold and it killed. Denisov stared at Devereaux.

They had been spies against each other. And one day, when there was no other way, Devereaux had "defected" Denisov. Denisov had been trapped in America because Devereaux had made it so. He had lived on his hatred of Devereaux for three years—before Devereaux came to him in his hidden lair in California and decided to use him. Devereaux had let him free because it suited him to do so after Denisov had been used.

Once, in a car in Zurich, he had the chance to kill Devereaux. And he had hesitated. Why had he hesitated? He still hated him but he saw there was no hatred on the other side. Devereaux did not hate; therefore, Denisov thought, he could only use. Denisov was in the arms trade now and he was a rich man and he pitied Devereaux, who could only use. And who had scruples, in an odd way.

"So tell me about these men if you have to," Denisov said, shaking out of his thoughts.

"They go to my apartment the following day. They are killed there."

"By you."

"By a woman. A woman who kills in the professional way. There is a picture of her."

Captain Boll of the Swiss army had commissioned a drawing of the woman based on the description by the unfortunate young thug who had been hired to break a window in a building and lure the concierge out of it. He had been arraigned on various charges and he would go to prison for at least two years and he said the likeness was very good.

Denisov stared at the drawing for a moment.

There are some faces—even captured in an imprecise drawing—that are unforgettable.

He felt a strange stirring. He looked up. His face betrayed nothing. His hand framed the drawing on the table. Alexa.

"She might be beautiful," Denisov said.

"Yes."

"It is she who killed those men?"

"Yes."

"Why?"

"I think she came to kill me instead."

"I don't understand this."

Devereaux stared at the Russian in silence. Denisov

was very good. The eyes hid everything. Denisov glanced again at the drawing. For a moment. But it was too long a time, Devereaux thought. And the hand on the table still framed the picture.

"Who is she?" Devereaux said.

"I don't know."

The silence shared the space between them.

"How are things?" Devereaux said.

"Well."

"Business is booming."

"Perhaps," Denisov said.

"Perhaps you are too busy."

"No." Carefully. "Not too busy." And his hand on the table around the drawing was still.

"I want to know about her—"

"You are the agent, not I."

"You're close to the trade," Devereaux said. "To old sources and new ones."

"Perhaps."

"I set you up. With Krueger."

"I am so grateful."

"I don't expect to pay in gratitude," Devereaux said.

"You have your sources, comrade," Denisov said. "Why do I become involved?"

Devereaux said, "I defected you in Florida because there was no choice. And I sprung you from your golden prison in California because I had to use you. You're free, Denisov, freer than you ever were in the old trade." He paused, the eyes gray and level and even mocking: "I need to know about her. About two other men. And I need to know about a nutcracker."

This was too much. Denisov started. His eyes widened.

He knew too much to hide it this time. It was the last word he had expected the other man to utter.

And then Denisov smiled, a strange and dominating smile that broke in waves across the cold harsh presence of the other man.

"Nutcracker involves you?"

Devereaux stared at Denisov for a long time. "A man I once knew called me twice in Lausanne. Before these things happened. He babbled to me and I have been trying to remember the things he said. He talked about old spies and fictional spies and he sounded deranged."

"And he told you something about Nutcracker."

"He said he had a nutcracker when he was a child. It was such a strange thing to say. Even in the context. I thought about it then and now. I wanted to see what you knew. And you know, don't you, Russian?"

"I heard a rumor. In London three weeks ago. You know we have our gossips in the arms trade. Something is up. But no one knows what it is."

"But Nutcracker. It means something?"

"Why should I tell you anything?"

"What moves you, Russian?"

But Denisov saw. He smiled and it was genuine. "You are outside, are you not? That is what this is about. You are outside and you cannot go back to R Section and ask them for help. Is that it? I feel so terrible for you, my friend. It is bad for you, is it not?" The smile was very good and wide and open. "Is someone to kill you and you cannot save yourself?" The syntax was breaking down. "I think it would be terrible to make your woman weep for you. But then, these things must happen."

"How much money?" Devereaux said.

"Let me enjoy myself for a minute," Denisov said. "It gives me pleasure to think you must need me. I owe you so much."

"Fifty thousand dollars," Devereaux said.

The smile faded. The blank face of the careful agent replaced it.

"There is an aerospace company in California. They are to award the contract. I mean, they will receive the contract for a certain plane. I think no one knows this now except your government. So for four thousand shares of stock, perhaps I will become even more a capitalist."

"That's insider trading, Denisov. It's against the law."

Denisov did not smile.

"You can't fix Wall Street," Devereaux said.

"There is no free dinner."

"Free lunch."

"Agreed," Denisov said.

"It will be done," Devereaux said. "Now tell me about Nutcracker."

"I know nothing. It was a phrase. A subcontractor in London who must think he knows everything but he knows nothing. He said there was chatter out of Cheltenham, the Americans were working on something called Nutcracker. That was all. Realignment of networks in Berlin. But it was chatter, even gossip, and you know that Cheltenham is a sieve. You cannot believe anything that comes from there."

Cheltenham was the mole-ridden listening post shared by the Americans and British in the English west country. Cheltenham eavesdropped on the radio "chatter" of the world and tried to make sense of all that it heard. Nutcracker was a name, something that had been dropped by computer or transatlantic phone or radio transmitter—it was an odd name of some odd thing that had struck Denisov in memory and now, in this damp and dirty public house in Dover, had been retrieved by a retired American agent.

"And you know this one," Devereaux said. He was pointing at the picture.

"I do not think so."

"When will you tell me who she is?"

"Perhaps I must understand what this is. What this is about. So there is no danger for me," Denisov said. "I do not trust you too far."

"This does not concern you."

"I will see if that is true."

"She came to kill me. Who is she?"

"Perhaps I do not know yet. Perhaps in a little time, I will know."

"KGB," Devereaux said.

"Perhaps."

"And these are photographs of the men she killed."

They were morgue shots, obtained from Boll along with the drawing of the woman. One of the faces had been obliterated.

"I do not know them."

"I do. They were KGB. Resolutions Committee."

"They wore cards? Did they tell you before they died?"

"They were identified."

"And KGB kills KGB?"

Devereaux stared into the eyes of the saint. "Yes. Think about it: KGB kills KGB."

"And R Section?" Denisov tried a shy smile. "Does R Section kill its own?"

"Perhaps."

"Someone called you. In Lausanne. And then these things happen. Do you kill R Section, my friend? Is R Section to kill you?"

Devereaux said nothing.

"You speak madness," Denisov said. "You say nothing to me but your quiet is madness. You want me to say that KGB kills its own and that R Section kills its own? Speak, my friend, and tell me why I should play this mad game for you."

"For four thousand shares of stock," Devereaux said.

Denisov sighed. "My weakness. It is my only weakness."

"It's greed."

"I am a careful man."

"You stole from KGB when you worked the Resolutions Committee. You steal now. I don't care. I want to know about this woman. And about Nutcracker—"

"Four thousand shares. Must I trust you?"

"I will call Krueger and make the purchase through him. Is that satisfactory?"

Krueger was a man in Zurich who kept all the accounts and knew all the numbers and was an honest broker for every side because he was on no side but his own. Denisov nodded.

"He holds them until you deliver," Devereaux said.

"Good. Be careful. Always be careful and do not trust too much," Denisov said.

17

FAMILY

Leo said he didn't mind. Leo was an easygoing sort of man, which suited Lydia Neumann to a T. They always drove in spring. Sometimes to Florida, sometimes to Canada for the last of the winter carnivals in places like Montreal and Quebec City. They brought their own weather with them, their mutual comforts, their sense of each other. It was hard to believe that after seventeen years of marriage they still wanted to be alone with each other. They had no children and yet they still expected children in the vague and rosy future.

They went to the Midwest this time because Lydia had to see the woman in Chicago.

"Besides," Leo had said, "I haven't been in Chicago since the navy. Took boot camp at Great Lakes. We went down to Chicago on Saturday and used to hang around the Walgreen drugstore in the Loop, right on State Street. Wait for the girls to come down and look for us. We had a lot of fun."

"Did you meet many girls, Leo?"

"Oh, some. I guess. I don't remember."

He did remember, of course. Lydia smiled fondly at her husband.

And yet she was not relaxed. She had to do this one thing. She probably should not even do this.

Leo was to spend the morning in the Loop, staring up at the tall buildings as though he had never seen such wonders. The day was bright, crisp, full of crowds on the wide walks of Michigan Avenue. The old elevated trains rattled around the screeching curves of the Loop. Leo had a Polaroid camera and took lots of pictures of buildings, monuments, the Picasso statue and the Chagall Wall, and of pretty girls on Dearborn Street who reminded him of all the pretty girls he had known as a sailor a long time before.

Lydia Neumann entered the IBM Consumer Product Center precisely at nine A.M. At 9:02, the attractive black woman, in businesslike attire from Saks Fifth Avenue down the street, crossed to her, smiled the automatic IBM smile, and took her to see the woman visible in the glass office beyond the carpeting.

"Hello."

The voice belonged to a breed of professional class raised in the last generation that has no regional inflection, no accent, no betrayal in voice of any background at all. The voice suited her surroundings and her looks. She was a white replica of the black woman with a different wardrobe. Her eyes were defined in a businesslike way by eyeliner—just enough—and her mouth by lipstick—not too much. Her clothes spoke of being a bit more expensive than one might expect from one so young. Her blouse was silk but not revealing. Her hair was mousey brown and broken up into swaths to reveal a $125 haircut.

Lydia Neumann patted her own spikes created by Leo every three weeks or so. She sat down and didn't smile and waited for the smile of the young woman to fade.

"How can I help you?" The voice was eager, formless, nearly a controlled squeal. It revealed nothing.

"My name is Neumann but you musn't mention that again," Lydia Neumann said. She felt the weight of what she was about to do. What did any of it have to do with her? And then she thought of Hanley.

"All right, Ms. Neumann." She was as uncluttered as her office. Her figure was slight and everything about her was what Mrs. Neumann hoped she would not find. Still, she had to try. It was all she could do.

"I work. In an agency. Of government."

She let the words sink in. They didn't. The young woman with the poised Mont Blanc pen and the unringed fingers and the recent Bahamian tan was not impressed because it meant nothing to her.

It was hopeless, Lydia Neumann thought.

And then she thought of Hanley and tried again.

Perhaps her face reflected some anger.

"He is all you have. And all he has," she said.

"I beg your pardon, Ms. Neumann?" At least she dropped the pen this time.

"Margot Kieker," she said, pronouncing the name of the young woman. "Your great-uncle I'm talking about."

The doll blinked.

It walks and talks, said Mrs. Neumann to herself.

"Uncle Hanley," said Margot Kieker.

"He has a first name—" began Lydia Neumann.

"It doesn't matter." For a moment, she caught the dull trace in the voice of the doll-face. The blue-rimmed eyes blinked, while precisely defined lashes met and separated. Her eyes were very blue, Lydia Neumann saw, clear and cloudless as though they had never seen any rainy days.

"We called him that. If anyone thought to speak of him. My grandmother ... Ten years older than he was. Cancer. And then, my mother. My mother died six years ago."

Lydia Neumann waited.

"Do you think it runs in families?"

"What?"

"Cancer," said Margot Kieker.

"Yes," she said, to be cruel, to break through to the doll. But it wouldn't work.

"So do I. There's nothing to do about it," said Margot Kieker, the voice becoming soft, intimate. But not with Lydia Neumann. It was the voice of herself speaking to herself. Her eyes were seeing far away on a bright Monday morning in Chicago.

Then she snapped awake again and stared at Lydia. "Uncle Hanley. You work with him?"

"Yes."

"How is he?"

"He's in a hospital," began Mrs. Neumann. She had planned what she would say to this strange creature all the way out to Chicago. They had traveled a while through the panhandle of Maryland, through the mountains that enclose the narrow valleys in the west of the state. It was the part of the state that lies beneath the weight of Pennsylvania coal country. The part where Hanley was being held in a hospital of a special kind.

Lydia Neumann had checked on Hanley's question. The drugs he was given were very powerful psychoactive

compounds and when she had asked a friend of hers
to describe them—a man who knew the secrets of
pharmaceuticals—he had been uncomfortable with the
question. At last, he had explained that knowledge of
such drugs constituted a breach of security in itself. He
wouldn't say any more. He had worked in the secret drug
experiments at Aberdeen Proving Ground in Maryland in
the 1960s and he had managed to stay out of trouble by
being discreet.

Lydia Neumann had felt terribly frightened. When she
had gone back to see Hanley the following week, her fear
had increased.

Hanley had been moved out of Ward Seven to Ward
Zero. It was a ward not listed in the organizational charts
of the mental hospital. He could receive no visitors. He
was reported to be terribly ill and terribly depressed.

"Your great-uncle is in an asylum. Against his will.
There have been no procedures to put him there. Nothing
very legal, I think. And I think he is in terrible trouble
unless you go to help him."

"But I haven't seen him since I was a baby. My mother
never spoke of him. There was some slight. Some family
business between my grandmother and him. They were
brother and sister and—"

"You are his flesh." She said it as well as any preacher
might have done. Mrs. Neumann, in her great raspy voice,
said things of certainty with a certainty of expression that
made no mistake about her beliefs. She was refreshing in
that, even to someone as cynical as Hanley had been.

"Flesh," said Margot Kieker as though the word did
not belong in this cool, gleaming room.

"Flesh and blood. It carries weight in law. You are his

relative and he has been committed against his will to an asylum. In Maryland. You have to get him out."

"But. I don't understand. Is he insane?"

It was the question Mrs. Neumann had pondered as well. Like an unfinished conversation, there was no answer. Let that conversation wait for a time.

"No," she said, without believing it. "The point is: He is very ill. He is very, very ill and I can't see him."

"Are you his friend?" she said.

"Yes," said Mrs. Neumann without thinking.

"Are you his lover?"

Mrs. Neumann laughed and both of them realized that laughter did not belong in this holy place full of holy things of a new age.

Margot Kieker tried on a smile approved by the company.

Mrs. Neumann responded. "No, dear, not his lover. I am...his friend." To say the word again, deliberately, seemed strange to her. She had never been in Hanley's home and he had declined all invitations to visit her and Leo. Hanley was the solitary man, enjoying his solitary nature. Or, at least, accepting it as a priest accepts the restraints on friendship and love in his vocation.

"That's very nice of you to be concerned about him," Margot Kieker said. It was the sweet butter sentiment of the prairies. Then her lips snapped shut like a purse. The sentimental visit was over. The workday was beginning and Margot Kieker was fresh and starched.

"You're not interested in a computer then?"

Mrs. Neumann blinked.

Margot stared at her, the mouth poised to register an emotion—if appropriate.

"Yes, I am interested in computers," said Mrs. Neumann, saying too much to a stranger. She felt angry and embarrassed. She had gone out of her way to save her "friend" and it was nothing more to this creature than if she had gone across the street to buy a newspaper.

Mrs. Neumann opened a paper file and pushed it on the desk. It was a computer printout that told most of the story of Hanley's life.

"Do you know what this is?"

"A résumé?"

"It is a print of Hanley's 201 file. I've made some deletions because there are . . . matters that do not concern you. What concerns you is the bottom line, honey."

The "honey" was intended to shock but it sailed over Margot Kieker. She didn't even blink. She guided her eyes to the place on the printout indicated by Mrs. Neumann. She frowned.

"This isn't our company's computer. I've never seen that typeface in our training modules and—"

"Look at what it says, honey."

This time, the edge of a frown. Mrs. Neumann figured she could get through in six or seven weeks of intense confrontation. It must be the same as deprogramming a Jesus freak: The intellectual argument never counted because there was no intelligence involved.

"I don't understand," said Margot Kieker. And she licked her lip, slowly and unconsciously, reading the words.

"His government insurance policy, his own insurance policy, his benefits, and title to a vacant bit of land in New Jersey he had acquired. It is his will. Every agent"—she almost bit her lip—"every employee in our section is required to file the will in the 201 file."

Margot Kieker looked up. "Why leave this to me?"

"Family," said Lydia Neumann.

"But I don't even know him."

"Flesh and blood," Mrs. Neumann preached.

"But I don't understand," Margot Kieker said.

"No." Softly. "No." Defeated. "You don't, do you? But you are going to have to. Or are you some kind of a monster?"

18

November Is Coming

Claymore Richfield, the director of research for R Section, gathered the signals (written on "yellow-for-caution" paper) and put them down neatly on Yackley's desk at 9:06 Eastern time Friday morning. He arranged the yellow three-by-five notices in such a pattern that they formed an outline of a Mercator map projection. The first signals—and sources—moved from the east to the west.

"He doesn't move at all unobtrusively, does he?" Yackley thought to say. He felt fear closing him in a bag. He stared hard at the photographs of his wife and daughter on the desk as though they might be obliterated at any moment.

"So it appears," Claymore Richfield said, tapping his stained front teeth with the eraser end of a Number 2 pencil. The tap had a beat—the exact beat of "Sweet Georgia Brown" in fact—but it just sounded like tap, tap, tap to Yackley. He looked up in annoyance at Richfield, who was staring out the window at the mass of the Bureau of Engraving across the street. Even old Engraving inspired Richfield: He had in mind a hard, holistic dollar to replace the paper dollar, just as various credit cards were now designed. The "hard dollar" would inspire public confidence in currency again, he reasoned, and make it more difficult to stash or make illegal transactions. A "hard dollar" would be harder to counterfeit as well. The people at Treasury were appalled by the idea.

"So it appears," Yackley repeated. "Does that mean the information isn't any good or does that mean we don't care enough to check on bona fides?"

"Not in this case," Claymore Richfield said. He had been pressed into temporary service as acting director of Computer and Analysis during Mrs. Neumann's absence.

"What do you mean?"

"There is unusual traffic. Some of it radio, radio computer, some of it routine filings. Devereaux left Switzerland openly on Tuesday, told the police his destination, used his own passport. He even contacted his lawyer. He made himself the talk of the town. On Wednesday, he appeared in London and used Economic Review facilities for all sorts of inquiries that are—at the moment—still secret. He paid for them in cash and ER has a policy about this sort of thing."

ER was the London-based research tank and resource center used by public and private intelligence agencies from countries on both sides of the Curtain.

"What could he be preparing for?"

"Perhaps nothing," Claymore Richfield said. "He's a good one, our November."

"He's not 'our' November. He's a goddamn renegade agent, he's killed two of our men—"

"Our chasers," corrected Richfield. "Casual laborers."

"Two of our men," repeated Yackley, trying to raise

his voice a tone or two, to impress the other man. It was pointless. Claymore Richfield wore Levi's when he met the President at the White House. He was a loyalist to Yackley but a difficult one.

"Thursday, he flew into Toronto on Air Canada out of London. That's been the end of it. Of course, he used his own passport. We picked up all the routine entries out of Toronto—as usual—and there he was. Using 'Devereaux' even." Claymore Richfield smiled at that. "He's coming our way. He's in Washington by now."

"How do you know?"

"I don't. We can't sweep the hotel registers as easily as the French used to do. But he's here. I sent along a couple of boys from Operations to do the police routine. For all I know, he's at the Watergate by now," Richfield said, referring to the famous hotel and office complex above Georgetown.

Yackley bit his lip and said nothing.

There were some things he felt he couldn't say to Richfield.

It was time to consult Perry Weinstein again. Quickly. About the matter of sanctions.

19

METHODS

Devereaux had been professor of Asian Studies at Columbia University in New York City when he had been recruited to R Section in 1966. The lure had been Asia. He would go to the land of blood-red morning suns and the eternal fog that hung over the endless rice paddies; he would go and squat down in the rich delta earth with peasants with wizened faces and flat and serene eyes and attempt to understand that part of him that yearned for Asia as for a lover. He would be an intelligence agent, of course, but that was the means; it was never the end.

The means became the ends. Then the means obliterated the ends. The Asian earth was pounded by death from skies, the paddies turned red with blood, the jungle crawled over all—over civilization, over conqueror and defeated, over the living and the dead. Over Devereaux. He had gone to Asia to find his soul; instead, he had lost it there.

Devereaux had learned to think during the years in school in which he had earned his doctorate in history.

He had always known how to think on the level of the street: On the street, thought was part of instinct, part of conditioning. It is thought that makes the fighter choose the combination that breaks the defense of his opponent and lets him come inside and tear away the flailing arms and land hammerblows on face and chest and belly until the weight of the other cannot stand any more; those who don't understand call it instinct, as though instinct were something that could not be developed as part of thought.

Devereaux knew the street and knew street thinking; he had just grown lazy in that regard in the idyllic months of Lausanne. He had allowed himself to be circled and nearly trapped.

The other part of thought was reason and the key was research. There was no other way around it. With a certain number of facts, a certain number of theories could be put together.

He had the facts now. Not all of them. It was not so difficult.

He sat in the glow of a single lamp in Hanley's living room. The apartment was unchanged from the day nearly three weeks before when two men had come to take Mr. Hanley away. They were described by the doorman and by the super in the building.

No. No one had seen Mr. Hanley again since they came to take him away in the ambulance. Yes, he had been home a lot; he had been ill. Yes, Mr. Hanley continued to pay rent on his apartment; probably part of some government insurance plan. No. No one had come to visit Mr. Hanley or his apartment after that first day. They mentioned the name on the ambulance that had taken Hanley away. He took down the name and looked it up.

The answers were so prosaic that they were undoubtedly true. Devereaux had very little difficulty in gaining entry to Hanley's flat. He had various badges and cards of authority; he had authorized papers to search the premises. Besides, people wanted someone to be in that flat again. It wasn't natural for a flat to be empty all this time. It just wasn't right.

Devereaux spent three hours in going through Hanley's life, scattered in the apartment, to find a clue. Not to his disappearance. That would be solved in time. But to Devereaux's part in it.

Once again he was the scholar on the trail of just a few facts. He was the student in study hall at the University of Chicago again. He was waiting as he pushed his way through graduate theses, through long-forgotten letters written by long-forgotten people, through books that had not been removed from the stacks for decades: He was waiting for first the one fact and then the second and then the third to fall from the pages in patterns and for the patterns to be seen at last in his mind.

Sometimes the patterns had come very late at night, in the room he lived in on Ellis Avenue down the street from the university complex. Sometimes they came in thoughts before sleep; sometimes, the pattern fell out with morning coffee. But the pattern was always apparent at last because Devereaux had prepared his brain to receive it.

There were insurance policies set out on Hanley's desk. Hanley had a desk as plain as the desk in his office. His whole apartment was furnished with plain and useful furniture, without regard for elegance, grace, even beauty. Perhaps all the furniture had been left here by a previous tenant; it had that feeling of anonymity, like the man himself.

The perfect spy.

Devereaux smiled. He read the policies and noted the name of the beneficiary: Margot Kieker.

The policies were laid on his desk because Hanley was thinking about death. In that sense, his telephone calls to Devereaux had been honest. And if he had not been in his apartment for three weeks—and had been off the job for weeks before that—then Hanley had not set the operation against him.

But who had? And for what purpose?

There was so little of Hanley in the apartment with pearl-gray walls and mournful tall windows and dark furniture and large bare rooms.

Save a single sheet of paper found in a spring-locked false panel beneath the last drawer on the right side of his desk. Devereaux would have missed it. He had shifted his weight in the brown leather chair at the desk and accidentally kicked at the drawer and the panel had dropped. After it dropped, he began to dismantle the desk and the other furniture in the room. He did the job as quietly as he could. He broke apart the desk and the bureau in the bedroom.

But there was only the single sheet of paper.

It was standard 16-pound typing paper, white, 8½ by 11 inches.

In ink, at the top, was written a single word in block letters, as though Hanley decided on the word as a title for an essay. (He could not be sure it was Hanley's handwriting; he had never seen it.)

NUTCRACKER

Below the single word were other words, lined up neatly flush left but in a slightly smaller handwriting:

January
New Moon
Equinox
June
August
Vernal
Winter

And below that, in a handwriting that might have been added later:

November?

The words fell out into his mind, formed patterns like falling leaves, fell wildly against the void of blackness. He waited for thought. He waited for the meaning of the words. He waited calmly in the light of a single lamp in the apartment. And after a time, he folded the paper, put it in his jacket. He turned out the lamp, closed the door, and left the building.

There were two approaches. They had been taught this at the training school in Maryland where he became an agent a long time before. The first approach is always best: To effect some sort of bluff of officialdom when approaching another for information. Most people are intimidated by those who appear to be officials or in charge, even if they are actually trained in the same business. No one wants unnecessary trouble.

The approach wasn't going to work.

The young man in steel-rimmed glasses had a wise,

mocking look to him and Devereaux waited while he read through the bona fides Devereaux had purchased in London. He wasn't going to buy any of it.

The ambulance garage was on Sixth Street N.E., in a shabby section of Washington just east of Union Station. The garage was made of brick. It was one story high and the few windows carried bars on them. The windows were darkened by soot. The entrance of the garage was barred by a large Doberman pinscher, who set up a racket when Devereaux entered.

The man in the steel-rimmed glasses was not alone. He wore a white uniform and his shirt was open enough to reveal most of a pale, muscular chest. He had the easy grace of an athlete as he walked across the oil-stained floor. Devereaux waited in front of the barking dog.

"Come on, Tiger," the young man said at last, waiting until the last moment to restrain the dog. "Go on over there, Tiger."

Devereaux said who he was and why he had come. The young man looked at the papers and looked at Devereaux and looked at the dog. The second man, larger and softer, was in a sort of office at the back of the garage. There were sixteen bays in the garage, four occupied by ambulances, three by private cars, and one by a brand-new black Cadillac hearse.

"For the ones you don't get to the hospital," Devereaux said.

The young man looked up, annoyed, turned, saw the point of the joke. He grinned without pleasure. "Yeah. Something like that. You don't leave anyone in the place where he dies."

Devereaux was thinking about the dog. It was a shame.

Because the kid wasn't going to buy it the easy way. And Devereaux didn't have all that much time.

Devereaux shifted on his feet and the dog sensed the shift and gurgled a growl. But the young man kept reading.

"I don't get it," he said. "So what do you want?"

"I want to see some of your records over the past two months. Delivery schedules, you might say."

"I'm not sure I can do that," the young man said.

"What's your name?"

"Sellers," he said. "What's your name?"

Cocky.

"It's on my identification."

"I never heard of identification like this."

"Maybe you've never had an insurance inspector come around before."

"We have insurance guys—"

"We're the guys who check up on insurance guys." The line had worked in the apartment, of course, because the people there wanted to believe in him. But Sellers knew. And it was too bad.

"Come on back to the office," said Sellers. "Let's talk to Jerry." Devereaux had not expected that.

It was late afternoon. Sunlight tried to fight its way through the dark windows but it was a losing battle. Caged lights hanging from the ceiling provided the only illumination.

The office was three stairs up at the back of the garage.

The walls were bright yellow and covered with graffiti and calendars. Miss National Hardware Convention held a wrench in one hand and showed her bottom.

The desks were butted into one wall and littered

with bits of paper. There was grease on the chairs. Jerry was taller than Devereaux but his eyes looked a shade slower.

And the dog was outside. That was just as well. Not that it would have mattered.

Devereaux figured they would have made a call by now.

He walked into the room ahead of Sellers and when Sellers was nearly through the door, Devereaux turned suddenly and flung him at the second man.

But Sellers was braced. He only stumbled. Jerry pulled out a pistol.

Just a shade slow in the eyes.

Devereaux fired up and the bullet caught him flat in the throat. It was a small-caliber pistol—the Colt Python .357 Magnum was in the custody of the Swiss army captain named Boll—but it was good enough.

The dog was barking like mad and flinging itself against the door.

Sellers was deafened by the explosion. He turned and stared at Devereaux. His blue eyes were very wide. Jerry slid down the wall.

"I don't have any time," Devereaux said.

"We don't keep the records here."

"Sure you do."

"I'm telling you—"

"When you do a job for an agency, you keep one copy of the records." It was said like a dead man was not in the same room.

"I don't know what you're talking about."

Devereaux said, "Take off your glasses."

Sellers removed his wire-rims carefully.

"Give them to me."

Sellers handed them to Devereaux, who stood with the pistol in hand.

Devereaux dropped them. He stepped on them and broke them.

"Glass," Devereaux said. "I thought everyone used plastic."

"I've got another pair," Sellers said. He almost smirked. He was tough enough, Devereaux thought. No one was tough enough to stand up forever but the tough ones could wait you out. Especially if they had made a phone call and they were waiting for reinforcements.

Devereaux put the pistol in his pocket. There just wasn't enough time.

"Come on," he said.

"Tiger is waiting," Sellers said.

"And I don't want to kill the dog," Devereaux said. "You see the way it is."

The voice was reasoned and Sellers saw the way it was. He'd get this guy, there was no question of that. But there had to be a little room to do it. And the guy sure had dropped Jerry. Jesus Christ, he'd dropped Jerry without even thinking about it.

There are slums in Washington very nearly as bad as those in cities like New York or Chicago. They are the best places in the country to conduct business without interference from people in authority.

Or people who might be looking for you.

It is true that most urban slums are inhabited by blacks and that the presence of two white men—like the two white men who now entered the house on Eleventh Street N.E.—might appear odd to the neighbors. But one of the

men—the man with the graying hair and the hard face—
that man had already turned the right color. He was green.
He had green and it came up front. And he was Syndicate,
there was no doubt about that. You can tell the Syndicate
because those boys look right through the back of your
head. So don't mess with the man—this was the advice of
Junius Falkner to his nephew—don't mess with the man,
let him have the room he wants, just you go 'bout your
business and you say none to him. Even if the other white
man was blindfolded.

It was not what Sellers had expected at all.

Devereaux tore off the blindfold. The room was illuminated by three lamps fed off a single outlet. The single outlet looked like an octopus with streams of wires
running from the core. There was a television set and a
linoleum floor and a single bed with a swayback mattress
covered with dirty sheets. There was a second mattress
on the linoleum itself. There was a wooden table, painted
green, and three chairs. Rooms like this always have three
chairs. The single window was bolted with burglar bars
and there were roaches above the sink on the far wall. The
far wall was only eleven feet from the entry door.

The room smelled of neglect, dirt, and fear.

Sellers thought, for the first time, that the fear might be
coming from him.

The gray man indicated one of the straight chairs. Sellers sat down. He was still blinded. He blinked and his
eyes teared.

"I suppose you can't see very well. Do you want me to
describe the room?"

Devereaux's voice was flat but it was not heavy. It was
the voice of a doctor asking a patient how he felt and

not really caring because the doctor already knew the diagnosis.

"Where the hell are we?"

"Where people don't look for other people."

"But we're still in the District?"

"Perhaps."

"Man, you made me ride around in a trunk. That's shit, you know, man?"

"Sellers. What do you do?"

"I drive an ambulance."

"That isn't what I asked you."

"I drive an ambulance."

Devereaux hit him very hard, probably as hard as he had been struck by Captain Boll on that warm spring morning in the Lausanne police station. The difference was that Devereaux had expected the blow; the room was bright; Devereaux knew where he stood with Boll... there were so many differences. And this blow came down hard on the bridge of Sellers' nose and broke it. They both heard the crack.

Sellers made a fuss. The blood broke down both nostrils and he tasted his own blood and his eyes teared because of the pain. He held his face, and when he tried to get up Devereaux shoved him back down on the chair at the table. He finally began to sob. When you taste your own blood, the reality of the situation penetrates.

Devereaux waited without a word for a long time. Sellers was such a small part of whatever it was that was happening. He was the corner of a package that had come unraveled and had to be worked loose before you could get to the rest of the wrapping.

Devereaux's code name had been the last name on the

sheet of paper in Hanley's desk. Why the question mark? And what did the other names mean? They were obviously the names of other R Section agents—but why were they listed together? And what was Nutcracker?

The questions nagged while he waited for Sellers to think through the pain. The questions made Devereaux impatient.

He pulled Sellers' oily black hair up until Sellers almost had to rise out of the chair.

"Oh, Christ," he screamed.

And Devereaux banged his face on the edge of the table again, breaking again that which had already been broken.

Sellers passed out.

When he awoke, he was on the floor, bathed in blood, and the swimming image of the other man remained. It was as horrible as the endless nightmare he had once floated through during a long and terrible acid trip.

"All right," he said. "Jesus, man, don't do that again, I can't even breathe, I'm breathing my own blood."

"Who do you work for? What do you do?" It was the quiet voice.

"I work for Mr. Ivers. I swear to God about that. I just work for a guy named Ivers who comes around every day and he tells me what to do. Sometimes it's a straight pickup. You know, an old lady in a nursing home finally stops straining the family budget and we pick her up—old ladies are light, you know, like birds—and we take them to the funeral home. Sometimes we do funeral work. You know, a pinch. All over the place."

"This isn't getting me anywhere," Devereaux said. His voice was very soft and it frightened Sellers to hear it.

"All right. All right, man, lay off, will you? Some-times. Sometimes we get a pickup order."

"What's a pickup order?"

"Special stuff. It's a government order. Got stamps on it. You know, all that tiny print and them pictures of eagles on them."

"Where do they come from?"

"Orders from all over. Orders from Defense, orders from Treasury. You'd be surprised."

"And what are the orders?"

"Man, I don't want to get in trouble, you know?"

Devereaux said, "If you tell me everything I want to know, and it's the truth, then I won't kill you. If you don't tell me everything, or you try to lie to me, then I will kill you but it will take a long time. And in the end, you'll still tell me everything I want to know."

"Who are you, man?" Sellers was sniffling because of the blood and the fluids in his mouth and nose. His sinuses hurt; that was the least of it.

"The last man you ever wanted to see," Devereaux said.

They waited. The building was full of sounds. There were children running in the halls, shouting and threaten-ing; there were television sets full of canned laughter.

"We get pickup orders. They use our service. We take them where we're supposed to take them."

"Where's that?"

"Couple of places. There's a place in Virginia, down near Roanoke, called the U.S. Center for Disease Isola-tion Control and Rehabilitation. That's for ones that got contagious diseases, you know. The ones you don't send to Atlanta. We got to wear masks and rubber gloves when we handle them. We don't get many of them but I don't like those cases."

"And who are these people?"

"I don't know."

They waited.

"I really swear to God I don't know. I mean, I got guesses, but I don't know."

"Go ahead and guess."

"Man, it's plain, isn't it? They fucked up with the government, man, didn't they? You got to get rid of people sometimes. I mean, nobody says that to me but what the fuck do you think it would be about? You gotta be a genius to see that or what?"

Silence. This time the waiting was exhausted. There was no menace to it.

"Tell me about the other places," Devereaux said. In another part of the building, someone was listening to a very loud rendition of *The Cosby Show*. The children were laughing. A warm spring night in the capital of the United States.

"St. Catherine's. That's out beyond Hancock in Maryland? You know where—"

But Devereaux knew suddenly. He was listening but he knew. The R Section had its training base in the rugged mountains of western Maryland, the same line of Appalachians that ran down from Pennsylvania and the deep mining valleys, down through the panhandle, down into Virginia and North Carolina and eastern Tennessee. He had heard vague rumors then about government contracts with various hospitals, to take care of mentally unhinged agents. And now, their directors.

Places that were secure.

Places that were under control.

Hanley was a director.

There are no spies. Hanley's words suddenly surged into consciousness from wherever they had been buried and floated like a leaf.

"You went to a building about five or six weeks ago. It was in northwest Washington. There was a pickup. A man about fifty-five or sixty, man was bald, had big eyes. A man with blue eyes." He began the careful description of Hanley, creating the photograph from memory.

Sellers waited again. "Is that what this is about?"

"Yes," Devereaux said.

"This is about that one old man?"

"Who gave the order? And where did it come from?"

"Mr. Ivers. Like always."

"Where did it come from?"

"I don't remember that."

"You see. That's where you fail me. You fail to tell me exactly what I want to know."

He saw the other man rise. He felt the pressure of Devereaux's foot on his left hand.

"No, man," Sellers said.

"Where did it come from?"

"All right. Let me think. Just give me a damned minute, will you? Let me think about it."

He closed his eyes and tried to see the order.

He opened his eyes.

"Okay."

"Okay," Devereaux repeated.

"I didn't remember because I never heard of it before. Is that okay?"

"All right."

"Department of Agriculture," said Sellers, "Isn't that a kick? How the hell does the Department of Agriculture have any secrets? Can you figure that out for me?"

"What section in the Department of Agriculture?"

"Man, gimme a break. I don't read the whole damned thing. It goes on for pages. You know, name and judgment and all that jazz. I just look at the place I'm supposed to take him and if I'm gonna need to use restraints. We had to use restraints."

"I suppose you did," Devereaux said. It was broken. At least the part of it that would involve Sellers. The problem was what to do with Sellers.

Sellers lay on the floor, blinded and gagging on his own blood. He never realized that Devereaux was deciding his life in that moment of silence. Sellers thought it had all been settled.

Devereaux counted on his own survival—alone—once. And there was now that unfinished conversation in mind with Rita Macklin. She would say:

And you want to go back to that?

And he would say:

I protect myself. I make decisions for my own survival.

And she would say:

The good agent. (He knew her tone of voice.) Well, maybe it's not good enough for me. No, not good enough at all.

They found Sellers on Saturday afternoon, locked in the trunk of a Budget rent-a-car parked in the crowded lot at National Airport, in the spaces reserved for Congressmen.

He was really upset and very frightened when they found him.

20

DEATH COMES TO THE TAXMAN

Kaplan died shortly after dawn on Saturday.
Hanley had been unaware of his death, though they shared the same room.

Kaplan had made a noise, started, been still.

Kaplan was the tax accountant who worked for IRS and had devised the Church of Tax Rebellion, also incorporated as the Church of Jesus Christ, Taxpayer. The death of the prophet went unnoticed for two hours.

Hanley had awakened suddenly at seven and pressed the button. The button was all-important. It was his last link to life. He was sinking away, into himself; he would be dead in a little while.

His arms were scrawny and his eyes bulged.

He did not read or watch television.

He would stare in the darkness at night; and into the light during the day. He would see nothing. His eyes seemed to react very badly to the things around him. He knew smells: The smell of Sister Domitilla, the smell of Dr. Goddard. He heard voices but they were from far away.

There was the voice of his sister Mildred. And his mother. And the voice, very deep and very slow and very certain, of his father.

There was the voice of the Reverend Millard Van der Rohe in the pulpit of the plain wooden Presbyterian church on Sunday. The smell of dust on summer afternoons coming through the plain windows. Women with paper fans from a funeral home fanning themselves. The sweat breaking in stains across their broad backs. Men sitting as solemn as the church, listening to the words of the Lord.

And sometimes, he heard the Lord as well.

The Lord explained things to him in such a simple and wonderful way that Hanley felt glad.

He freely confessed his sins to the Lord and the Lord was as kind as the face of his mother. The Lord reached for his hand and took it and made it warm. The Lord spoke of green valleys.

Hanley became aware again.

They were closing the curtain that divided Mr. Kaplan's bed from his own in the small white room. The room did not have a couch. No one in the room was expected to stay for a long while. There were no restraints. No one needed them. Age restrained; illness restrained; the weakness that comes at the end restrained.

Hanley waited for them to feed him. He felt like a baby again and that was comfortable. In a little while, he would go to the Lord, who had the face of his mother. The Lord smelled of his mother's smells. The Lord comforted him. He would lie down in green pastures. There was a summer storm coming across the meadows and he was a child in the pasture, watching the magnificent approach of the high black thunderclouds eating up the blue sky, tumbling up and up with power and majesty and glory.

He had never felt so close to God.

21

NOT MONSTERS

William said she did the right thing. Of course, she called him by his nickname but when she thought of him, she thought of him as William.

William was a software programmer and he wore very white shirts to work every day.

They had met at one of those little group parties that form after computer conventions. She had been attracted to him by his stern face, his light brown hair, and the expanse of white covering his chest. He seemed very serious and sincere. They had shared Virgin Marys together and made a date that first meeting.

They both liked music in the little clubs on Lincoln Avenue. They both lived in the Lincoln Park neighborhood and cared for plants that insisted on dying anyway. William had a cat named Samantha, which Margot Kieker thought was real cute, and it was rather touching in William to have a cat at all. The cat didn't like Margot. She was used to that. At least William liked her.

He had theories about the seriousness of the world. He didn't like black people very much because he had never met very many of them; but he wasn't prejudiced at all. He once voted Democratic and then stopped voting until Reagan. He was twenty-eight and he owned a condo and a BMW.

William said Margot did not owe a thing to some distant relative she barely remembered. Someone named "Uncle Hanley."

For two days, she carefully cleaned her apartment, thought about William, sold $32,000 in hardware and software for the new PC line of computers, played her complete file of Boston Pops records, and thought about an old man named Hanley.

Lydia Neumann met her at 8:30 in the coffee shop of the Blackstone Hotel, where the Neumanns were staying. Leo was up and about already but he was not involved in this; it was better to keep it separate. Leo and Lydia had a lot of separate compartments and that kept them together.

Margot Kieker was drinking a Coke. Actually, a Diet Coke. And carefully applying strawberry jam to her whole wheat toast.

Lydia Neumann sat down heavily and saw no change in Margot Kieker. The hair was precise, the makeup muted, the face unlined, the eyes unclouded. No worry, no sleepless nights, no fears of tomorrow. The future was perfectly assured. Lydia Neumann felt disgust for the creature in front of her. And yet, there was curiosity as well.

"You don't understand me," began Margot without looking up from her toast. She was saying words that were unpleasant and she never wished to be unpleasant. There had been unpleasantness last night when she had explained to William what she was going to do. Well, that was unpleasantness enough to last for one week.

"This really is too much," Lydia Neumann said in her best voice. It was the voice of her Aunt Millie. It defined the world with a series of boldly drawn lines. "Do all conversations you have begin with yourself?"

Margot looked up. "I beg your pardon?" She was really puzzled.

Lydia frowned, let it go.

"You don't like me," Margot said. She had given it a lot of thought. "You don't understand me though. That's what I meant. It took me a while. You have to be careful, someone like me. I mean, I have to be careful."

"I can see that," Lydia Neumann said.

"You don't even understand. You think I can't think about things or that I don't know what I am or what my limits are. But I do. Everyone does. Everyone my age does. We know there are rules and rules and rules and God help us if we don't learn all the rules the way we're supposed to."

It was the first bitterness in her voice, the first crack of the façade.

"Do you know how many people would give their life for a job like mine?"

"And how many have," Mrs. Neumann said. Her throaty whisper made Margot shudder.

"I worked very hard. I think you have to understand that. I'm not pretty but I can look pretty. And I am willing to work very hard, even if I have to work harder than others just to stay up. You came into my life two mornings ago and you talk about flesh and blood and you expect me to enter into a very complex thing for the sake of someone

I haven't even laid eyes on for more than twenty years. And you called me a monster."

Lydia Neumann stared at her.

"I am not a monster," Margot Kieker said. "I am alone in the world and I am making my way by myself. I close the door of my apartment at night and it is my apartment— that's a good thing—but that's all I have. It reminds me that anything I have and anything I am still means I am alone. That doesn't seem to mean much to you. You said you were traveling with your husband. And naturally, you work for the government. No one in the government has to worry too much about working too hard."

"Don't bet on it, honey."

"Why do you patronize me?"

Yes, Lydia Neumann thought with a start: Why was she hostile to this pathetic creature with her too small nose and wide eyes?

Because of Hanley, came her own answer. This was Hanley's legacy, all he had in the world to leave his world to. It made her mad. She and Leo might go to the end of their lives without children and there would be no legacy but it didn't matter to them.

They were not alone. Until they died.

"Why did you call me?" Lydia Neumann said.

"You left your number. At the hotel that day. You said you would be here until today. I wanted you to go back but then, last night, I realized that I couldn't let that poor man, whoever he is, just die."

"Whoever he is is your great-uncle."

"Some stranger who came to the house once. Do you know my mother was thirty-seven when she died? Breast cancer. I'm twenty-eight. My grandmother was fifty-one.

The same thing. Do you know what I think about at night alone? Just the thought of being alone. I never smoked, I don't drink, I take care of myself. I had a mammogram last month. Every year. The doctor said that in view of my history, it might be a better idea for me to have my breasts removed surgically before any sign of disease appeared."

She said this in her mechanical, computer voice. It was the only voice she had. It was borrowed, without accents and with rounded consonants to sound like vowels. She was crying when she said these things.

Lydia Neumann stared at her.

Margot wiped her eye with a handkerchief of white linen. The handkerchief had her initials sewn in blue. William had given her the handkerchiefs at Christmas; it was the last gift she had expected.

"I can arrange this for you," Mrs. Neumann said.

Margot looked up.

"With your company, your supervisor. It'll only take a few hours; a few telephone calls. It won't appear to be what this is about at all. I am quite well known in some very upper circles in the wonderful world of computer science," said Lydia Neumann. She touched Margot's pale, ringless hands. "Leave it to me."

22

THE GOSSIP OF BERLIN

Denisov learned enough in three days to understand the direction of things. He merely didn't understand the sources.

He had tapped the informal network of private intelligence operatives (called "casuals" and "contractors" in some jargon); he had caught the thrust of Alexa's trail. It was dangerous for Alexa. She was "going into black" in the citadel of the West to kill an American agent. "Going into black" was to go illegal, off the charts, into enemy lands, into illegal jobs that no one would vouch for.

Why was it so obvious?

Denisov was a careful man and he was appalled at the carelessness of the information sources he tapped. Everyone seemed to know about Alexa's mission; everyone seemed to agree that it was going to be very dangerous. It was as though information were suddenly free and intelligence had become a sieve. There was so much that so many knew that it was like a story agreed upon before the telling by both sides.

The last source had been Griegel, the "wise old man

of Berlin." Griegel was— How could you explain him?
He was the go-between and lived quite undisturbed in his
three rooms on the top floor of an ornate old residence off
the Unter den Linden. He was an old man who had always
been old, who smoked American Chesterfield cigarettes
in a long black holder.

Griegel was alone now. His wife had died two years
ago, about the time that Denisov had finally met him
through Krueger in Zurich.

Griegel was one of the honest go-betweens. What
information he had was given to him. He offered no bona
fides because none could be given. He fulfilled the role
of an international neighborhood gossip. He lived undisturbed 1.4 miles east of the Berlin Wall at the point of the
Soviet War Memorial.

"Birds of peace," said Griegel, pointing with his cigarette holder at the pigeons wheeling in the bright spring
air. "East or West. All the same to them."

The trite sentiment was expected. Griegel was a man
who liked company. He held on to the company of others
by delaying the inevitable moment when he would have to
reveal all of substance that he knew. Like many gossips,
the facts were less important than the talk; he kept stok-
ing the talk with prods of unimportant comments.

The two men sat at a table by the balcony and looked
down. At the corner of the narrow street, they could see a
few of the famous linden trees for which the great Berlin
street is named.

Denisov said nothing. He watched the street.

"The next summit meeting is to be in Berlin," Griegel
said. He had the sharp accents of the Berliner and Denisov raised his hand in protest—his German was too slow.

"Would you prefer English then? Or Russian?" Griegel smiled. "Unfortunately, I cannot speak Russian very well. This makes it difficult when they want to tell me things." And he smiled. He had the wizened flat German eyes of the kind seen on some old men, with Oriental corners and merriment that is kin to mischief.

"I came to see you," Denisov began because the old man would not start the conversation. "I am not concerned with the summit meeting. I am concerned with my own business."

"And what is your business now?"

"I am in trade. Commercial trade."

"Ah," Griegel said. He smiled at the shadows on the street. "What do you sell?"

"The things that people need," Denisov said.

"Ah," Griegel said again, catching his breath and bobbing his head as though he understood.

"Why does the community speak so openly of intelligence? Of exchanges?" Denisov began again.

"The community," Griegel said. "The community lives on gossip."

"And you are the greatest gossip of all," Denisov said.

Griegel cackled. He ended his laughter with a fit of coughing and placed a new Chesterfield cigarette in his holder.

"The summit interests me," Griegel said. "It is such an important thing. And to have it here, in Berlin. There is talk these days about the summit and the air is filled with hope." He puffed the cigarette. "Hope like pigeons who are the symbols of peace, flying freely over poor Berlin. Holy doves."

Denisov frowned. "Flying rats," he said. He would prefer the conversation to end within a week or two. He shifted his bulk uncomfortably at the table. Even the saintly eyes seemed irritated. He had done his work in Europe, tapping into old sources and networks, feeling his way around the dark room of espionage without bumping into any unexpected pieces of furniture.

There are rarely facts found in such a search; Denisov had merely discovered a sentiment, a feeling of change to come. Griegel was useful because he was a parrot—he repeated the lies told him exactly as they had been stated in the first place. A useful parrot, used by both sides and by independents—like Denisov.

"How can you say such things about birds? They are God's creatures, even in this godless state," Griegel said. He was smiling still. "You are such a cynic, friend. Reality should not cloud your vision." The smoke drifted out the window. The old man sat in a wooden chair beside a wooden table butted against the iron balustrade that formed a small, crude balcony. He never moved from the chair. The street—narrow and in shadows—was his world. Up and down the street they came to the gossip of Berlin.

The old man sighed. He took the cigarette out of the holder and threw it out the window. He stared at the holder for a moment and then put it down.

"All right," he said.

Denisov said, "What about Switzerland?"

It was automatic, like pressing the button on a jukebox. Griegel played the record triggered by the words.

"They talk about action in Switzerland," he said. His eyes glazed over. "Soviet agent, one of the best, goes mad and kills two of her comrades. It was a quarrel, they say. She has fled to the West, they say."

"She."

"She," Griegel said.

Denisov put the money on the table. Not overvalued East German marks but Swiss francs. Hard money. The amount never varied, was never haggled over. The information retrieved from the old man was all alike to him, like so many songs on so many recordings.

"Who controls her?"

Griegel blinked; again, the eyes seemed glassy, as though he were drugged. When he spoke, the voice was automatic: "They say there is an old man in Moscow who is old and diseased and who wishes to live forever. Although, in a way, he is already immortal because his name lives forever."

"What about him? Is he in control?"

"In control? Who can say about that old man who wants to live forever." Griegel frowned. The wrong record was chosen. "Who can say." The frown deepened. "Some say the old man will go."

Go. Defect.

"Alexa," Denisov tried. He was operating in darkness. What buttons had to be pushed to retrieve information?

"She went to kill a man in Switzerland and killed her own comrades." He was silent; it was all.

Denisov was sweating though it was a cool day. The sweat broke on his forehead and beaded and fell down his face.

"November."

Griegel closed his eyes. The machine of memory whirred. He opened his eyes and saw nothing. "November is dead," he said.

"November in Switzerland."

"There is no November. November is dead," Griegel said.

"Who did Alexa go to kill?"

"Alexa killed two comrades in Switzerland. She went mad."

Denisov wiped at his face because the sweat stung his eyes. Outside, the rumble of Berlin filled the air. Pigeons fluttered above the low buildings and thought about East and West and where to eat next. The Wall was a good deal safer these days for pigeons because it was difficult to recruit soldiers to man the Wall and some of the watch-towers contained machine guns and cardboard cutouts of soldiers. The pigeons knew these things.

Devereaux had wanted information. Had wanted Denisov—for a considerable price—to tap into the "Community" of shadows that existed in Europe—the soldiers of fortune, the mercenary agents, the contractors and private intelligence sources, the arms dealers who knew many things about many countries. He had tapped, probed, prodded: And all he had was this vague feeling of momentous events yet to come.

"Who is the old man in Moscow?"

Griegel snapped out of the trance. He smiled. "Who can say?"

"Her control?"

"Who can say?"

"Gorki," Denisov said. The man in control in Resolutions Committee was always code-named Gorki. Was it the same man who had controlled Denisov long ago? But it had to be: He controlled Alexa, he had controlled Denisov when Denisov had been in the trade.

Denisov watched Griegel.

Griegel closed his eyes.

Denisov wiped at his face again.

"Gorki," Griegel said. And opened his eyes. He smiled at Denisov. "That reminds me of an absurd thing. It is too absurd."

"What is it?"

"A nutcracker. A wooden nutcracker."

"A nutcracker?"

Griegel blinked. He was back in the present. "Did you remember the case of the Soviet agent who defected to the West in Italy and then redefected back into the Soviet embassy right in Washington in the United States?" He laughed in a dry voice. "Do you ever wonder that perhaps it is all a great game and that none of the players understands it?"

"What is Nutcracker?" Denisov said. His voice rose. And Griegel went into a trance again and this time, the voice was dull and slow:

"Nutcracker is an operation which involves the suspension of certain long-held beliefs: Nutcracker assumes the truth of the game. The truth of the game, which cannot be admitted, is simple: There are no spies. The game exists for its own sake."

Griegel shuddered and seemed to fall asleep in the wooden chair. His mouth gaped. His hands were slack on his lap. Was it a trance? Or was it a game played within a game, a little show for Denisov's money?

Denisov sat still for a long time, trying to catch his breath. His face felt flushed to the touch of his cold hand. He thought of Alexa then and he was almost feverish.

He had known her, of course.

He had slept with her.

They had been under control of Gorki, together, in Finland. She was Gorki's pet, it was obvious. She deferred to Gorki when they spoke of the man. Denisov had never been under illusions—about the trade, about Gorki, about the system he served. Denisov had been faithful in his way but he saw the true believer shining in Alexa's eyes and it had made him wary for a long time. They had business to do in Finland and it was a dirty job and she had been good enough and Denisov had been better. Denisov had shown her certain ways of doing things that had impressed her.

He was not a beautiful man and he was large and his manners were too shy. He was not at all in appearance what he really was, in his heart, in his mind. Alexa had been like the others—like his old wife even, whom he remembered less and less—she had seen only the external Denisov at first, the clumsy and amiable bear. But then, in the business in Finland, when he had been quite ruthless, she had seen the power and sureness in him and she had loved the power of him and he had taken her as simply as a man takes a streetwalker.

He had slept with her. He made love as never before. When it was over, the smell of her filled his memory. Back in Moscow, in the small and noisy flat, he had made love to his old wife after the assignment and he still remembered the smell of Alexa. He had made ferocious love, hard and cruel, demanding. He had moved over his old wife and felt her under him, her big belly and sagging breasts, and with his eyes closed and the smell of Alexa in memory, he was making love to Alexa again in Helsinki, before they had parted. He closed his eyes in Moscow and remembered the smell of Alexa beneath him, the firm, straining belly that pushed against his belly until he had to explode, again and again, into her.

The breasts were firm, and he had felt suspended above
Alexa and felt her long, cat's tongue drag across the flesh
of his throat and reach his ear and lick into it like a sau-
cer of milk. His head exploded and this strong woman
beneath him—he had been thinking of Alexa—moved
and moved and he grasped her buttocks, her back, every
beautiful part of her perfect body...

He was sweating in the coolness of morning in the
shadowed street in Berlin. He remembered: He had
opened his eyes in the darkness when he made love to
Alexa and she had been watching him. He was above her
and her body was moving beneath him but she was watching him with an apartness that frightened him.

Griegel's voice intruded.

"No. Nothing," Denisov replied, though he had not
heard what the other man had said. He closed his reverie
and looked around him.

"Quite beautiful," Griegel jeered. The Berliner always
attempts humor, even when it is most inappropriate.

"I was thinking about Nutcracker."

"Ah, she's cracked a few nuts in her time," said
Griegel. The English pun startled Denisov. It was something he wished he had the skill to say. Even the puns
of Gilbert had to be studied and had to be explained for
Denisov.

His head filled with music then. He rose.

He nodded in a correct German way at the old man
at the table and saw, from his height, the East German
agents in the street below. Berlin was not so difficult and
neither was Prague; the past that had been an agent named
Denisov had been obliterated long since. No one looked
for him anymore or even suspected he existed.

If you think we are worked by strings,
Like a Japanese marionette,
You don't understand these things:
It is simply Court etiquette—

The music pounded as he pounded down the stairs, round and round the balconied marble stairs. What was the reason for so much music?

But Griegel had made a pun.

The pun had given him Gilbert and Sullivan's wonderful tunes.

He saw the players again of the old D'Oyly Carte company before it disbanded in London. He saw them go round and round with the music. He saw the strutting English actors in Japanese costumes and the strains of the opening of *The Mikado*.

He was on the street, hurrying along to his car parked illegally at the corner of Unter den Linden. He would be in West Berlin in ten minutes; he could be in Washington in ten hours.

Did this matter affect him?

Yes.

He saw it clearly now. And the danger to Alexa, the danger so palpable that he was certain he could see her dead in the streets.

It was a price worth paying, to save her. To have her gratitude.

He saw the images and rushed past the security forces in their trench coats loitering in dark doorways.

When he reached the car, he had a ticket.

And he thought—in one blinding moment—he had the key to Nutcracker. If only he could keep it in his head.

23

REPORTS

You are a busy little fellow, Yackley thought. The reports were coming on a regular basis now. They had picked up on him at the border when he crossed from Ontario into upstate New York at Niagara Falls. But the report from U.S. Border Patrol had not been correlated into Devereaux's running file (NOVRET) until Sunday morning. He had been granted two days of mischief.

There had not been any luck involved in finding Sellers in the trunk of the car at National Airport. The arrogant bastard had parked the car in one of the stalls designated for use by Congress and staff. Obviously, it would have been found as soon as a Congressman complained about someone using a privileged space.

By then, someone thought to secure Hanley's apartment. It was too late. The place had been wrecked. Devereaux must have gone there sometime Friday.

The problems were multiplying as well. Mrs. Neumann had apparently pulled a copy of Hanley's 201 file. That was discovered Thursday night by Claymore Richfield, who hadn't even been looking for it. She had left a trail in the computer and she had been gone on leave for four days. She would be back Monday. There would be questions to be answered Monday.

Yackley felt the Section was falling away from him and that Devereaux was suddenly on the periphery of every action, waiting for Yackley's move. Yackley knew he was the target.

There was a name in the 201 file—the will section. Margot Kieker, whoever she was. They had run that through the National Credit Center in Virginia and the information was thin. She lived in Chicago, she was a salesperson for IBM—she sold computers.

Computers, for Christ's sake.

Two agents from the Section hit the sales center in Chicago on Thursday. They were told that Ms. Kieker had been called to Washington. They said it like that, very proudly: She had been called to Washington by the director of a top secret computer design program and would be gone for several weeks. It was quite an honor for everyone in the sales center.

Yackley read through the reports, fingered them as though they might speak. He glanced at the photographs on his desk. His wife still smiled at him as she always did, even in life. She thought none of it was terribly serious. He had tried to impress upon her the changes going on in government, the changes going on in the business of intelligence. He was on the cutting edge of those changes. He always used terms like *cutting edge* in trying to explain to Beverly. She would have none of it. She made apple pies from scratch and read *USA Today* and thought baseball was boring and wore cotton dresses during the week. She didn't understand a damned thing. If she hadn't supported him through law school, he would have felt he owed her nothing.

The reality of the White House is always so much less. A thousand books and movies have given the public the image of a great manor with a full staircase that reaches and reaches upward to a heavenly second floor. The Oval Office—which had begun life as the presidential library—is a gigantic room in image; in reality, it is very much of the eighteenth century, small cozy and able to be heated by a single fireplace.

Perry Weinstein considered the vulnerability of the place every time he crossed the underground corridor to the White House proper from the Executive Office Building.

He was coatless with his tie askew. His glasses had been patched that morning with a paper clip inserted at the place the screw fell out. He looked like a man on fire. His eyes were wide with interest in some idea percolating inside him and when he talked, he brushed at his rep tie with nervous fingers, as though the fire had spilled ashes on him.

The man on the other side of the narrow desk was Reed. Reed was about four or five in the hierarchy, if anyone paid attention to numbers like that. In fact, a good-sized forest was felled each week to print just such speculation.

Reed was Eastern, which was unusual; he was old money but he made more of it in new ways; even though his funds were in blind trusts, it didn't matter because what was good for Quentin Reed was good for the U.S.A.

"We need some orchestra music for this one," Reed

was saying. The room was modern, dull, white, window-less, and devoid of charm—exactly like Reed.

"We've worked OT," Perry Weinstein said. It was not his style at all. Clichés fell by the bushelful in this administration. Jargon clogged the corridors of power. Everyone had slang or invented it. Yackley was probably chosen to head R Section because of his inability to speak in anything but clichés.

"Play me some," Reed continued. He assumed a pose of power that required him to lean back in his swivel chair and feign defenselessness.

"I'm coordinating with Section, Langley, Puzzle—" He stopped. Was it too much jargon? But Reed nodded as though he understood. "We have a scenario ready for a road show three weeks before the Pow-Wow."

Pow-Wow was Summit; the leaders of the United States and the Soviet Union were scheduled to meet in one month's time in Berlin—in both sections of the city to symbolize a new beginning to peace. Peace was full of new beginnings.

"Two years ago, we started our exchange program," Perry said. He lapsed out of jargon, to Reed's annoyance:

"We picked up their agent in Italy and the Brits picked up one in the Isles; they defected two West Germans into the East. I think we rattled our sabers effectively. It set the tone."

"But the one from Italy—what's his name—that was badly handled by Langley. He redefected into the Soviet embassy right on Mass Ave."

Perry let that one go. Reed sighed, shifted the swivel, tapped his fingertips together to make certain they were still there, and continued:

"I don't want a fuck-up like that this time. That's why you're in place on coordinating this thing. And I don't want to see the Red Machine come back as quickly."

"I've tried to explain to you, Quent," Perry Weinstein said, brushing at his rep tie again. "We can't absolutely control the Opposition. All we can do is hold our own."

"I'd like to see a better scenario than that."

"It can't be guaranteed," Perry said, his voice on edge. "We have identified nine agents, all very top drawer, very KGB and GRU upper echelon. Including, I might add, the director of the Resolutions Committee."

Quentin stared at him. The eyes had no comprehension.

"His code name is Gorki. He's an old man, he made contact with us in the last eighteen months through the CIA. He wants to come over to our house. He has some health problems and he needs us. I think it's less a matter of ideology than just wanting to live longer."

"I like this—"

"It's timed for the summit exchange."

"I like this very much, Perr."

"We have our little Indians all lined up. There's a cipher clerk in SovEm in Rome, there's an East German intelligence director in Potsdam, there's—"

"More and more," enthused Reed, cutting off the litany. "How do we begin?"

"The best one is a Resolutions courier named Alexa. Really attractive. I thought you'd like this." And he slipped the photograph out of his pocket and dropped it on Quentin Reed's empty desk top.

Extraordinary face, without any doubt. The eyes held you.

But the body. The sheer, voluptuous nakedness of that body. She stood quite naturally, not posing at all, not hiding anything either. Reed felt an urge and hid it by slamming his body forward into the kneehole of the desk and plunking his elbows on the desk top. The picture required several more seconds of careful study.

"This girl is naked," said Quentin Reed.

"Her name is Alexa. Rather, her real name is Natasha Podgorny Alexkoff. But she's Alexa, which is a good name for a killer. She seduced that security guard in Silicon Valley a few years ago. She's been active. Considered their best 'Resolutions' courier."

"And she's here?"

"Reasonable supposition. She crossed the Canadian border into Niagara Falls three hours ago."

"We have her?"

"Not yet. It's better to bait your trap. You see, she's sort of a gift to us. From Gorki. The old man who's coming across on Summit eve."

"That's one helluva gift," Reed said. His tongue licked at his dry lips. He had gray eyes to match his suit, and right now he felt he could take on this Alexa-Whatever. It was only ten in the morning and he was thinking about the bedroom. Hell, the top of his desk.

Perry Weinstein appreciated the spectacle of Quentin Reed. Reed was looking at the photograph of Alexa and could not see the contempt in Perry's eyes.

After a salacious moment of silence, Perry spoke again: "Gorki took that. He had her. About five years ago, in his dacha."

"But what does she do? Besides this, I mean?"

"She kills," Perry Weinstein said.

The cold word fell between them. Perry dropped the photograph on the desk top. "What does that mean?"

"It means she kills. She's a courier. That's their slang for Resolutions agent. She killed a man on a ferry in Helsinki two weeks ago. She killed three people in Lausanne a week ago. She kills people, that's what she does."

Perry repeated the word because of the effect it was having on Quentin Reed. The spirit was drooping. The gray eyes became old again. The hands left the desk top. The photograph was an orphan.

"I can't believe it."

"Yes. Apparently, that's one of the reasons she's effective. So many can't."

"Why is ... why has she come here?"

"We guess she's here to kill somebody." Perry Weinstein said it without emphasis and watched the effect on Quentin Reed.

"My God, this doesn't involve the President, does it?"

"No. That would be so unlikely, so crude, so—"

"It wasn't so goddamned unlikely when they put those assassins on the Pope, was it?"

"We are monitoring her constantly."

"Why not just pick her up?"

"We'd like to see what she had in mind."

"How did you get this photograph, Perr? How do we know about her?"

"That's why we have spies, Quent," Perry Weinstein said.

"Spies? Spooks?" Quentin smiled. "Are you going to give me that booga-booga stuff? You're coordinating Changeover, aren't you?"

"Joke, Quent."

"Changeover. I think the budget director outdid himself. Save five bill over five years."

Perry nodded. Changeover was the newest idea in intelligence since the invention of invisible ink. Cost analysts had figured out that information gained through fixed investment enterprises—satellites, computers, machine analysis—was far more cost efficient than information gained by agents in the field. The agents would be cut back over five years to avoid the sort of bloodletting that had crippled CIA during the Carter administration.

"But what about this dish of Russian ice cream? Tell me about her."

"There's nothing to tell—so far. She's a gift from our man in Moscow Center. She's already cut off from her control, she's flying blind. She has some sort of S&D here—"

"S&D?"

"Search and destroy, Quent," said Perr.

"Right."

Silence.

The jargon machine was on hold. The room was silent. Being this close to the most powerful man in the country—he was 150 steps away at the moment, sitting in the Oval Office, reading briefing papers for tonight's live press conference—awed them both, awed everyone. The reality of the presidency was borne by the sense of awe.

"I think this is going to put the President in a strong position. At the summit."

"It did at the first one. We had spies and they had spies and there were defections all over the place. They started it with that couple pulled out of West Germany. And we aced the game with the agents in Italy and Britain. We won the battle of the magazine covers."

"It was like war," Quentin agreed.

"A lot of war is trading prisoners," Perry said.

"Is that what's going to happen?"

"I don't know. You can't always predict the Opposition."

"I thought we could," Quentin said. "Isn't that why we have intelligence services and why we finance estimates?"

Perry cleared his throat. He got up.

"I'm fifteen minutes behind as usual," he said to Quentin, who had not moved at the desk. He reached for the photograph.

"Don't you have a copy?"

Perry smiled.

He left the picture of the naked Soviet courier on the desk.

24

STRANGER IN THE HOUSE

The car was streaked with dirt and road salt. The suit-
cases in the trunk were crammed with dirty clothes.
Ends of vacations always look like this. The car growled
up to the garage door in the last of the afternoon light—
the muffler had been pierced by a rock on the road somewhere in Pennsylvania.

The garage door opened automatically and the car
crept into its space.

Leo Neumann turned the key in the ignition and the
engine dieseled into silence with a few sputtering coughs.
For a moment, no one said anything. There had not been
many words in the last five hours, in the last 150 miles.

Lydia Neumann sighed and reached for the door handle and pulled herself out.

Margot Kieker took it as a clue. She pushed at her
handle, was confused a moment, and then found the right
lever. The rear door opened with a groan.

"I'll bring the bags in," Leo said.

"Leave them for a moment. Let's open the house. I
could use a beer," Lydia Neumann said. She really meant

it. Her voice was more hoarse than usual; she had been fighting a cold. And now this. This thing that had happened in the morning, at St. Catherine's.

A great fuss. Sister Mary Domitilla had to consult with Sister Duncan, and then Dr. Goddard himself had come into the matter. But the matter had been settled by Finch, a small-faced man with large ears and a way of talking through his nose that made everyone around him want to offer him a handkerchief.

Finch was clearly in charge, though no one deferred to him. He was like a janitor in a corporation who has executive pretensions. He had to interrupt conversations to be heard.

But he was heard.

It didn't matter about Miss Kieker being next of kin or not next of kin. Yes, she had proof. Yes, she had rights. Get a lawyer, Finch said at one point. It didn't matter. Not to Finch and not to the good ladies who ran St. Catherine's.

No one could see Mr. Hanley.

Not at all. Not at this time. Not at all.

But Margot Kieker was his only living relative.

Mr. Hanley is in a bad way, miss.

But I want to see my great-uncle—

You wouldn't want to see him the way he is now, miss.

Finch went on and on, reasonable and wheedling and talking wetly through his nose. His little eyes shifted back and forth across the globes of white and watched the faces of Leo and Lydia Neumann.

They were all travelers, all tired by the eight-hundred-mile journey from Chicago.

And somehow, Mrs. Neumann had expected this. She

had expected it because she had this very bad feeling about what was really going on in St. Catherine's.

They entered the house like burglars. As though they did not belong there. Then Mrs. Neumann shook herself out of the gloom. She went from room to room, turning on the lights. She turned on all the lights. The house looked so unlovely because it had been closed for nine days and everything in it was too perfect. She and Leo had lived there for twelve years and it fit them to a T.

Because Mrs. Neumann led the way, lighting the house, she saw him first.

He was not at all changed. She almost smiled. She knew him, had known him; and then the absurdity of it struck her. He had intruded on her house.

"What do you want?"

He said nothing. He sat on a plain wooden chair near the front window. His hands were on his knees, he sat very still. He put his finger to his lips and looked up at the chandelier.

Leo came in then. He didn't know the man. He reached for a poker at the fireplace and took a step.

"Leo," Lydia said in annoyance. He paused.

"Put the poker down," Mrs. Neumann said. "He's not here to do anyone harm." She looked carefully at Devereaux. "Are you here to harm anyone?"

Devereaux shook his head no. It was like a game. They were real; Devereaux was the ghost. The spook who sat by the door. Devereaux got up then and walked to the telephone on the side table and pointed to it. Mrs. Neumann watched him. Devereaux looked at her. She nodded. She understood. The other two merely gaped. It was like a game suddenly going on between two people in a crowded room that involved no one else.

Leo Neumann put down the poker into the holder next to the brick fireplace. Margot Kieker stood at the door, uncertain about what to do with her hands. She stared and would have been surprised at how young she looked. There was a natural grace to her, beneath the clumsy artifice, and it was clear in that moment.

Mrs. Neumann pointed to a door. They crossed the room. The door led to the paneled basement. Devereaux smiled to her and she flicked on the light at the top of the stairs. They went down to the basement, the two of them.

Basements are secure, packed with earth and surrounded by a moat of concrete. Even the sophisticated listening devices trained on houses are not made to work efficiently on basements.

There was a telephone in the basement room and Devereaux unplugged it from the wall. And then Mrs. Neumann spoke to him:

"Do you know what has happened to Hanley?"

"Yes," Devereaux said. "Part of it."

"He called you, didn't he?"

"Yes."

"His telephone was tapped. He told us that. He implied all our telephones might be tapped—"

"They probably are," Devereaux said.

"You get accustomed to this, in the field. I am not accustomed to this. I understand secrets; I do not understand spying. Not on your own people. Not on Hanley."

Lydia Neumann went to the stairs and called up. "Go on, Leo. Get the cases out of the trunk, show Margot the spare room, will you? And get her towels?"

Leo said, "You just said—"

"Please, Leo," Lydia Neumann said.

They even ate in the basement, for the sake of their visitor.

Devereaux and Lydia Neumann sat at a cardtable at the south end of the basement, in the direction of the highway. There was a reason for that as well.

All was secure. The room was paneled and dominated by a large felt-green pool table with carved legs. It had been a gift from her to her husband six Christmases ago. He had expressed a vague interest in the game, which he had played in his youth. Now they used it to store things on.

Lydia Neumann thought about security: Devereaux was an agent in the field, retired, and Yackley said he had killed two chasers in Lausanne. Lydia Neumann had thought about that for a long time, as she prepared a dinner of sandwiches and coleslaw and beer in the kitchen. They ate in silence—for a while. Margot Kieker came out of herself enough to talk about her mother and what life had been like in the Nebraska of her growing up, so different from Hanley's Nebraska.

Devereaux had watched her during the meal.

There is a way a man can watch a woman which does not frighten her. It is a watching that implies interest, even attraction, but it is not dominating. It implies that the man is watching out of some respect, some physical attraction, and he is attentive to the words of the other.

Devereaux had the trick of watching like that. It can be acquired and practiced, like all tricks.

Lydia Neumann would glance at him from time to time and then at Margot and then at Leo, who was enjoying the mystery of it all.

No, there was something wrong with security that put Hanley away, that denies him visitors; something wrong with the way things were going inside Section. She said this to Devereaux. It was a matter of making a judgment about Devereaux.

They sat at the cardtable with the flimsy top and rickety metal legs and she began her story, which began about six months before, when the new budget message came down from the National Security Council. There was to be an increased emphasis in the coming years on electronic intelligence gathering. And a think tank study—coming from one of the vaguely conservative institutions—had concluded that the weakest link in the chain of intelligence security was the case officer.

"Machines don't lie," Lydia Neumann rasped. "Machines cannot do anything but tell the truth."

Devereaux stared at her a moment. "Is that true?"

"No, of course not. 'Garbage in, garbage out.' But if they think it's true, it's true. Yackley had everyone in and we talked about Section, about how much a field agent costs us. A half million a year in Section. Do you believe that?"

"As much as I believe in thirty-seven-thousand-dollar coffee pots," Devereaux said.

"The point is, it got to Hanley. I mean, it was his division they were talking about."

"Operations."

"The director of spies, chief spook. They were talking about heavy cutbacks over the next five years. Not the kind of bloodbath that Stansfield Turner did at CIA, but the same sort of cutback. He was supposed to start a list and—"

Devereaux started. Just for a moment, he betrayed himself. Lydia Neumann saw it.

A list of names of agents.

"It got to Hanley, as I said," she said in a hoarse voice. "Poor Hanley."

"What got to him? You mean, he had a breakdown?"

"Of course. That's why he was committed to St. Catherine's. Except it gets worse and worse. I'm afraid. I'm afraid he's going to die."

"Yes," Devereaux said. "I didn't understand it. I thought it was Hanley. But it wasn't Hanley at all. That means he's going to die."

Mrs. Neumann blinked, stared. Devereaux's voice had not changed at all; the pronouncement was routine. It was a matter of life and death all along and now the verdict was death.

"What is it?"

" 'There are no spies.' I remember he said that to me. His line was tapped. He was babbling and I thought he was drunk. Perhaps he was drunk; perhaps he was drugged."

"Drugged?"

"He complained about the doctor. About medicine. I didn't quite understand it because I thought he was drunk at the time. Two men came after me in Switzerland. Chasers from Section."

"Yackley said you killed them."

Devereaux almost shrugged. His eyes never wavered. "There was an accident on a country road. The point was: They were chasers. I was asleep. Let sleeping agents lie. That's always a good policy."

"What is going on?"

"What is Nutcracker?" Devereaux said.

She stared at him.

"Is there an operation? Is there something called Nutcracker?"

"No. I'm not aware—I would be aware of it if it existed in Section."

"Perhaps," he said.

"Damnit, I would be aware of it—"

"If it existed in Section," he said. The voice was quiet. The furnace thumped on and the fan began to send surges of warm air through the vents. They felt the chill first and then the waves of warm air. The house was absolutely silent, save for the sounds of the furnace.

"Why did Yackley have Hanley committed?" Devereaux said.

"I don't know. He said it was on the advice of the house-man. Dr. Thompson. But Thompson is a fool; I mean, he's not a shrink even. Hanley went home in February. He told everyone he was tired."

"He was on medication."

It was not a question.

"I don't know," she said.

"He was on medication. It explains what he was saying to me." He paused, thought of something else. "Who runs Operations now? On a day-to-day?"

"Yackley. I mean, there are the sub-directors. A lot of it is automatic."

He said nothing. He seemed to be looking beyond her. "They're killing him," he said. Then he paused. "Perhaps I should prepare him for his death." And smiled.

25

WATCHER

Alexa adjusted her length in the car. The car was large, larger even than a Ziv, but she had been waiting for four hours.

Her muscles ached across her back beneath the silken shirt. She wore very dark slacks stuffed into the tall leather boots she had purchased in Stockholm. The day that she had gone to kill November; it seemed a million days ago.

The night had stars.

She stared at the stars and felt pity for the child from Moscow who had wanted to count the stars and contain heaven.

She felt pity for herself. As she had been, as she was.

She felt pity for her own fear. She was bereft, alone in the West, adrift in a foreign place she would never escape from.

Even after she killed the target tonight.

He was contained in this suburban house that was grander than Gorki's dacha outside Moscow. The Americans lived like such profligates. Every home was an estate. Yet she saw the people in Washington, in the city, at night: They came with cardboard for warmth and also newspapers and they bedded down under the bridges and in alcoves of doorways, in alleys where there was some warmth. She had contempt for Americans and their ways.

And fear for herself.

The target was at hand and there was nothing more to be done. She had delayed the inevitable too long. She had not wanted to decide her own fate while deciding the life of another. Gorki had abandoned her and done it cruelly. He had not transferred her, not posted her abroad to another assignment, not banished her from Moscow. He had decided she would die. She was sure of it and could not understand the wrath of the man who had been God to her.

She had danced for him.

She had been naked for him.

Not for any favor from him. Because he had so much power in him and she had been attracted to the power in him. It was a palpable thing to her.

Four times in two days—four times in forty-eight hours exactly—she had seen Devereaux. He was the target; the second November that came once in a blue moon. And when she killed him, as she would do tonight, she would have killed herself. Somehow, this was implied in the assignment. There would be no escape or there would be a botched escape; in any case, she would die when November died.

Once every six hours, she contacted the source at a phone with a New York City area code. The voice assured her this last time that the target was in this suburban house in Bethesda, Maryland. The voice was always right. He knew everything, Alexa realized: He really knew.

Which made it so sinister.

This was a script, she thought. This was a play with Alexa as an actress in a role assigned long before to her. It was all made easy for her. Which meant that it was all a trap—a death for November, a death for Alexa.

Gorki had ruled her passions but not her mind. Gorki thought he could pat her hand at a table in a restaurant in Prague and tell her that everything was all right. That she would believe him.

She was not a fool. Not even when she had danced naked on the Afghan rug that night, before the crackling fire, the fire lighting up her loins and her breasts and making her skin a tawny color. Not a fool when she had heard music that was unplayed and danced to it, intoxicated by drugs shared and the wine and all the making of love that had gone before. Danced in bare feet on the Afghan rug and showed him her power to arouse him. But in that mad moment, she had not been a fool. Not that.

Gorki treated her so. But what choice did she have now. To perform the assignment, she would die; to not do the job, she would betray her commission. And die as well.

She was strong; she had power because she was beautiful and men desired her. Also, because she controlled herself and those around her. She was aware of everything around her and she was cunning and intelligent.

And Gorki was so much more.

Power was the aphrodisiac.

He had commanded her as easily as a child commands its doll.

Now he commanded her death.

The moment she killed November, she was dead.

His death carried her own inside him.

She blinked. Her eyes had made tears and that had made her eyes irresistible.

She sat in the darkness, under bare trees, beneath stars. She sat in a rented car with a borrowed pistol on her lap. She sat very alone and still. Her shoulders ached. Beyond those yellow-lighted windows were homes of strangers where strangers were warm, familiar with each other, at some sort of peace, even for a moment. Alexa let tears fall on her perfect, taut cheeks because she was so cold and alone.

And then he was there.

On the steps of the house she had watched.

She put her hand on the pistol. Her long fingers crept over case, housing, trigger guard, trigger—they were like snakes creeping over stones. She held her breath—not that he could hear her.

November.

He was bright against the darkness because of the street lamp. His jacket was light blue, his sweater was black. He wore tan trousers.

He was a large man and he paused at the curb to look around him. He stared right into the darkness where she was hidden. It didn't matter; he didn't see her.

It was important to take care of him away from the house of spies where he had spent Sunday afternoon.

His image flashed beneath the street lamp.

Tall, long legs, a certain strength in the way he walked. It was the way a lion stalks in the veld.

She blinked her eyes to blink away the tears. She was aware her life was coming to an end very soon, even as his life was ending.

She pushed the car into "drive" and let it slide forward

into the street. She turned toward Wisconsin Avenue at the end of the street.

She came abreast of him.

Was he a hundred feet away? It would not be difficult.

She rolled down the window.

Because Alexa was careful, she wanted all the advantages. Let him step toward her on this quiet street.

"Can you help me?"

So small a voice. Her mother said she was given the gift of a small voice in a beautiful face. A strong woman's deception.

"Can you help me, please? I am lost, I think."

He stopped. Turned.

Stared at her.

She brought the pistol up beneath the window.

And he smiled at her.

What man would not smile at a beautiful woman in distress?

From that moment, doubt ceased. There was no thought of Gorki. She must obey because obedience was the way taught to a courier in the Resolutions Committee.

Take a step toward me.

And another.

She spoke to the target without words.

It will be very easy for you, dear one. She crooned to the target in her mind.

She had once stroked poor Tony's hair. His face was between her thighs and he pleased her and she thought to blow his head off in that moment. Poor Tony.

But he did not move, the one on the sidewalk.

She brought the pistol up and rested it on the sill of the window.

He was half turned toward her now, almost in profile.

"Be careful, Alexa," he said. In very soft English. "They want to kill you as well. When you kill me."

The English words had no emotion but a sort of wonder to them.

Her hand trembled. The pistol shook.

"Please," she said. In English.

What did she want to say?

She had to kill him.

"Please."

But he was gone, between the buildings opposite, into absolute darkness beneath the stars. The street was empty.

She was crying.

He knew. He knew her, knew the danger she had felt. It was like another man knowing your secret belief that you were going to die soon. It confirmed everything.

And all her courage was gone.

26

SPIES

Devereaux grinned when he saw the sign on the door.
    But he removed the pistol from his belt anyway.
He unlocked the safety—he detested automatics but it
was the only reliable piece he could acquire quickly on
the hot market—and he went to the door.

On the knob, a *Do Not Disturb* sign printed in four
languages—presumably for the benefit of the staff, rather
than the room resident—hung like a signal flag.

It was Devereaux's room.

He had not hung out any sign at all.

He turned the key and opened the door with a slight
kick from his right foot. It is exactly the way it is taught in
all the training classes. The pistol surveys the room from
right to left as the door swings inward.

Except it was on a chain and the chain held.

"Who is it?"

Devereaux did not put the pistol away but he held it
loosely at his side. "Come on," he said.

Denisov opened the door. His shirt was open, revealing

an expanse of chest and curly black hairs. A bottle of vodka and a small ice bucket sat on the sideboard.

"Make yourself at home," Devereaux said. He entered the room.

"I didn't want you to shoot me if I fell asleep," Denisov said in his heavy accent. He was in good humor.

"I didn't expect you until tomorrow."

"The work was satisfactory." He frowned. "As far as it went. You were right about a few things. Do you know the woman is here? Is waiting to kill you?"

Devereaux took off his corduroy jacket and threw it on one of the double beds. He went to the window and looked out at the winking red lights set in the obelisk of the Washington Monument. The lights looked like eyes and the Monument resembled—at night—a hooded Klansman.

He had his back to Denisov and he replaced his pistol in his belt.

Denisov smiled. "But you can see me in the glass, is that it?"

"Of course."

"Good. Do not trust too much."

"No. That wouldn't do for either of us."

"The woman is here."

"I know."

"You know this? You have seen her?"

"At least three times. I saw her tonight. I think she was finally going to kill me. She's very confused." He said it mildly. "I told her to be careful; I said they wanted her dead."

"Then you did nothing?"

"She caught me the first time. In the morning. Yesterday morning. She was in a car and I was careless. I guess

I have learned to retire from the old trade too well." He turned back to face Denisov, "Smirnoff vodka?"

"Actually, I had great trouble. I ask for Russian vodka. I ask for Polish vodka even. The man in the store said he refused to carry Communist vodka. As though vodka had a political party. He says I have an accent and he accused me of being a goddamn Russian spy."

"But you are."

"Not anymore. Thanks to you." He paused again. "I was in Berlin."

"You saw Griegel. How is Griegel?"

"As boring as ever. He said there is a control inside Moscow Center who wants to defect. Do you know who it is?"

"Gorki," Devereaux said.

Denisov frowned. He didn't like this at all. He was tired as well. The Concorde from London had utterly exhausted him. "Perhaps I should not ask you questions. Perhaps you know all the answers."

"Perhaps," Devereaux said.

Denisov poured some vodka into a water glass. Devereaux removed the Saran Wrap seal over a second glass, sniffed it, and dropped in some ice. He took the bottle from Denisov. They sat down. The hotel room was like a thousand others strung around the world and they were like the thousand others who hung their trousers on hangers and washed their shirts in the basin and set chairs against the door at night and always left a light burning and kept the television set on to an empty channel to produce a certain, soothing amount of "white noise." The white noise protected against eavesdropping and the chair on the door against surprises.

"She surprised me in the morning," Devereaux said. "She could have taken me out then. I was an open target, the street was empty."

"She is cautious," Denisov said.

"I don't know. But she's thinking about the setup. She was set up in Lausanne. And I just wanted to tip her a little. If I know her name and what the business is about, it will scare her. I think it will. Maybe you can stay on her and find out who she's dealing with."

"Yes. That would not be so unpleasant. She is beautiful. But what do I do when I discover . . . her associates?"

"I don't know."

"You fail at the end, comrade. You fail when I ask you for the last answer. Why do you always fail at the end?"

"Because I don't know."

"Take her in," Denisov said. "It is not so bad."

"Yes. You read the *Wall Street Journal* now."

"It is not so bad," Denisov said. "But even freedom cannot replace memory. An exile is an exile, no matter how great the freedom of the exile." He said, "Perhaps you will survive this matter. I think you will. You have lives like cats." He drank his vodka neat and harsh in the Russian manner.

"She's afraid of us as well," Devereaux agreed.

"Yes. We have proof positive in KGB that CIA agents eat defectors and flush their remains away in sewers."

"We have such proof as well," Devereaux said. They had automatically assumed their old sides for the sake of speech. It was easy to be against; it was familiar, like friendship. But it was easier than friendship.

"I knew Alexa," Denisov said.

"I thought you did."

"I betrayed nothing."

"Yes. That's why I thought you knew her. You saw her picture and you weren't even struck by her. By how she looked. You're not so much of a saint as that."

Denisov blinked behind the saintly rimless glasses. "I think of how to save her."

"For yourself."

"I knew her. In Finland. There was a business there and we worked together."

Devereaux said nothing. To say anything would be wrong. He wanted Denisov to think about the business at hand.

"I came to settle with Hanley. And Hanley is the key to this thing. If he's alive."

"You have killed him?"

Devereaux told him about Hanley then, as though there were no secrets between them. The spy withholds; it is part of training. He withholds from control, from his friends, from his co-workers, from his network. A spy's reserve is knowledge that is not shared. And yet there was so much they did not know that everything Devereaux had learned seemed no more than two or three interlocking pieces of a puzzle.

The two men talked into the middle of the night and the words opened into other words.

At three in the morning, Devereaux got up suddenly and went to the window again and looked down at the utterly silent, utterly empty streets of the city.

"Why do we know all this?"

Denisov stared at the back of the other man. He considered the question. He stared at the empty bottle of vodka they had shared.

"Because we are professionals," Denisov said.

Devereaux did not turn to look at him. "Because it doesn't matter. This is a scenario. A long and involved scenario and the answers are all written down long before it started."

"Yes." Slowly. "I thought about that, too. But this Hanley, this man is in an insane asylum which—"

"—which is where we put our actors who refuse to play their parts," Devereaux said. "What is Nutcracker?"

And Denisov started so violently that Devereaux thought he would fall off the straight chair.

"The word was used. By Herr Griegel in Berlin when I saw him. An operation. But it seemed to connect to nothing at all, I nearly forgot it. What is it?"

"I don't know. No one knows. Except that I think Hanley knows. Or he knew. Somehow, Hanley had to be taken care of and it was the easiest way to do it. He had to be put in a secure place where he could be examined to see what he knew, whom he had told—"

"You, my friend," Denisov said.

They both saw it in that moment.

"He called me. He was raving or drunk but he called me twice and his telephone was tapped and someone was afraid that I shared Hanley's secret. Whatever the secret was..."

"Except that you didn't. When you came back, when you started searching Hanley's rooms—they knew you didn't know a thing about—"

"About the only thing worth knowing, Russian," Devereaux said. "We are caught up in words and secrets and agents dancing around one another and it doesn't mean a thing, none of it. The only thing worth knowing is what Hanley knows. Or what he guessed. And they've kept him alive long enough to find out what that was and to find out if I knew any more than Hanley did."

For the first time, Devereaux's face clouded.

He closed his eyes, heard Hanley's words, heard his responses.

Yes. There was enough. To make someone think that he and Hanley knew more about something than they did. He had been involved because of a mistake; because someone misinterpreted the raving conversation recorded on tape on a tapped phone line.

"You can go back to sleep now, my friend," Denisov said.

"But it doesn't explain Alexa—"

"There was a man killed on the *Finlandia* who has not been identified. He was November."

Devereaux waited.

"Was there a second November?" Denisov asked.

"You didn't tell me this before—"

"Alexa took care of him. Two Novembers. Once in a blue moon, that is what Alexei said. It was the only unfortunate part of my journey. You see, it was necessary to retrace her steps and they led back to Helsinki and I had to see our stationmaster there. His name was Viktor. I had known him from days in the chess union, in Moscow, after I came out of Madrid embassy. His code name was Alexei."

"Tell me about the other November."

"On a boat in the Baltic. You know it, the *Finlandia*. A November with a scar on his face and gray hair who was to defect. Do you understand this?"

Devereaux betrayed nothing. He thought of Colonel

Ready. So they had caught him at last. He had tagged Ready with the code name and his own identity so that the wet contract on him would be shifted to the other man. Somehow, the Opposition had finally understood that Ready was not Devereaux. And that meant that someone in Section had told the Opposition. Only Section knew the truth—and only the top people in Section. So there was a mole and he was in Section. Or she. And he thought very suddenly and painfully of Mrs. Neumann and of Alexa waiting outside Mrs. Neumann's house.

Denisov frowned at the silence. But if Devereaux would not talk, the silence would last forever. Denisov frowned again, like a misunderstood child. "I had to finish Alexei."

"Don't you ever call it by what it is?" Devereaux said.

"No. It's only business. Killing is not business, it is some mad act. When you finish something, you are only taking care of business. Alexei must not know about me, not enough to tell anyone again." Denisov frowned a third time, then erased the thought from memory. "But I learned about Gorki. Why does he know so much about you? Why can he follow your movements so easily? I tell you, we don't have that capability. Not in the U.S.A."

"No," Devereaux said. "I wish we had another bottle."

"So do I. But the night is not so long from here now, is it?"

Devereaux was struck by that. Denisov had become entangled again in intricate English construction but it was appropriate. *The night is not so long from here now.* Whatever was going to happen, whatever had been set up, would happen quickly.

"You don't have the capability and neither would we.

No one predicts everything so easily except in spy novels. All the satellites and agents in the world only give us a clue, not the whole story. But someone has the whole story. About me. About Alexa."

"Who is it?"

"The man who tapped the phones. The man who listened to Hanley's conversation with me and decided I was dangerous."

Denisov did not speak. His hands were flat on the creases of his trousers. When he breathed again, his breath came in a whiney rush. "You have a mole in Section."

"More than that," Devereaux said.

"What is more?"

"Hanley knew. Somehow, Hanley had it figured out. Not all of it but parts of it. There is something called Nutcracker and it worried Hanley. Maybe it sent him off the deep end. I don't know."

"But Hanley. You know what you will do?"

"Yes. Part of it. No one knows everything."

"Except God," Denisov said. It was the voice of icons and incense; even a rational man, even a man such as Denisov, had these moments of automatic piety, gained from childhood.

"Except God," Devereaux said. "So let us pray tomorrow for guidance."

And Denisov was shocked to see that the other man was smiling.

27

FATHER PETERSON BRINGS SALVATION

They left a little before five in the morning. This was due less to the need to get an early start than the fact that Devereaux and Denisov felt there was too little night left for sleep.

Devereaux had made preparations.

In the small black bag were vials and vestments, the working tools of the Roman Catholic priest. He showered for a long time—the water restored him in a way that the vodka could not—and then he called Lydia Neumann's home. She didn't answer. The signal was not verbal: Three rings. Silence. Three rings.

Denisov was shocked.

Devereaux put on the clerical collar and fastened it with a stud. He slipped on the black blouse that ties in the back. He slipped on the black coat. He took the .32 Beretta police special, checked the action, and slipped it under the blouse into the belt of his black trousers. He looked at Denisov and smiled.

"I don't like this at all," Denisov said.

"You've become superstitious in old age," Devereaux

said. "I'm going to leave by the back entry. The car is in the parking garage. I don't suppose she's stayed awake all night watching it, especially since she can get information whenever she wants from our mole. Only this time, I really want a couple of hours. I'll shake any tail but you've got to cover the rear door."

"What is the gain again, exactly?"

"A chance to play the old game," Devereaux said.

"Substantially more than that."

"Seventy-five thousand."

"I'll leave you a poor man."

"I don't intend to take it out of my account," Devereaux said.

"No. I didn't think so."

He was not followed. Even spies sleep. Denisov had followed him out of the hotel and watched the back door while Devereaux took the rental car out of the garage.

Devereaux pulled into the driveway in Bethesda and the garage door opened and he slipped the long gray Buick into the second, empty parking space. It was typical of Leo Neumann not to have allowed junk to clutter up the second space.

He turned the ignition. The car fell silent. He had liked the idea of a Buick; a priest's car.

They waited at the kitchen. There were no lights on in the house. Dull dawn crept across the fog and lit the field behind the house.

Margot Kieker was as ready as she ever was. Her eyes were made up in that careful way that can be jarring at six in the morning. Her palms were wet and cold and she held them pressed together. She didn't quite believe all this was happening to her and that she had allowed it to happen.

But, in a strange way, she felt just fine.

He talked to her in a soft voice, explaining what they would do as though it were nothing at all.

"I only want to locate him. When I find him, I'll do the act and then we leave. That's all. I just want to know where he is. I can get him out myself."

"But what if they won't let you in?"

"I'm a priest. He's dying."

"But what if they say he isn't dying?"

"Don't worry about that."

Of course, Devereaux had thought about that since the night before, from the moment he had studied the girl at the supper table. He had acquired the clerical garb from a religious supply house in the afternoon and the plan had been to replace the regular priest who said mass on Sunday in the chapel inside the grounds. Once inside, he would have improvised.

Using the girl seemed safer. Especially for Hanley.

Mrs. Neumann spoke as softly as the morning.

"The problem with what you want me to do is that it alerts whoever it is that—"

"The mole," Devereaux said. "It has to be a mole in Section."

"Yackley," she said.

"Perhaps. Perhaps it is Richfield—he would have initiated the actual hardware part of the tap on Hanley's phone. He would have seen the transcript. It doesn't matter. Whoever it is has had it his own way and you have to flush him. Maybe Nutcracker will do that—"

*   *   *

The fog on the road made the going slower than expected. It was nearly 8:30 when they descended into the steep valley in western Maryland and then took the old road up to the south rim, where St. Catherine's stood.

Two and a half hours in a car can create a suggestion of intimacy between passengers.

Devereaux drove without much thought. Sunday morning was without traffic and the white fog that clung to the hills, to the meadowlands below the roadway, to the road itself—all hushed the outside world so that it ceased to exist.

"What is my great-uncle like?" She had tried once.

Devereaux glanced at her. She was on the edge of fear, like a doe in autumn at the edge of an Interstate Highway, deciding whether to cross. Her eyes were wide but steady. She had guts, Mrs. Neumann said. Maybe Mrs. Neumann understood these things well enough.

She was dressed in light blue, in a soft business suit that permitted a frilly blouse instead of an old school tie. The blouse had no color and it allowed the color of her face to define her face. She had a round face that might grow rounder with age. Her eyes were good and when she stared straight at you, you had to respond in the same way. She was good at silences.

"I didn't really know Hanley," Devereaux said at last.

"You worked with him."

"In a sense."

"You don't anymore."

"No."

"Why do this? For him?"

"It's for me."

"What did you do?"

"I worked for the government. At jobs." It wasn't enough. "Estimates. Field work. Department of Agriculture."

"No," she said.

Devereaux glanced again at her. The Buick clambered over the rise and there was a long, blind descent into white fog. Above them, the sun was trying to burn it off.

"No what?"

"This Department of Agriculture stuff. And Mrs. Neumann said that, too. This isn't about the price of soybeans."

"In a sense, everything is. About the price of soybeans," Devereaux said. But with gentleness.

"I ought to be told," she said.

He thought about it.

There was no more speech for two miles. And then:

"Your uncle is an intelligence officer. A director. In an agency that you have never heard of."

"Like the CIA?"

"Like the CIA."

"But I thought that was all there was."

"No. There are others. And he knows a good number of things. And secrets. So, I suppose, he was committed here for his own good and the good of keeping his secrets secret."

"But that's not right," she said. "I mean, I'm not being naïve. But what's the point of doing things wrong for all the right reasons?"

Because that is the way things are done, Devereaux thought. Because there is no morality in this, any of this; that morality is something for afterward, the sermons and soda water that follow the frenzy of the game. The politicians who preach about the amoral code of the intelligence establishment don't believe in what they say but like to hear themselves say it. The morality comes at the end of the game; when it is won.

No, not won.

Merely not lost.

Devereaux drove and said none of these things. The fog pressed against the car and intensified the silence.

"Why would he leave everything he had to me?"

"Because you were all he had."

"That's really pitiful, isn't it? Someone he doesn't even know? All he had."

And Devereaux thought of Rita Macklin. There was a conversation they were going to have to have. They both knew the form of the conversation but they never let it play out to the end because the end might really be too bad. What would Rita Macklin think of the morality in this? About rooting out a mole inside R Section for the love of government and country?

She would see through that.

When they had the conversation, they would have to be honest at least. He could never fool her anymore; that's what made it so good to be with her. Pretense was down and the careful agent could be careless. It was just that good between them.

He rehearsed in his mind: I had to do this. To save myself, to find out what had happened—

And she would say: What will you do now? It's not enough to go back, is it? You're going to have to stay inside, aren't you? Everything we arranged—it's not enough.

And he would say:

What?

What exactly would he say?

The silences in the car lasted the rest of the morning.

Finch looked at the priest. He saw the nuns on the steps already.

"Look, Father, this is a restricted area here, we are talking about the government—"

"I am a priest. I understand you have a dying man here, and his niece has called me."

"We don't have a religious preference on his card and—"

"He's a Catholic," Margot Kieker said. "Sister, Sister!" She shouted to the fat nun who waddled over. She saw the nun had cuts on the ends of her fingers and she wondered why.

Finch thought: Terrific.

"Sister, my uncle is dying and I want him to have the last rites. Extreme unction. Father Peterson was his priest, his friend, I had to ask him—"

"I hadn't seen Mr. Hanley for months, I thought he was out of the country, if only I had known—" Devereaux dithered. He stared hard at Finch and thought about how much Finch knew about anything going on around here.

They were at the main house and the morning fog was still thick and white around them. They might have been ghosts in a Scandinavian film.

Sister Domitilla looked confused. She looked at Finch—a man lately attached to the establishment by the government—and then at Sister Gabriella. "I don't want... I don't want to be responsible for denying the last rites to Mr. Hanley." She bit her lip. "Why can't they see him, Mr. Finch?"

"There are orders—"

"There is God's order, which is greater," Sister Domitilla blurted, surprised by her eloquence. She had felt very badly about Mr. Hanley. He had deteriorated so quickly, especially in the last week after Dr. Goddard began the electroshock treatments. The treatments were designed to help "resettle" the random electrical patterns in the brain. Hanley was sliding now; he would be dead in a matter of days.

"Look, I don't take orders from anyone but Mr. Ivers—"

Devereaux looked up at mention of the name. Who the hell was Ivers? It was the same name Sellers had mentioned.

"Mr. Finch," Devereaux said. "I am a priest. I want to help my old friend in his last moments—if these are his last moments. You can come with me. I am a man of secrets, as you are, as poor Hanley was." He paused, looking at Margot. "This poor creature is worried about her family. I am worried about my friend. But God is worried about his soul."

Devereaux's eyes were mild and he nodded solemnly to Sister Domitilla, who looked as though she might fall on her knees in prayer at any moment. Instead, she did something else.

"Come with me, Father, child," she said. "And don't interfere with me, Mr. Finch. This is St. Catherine's and I am in charge here and not you. You take care of security and Dr. Goddard will take care of the medical ills but I will take care of souls. Even the least of these, the most demented, is a creature of God."

"Let me see what's in the bag—"

It was all right, Devereaux thought, as Finch sniffed at the vials and replaced the tops, as he felt in the purple confessional stole for a hidden pocket. It was going to be all right.

Hanley had awakened after dawn and the room was vague in the watery morning light and he thought he might be dead at last. And then he had managed to focus well enough to see the crucifix on the opposite wall, above the place where Kaplan had died.

He felt unusually clear. He had felt this way for days. Ever since the beginning of the electroshock treatment. He was quite certain that he had been in this room all his life. He was now six or seven years old. Kaplan had been an old man. For some reason, he was supposed to die very soon, though he was quite young. His mother was due to visit him any day now. He was in Christ Community Hospital in Omaha and they were going to remove his appendix in a little while. They explained to him that it would hurt afterward but it would hurt much less than the hurt he suffered now. He had tried to explain yesterday—to Dr. Goddard—that he was feeling no pain at all. But Dr. Goddard only smiled at him.

He smiled when the door opened.

It was his sister, Mildred.

"Hello, Mildred," he said.

His sister seemed strange. As though she had something to say and didn't know how to say it. That was Mildred. The quiet one. And what was wrong with her eyes?

"Mildred? Is there something wrong with your eyes?"

"What?"

"It looks like someone has given you a black eye," Hanley said

"He thinks you're his sister," said a nun.

Of course this was his sister. Who did she think it was? He was six years old and he was having an operation tomorrow.

"Hello, old friend," said a man.

He stared at the man over him.

He blinked and could swear he knew that man. He saw that man and part of him knew him. The man was a reverend.

"Reverend Van der Rohe," said Hanley. "You came all the way to Omaha for me? Am I going to die?"

"No. You're not going to die, old friend."

"I was good. I missed Sunday school that one time but I was really sick, I wasn't just playing hooky."

"Go ahead with it," said another man. He was at the back of the room. "The guy's crackers."

"Mr. Finch," said the nun.

He had not seen a nun until he was twelve. He was certain of that. So how old was he? He couldn't be seeing nuns now. He was only five or six. No, at the time of the operation, he was seven. A terrible pain in his belly, they had been at the state fair, which is how he came to be in Christ Community Hospital. He didn't know anyone. They were so kind.

Hanley blinked.

"Mill? Are you there?"

"It's me, it's Margot."

"I don't know Margot," Hanley said. He thought of a name on something. What? A form of some sort? Margot Kieker. But this person was Mill. Mildred Hanley. She would marry Frank Knudsen and have a daughter named Melissa and up and die. Cancer. So young. It broke your heart. And then Melissa died. And then there was Margot. Now, was this Margot?

Hanley's eyes went wide in that moment and the priest leaned close to him.

"Make an act of contrition, my friend—"

Close. So close. He could see the gray eyes above him, feel the sense of power so close to him. He knew that face, he knew the sense of power. The face grinned hideously.

Like a nutcracker.

"Devereaux."

The name echoed in conscience. What does the brain know?

"Devereaux. I wanted you to come. I called you, damn you! I needed you!"

And the priest did a strange thing. He rolled on the floor and he came up with a pistol in his hand and the man at the door fired into the room.

Can you imagine a reverend shooting a pistol? There were more shots and the room shook.

The fat nun fell down. There was blood and Margot was pulling his arm. It hurt. Was it really Margot?

He was dragged to the floor, atop the woman who looked so much like Millie.

"Get out, get out, get out," she said, making a litany of the same words.

And he thought he really understood.

There was more firing and the man in the doorway screamed. He screamed and screamed. It was probably one of the patients. They were always screaming. He had to get out of here.

He had to get out of here.

He was up and it was absurd because he was nearly naked, he shouldn't appear this way in front of his sister. Once, in a bedroom in the old farmhouse, two children of intense loneliness, brother and sister, surrounded by emptiness, filled in by only each other: He had opened her blouse to see her breasts and she had let him and that was all they had done but they had been deeply ashamed for a long time and been bound to each other by the secret.

One man was dead. He was a small man with small eyes and there was the reverend standing at the door and Margot Millie was pushing him—

They were on the grounds and it felt good to be in the air. Hanley blinked at the ghostly fog and inhaled the air and felt lightheaded and nearly fell. The girl held him around the waist. He was so weak and it was cold in the milky-white morning.

Shouts and sounds and sounds of ghosts in the fog.

There were shots again.

Dr. Goddard was on the steps and he had a shotgun.

They heard the blast. The sound of the shotgun firing filled the dense air and exploded so that it hurt their ears. Hanley fell again, this time dragging the girl to the ground. He was so sorry.

"I want to apologize, Mill—"

"Come on, goddamnit!" the girl said with such savage zest that Hanley scrambled up eagerly. She shoved him in the back of the gray car and he felt the seat close to his face and the car was moving, there were shots and the side glass above his head was splattered by gunfire. The glass fell on him. The car shot through the closed gates, driving them off their hinges.

Hanley felt the razor cut of glass on his cheek. He opened his eyes. He sat up. The girl was next to him. He glanced around. The driver was the same; the girl was the same; he was in a car and it was plunging down into a valley and the fog grew around them.

"My face. I cut my face," he said. His voice sounded numb and strange to him.

In the rearview mirror, he saw the face of the driver.

"Devereaux," he said. "Devereaux."

The driver glanced in the mirror once. He saw the gray eyes. He knew the face, the eyes, the voice of that man.

"November," he said.

It felt such release to say that.

"November came back," he said.

28

DAMAGE CONTROL

Lydia Neumann sat in her office. Her fingers were poised above the cream-colored keys. The screen was blank save for a flashing green cursor.

The floor was nearly deserted because this was Sunday and her office was in the suite at the west end of the floor where R Section hierarchy had their private rooms and private showers and executive washrooms. Her presence was sometimes inconvenient, especially in managing executive washroom privileges, but there was nothing to be done: She was a woman, and she had risen very high indeed in Section.

The door to her office was open, as always. The office did not have a window; she was the only one of the four division directors without a window. But it was the most cheerful office of the four. There was a sampler on one wall, above the computer screens, that advised: *Garbage In, Garbage Out*. It had been a gift from some of the staff in division when she made the grade; it was a little joke the women shared and the men in the other divisions would never understand.

Lydia Neumann sat at the keyboard like Stravinsky. She summoned Tinkertoy to life on her screen.

She knew Tinkertoy so well.

Tinkertoy was the computer system used in R Section. It was named for the child's building toy. Link by link by link. The endless links fit numberless pieces of information together. Tinkertoy reconstructed the universe every millisecond as information poured into the computer from a thousand sources. Each bit of information was not merely added—it was indexed, categorized, fitted with other bits of information. Tinkertoy contained all the secrets of the spies, living and dead.

Tinkertoy was secure. It required a voice print, face print, fingerprint, and heat print.

When Tinkertoy's monitor flashed: "READY," she began.

She approached the information she wanted in three ways. Each approach was cautious and it allowed her time to retreat.

In each approach, she signed on at her level but then changed level of access by inserting the correct "add-on" code. This was only possible to her because she had designed the system with the safeguards. Even locked doors in secret buildings have to have keys and, generally, the lowliest worker in the building—the cleanup man—is given all the keys.

In each of the three approaches, she added on at a higher and higher level, to see how high the level of the secret of Nutcracker was kept.

She did not see Claymore Richfield walk into the room.

"Back on it already, Mrs. Neumann?"

She struck "BLACK," the key that cleansed the screen.

She was annoyed; she would have to start over. She turned to Richfield.

Richfield lounged in his jeans and sweater at the door.

"I hope I kept everything in order."

"I hope you did, Clay," Mrs. Neumann said.

"I wouldn't expect you back until tomorrow."

"Yes. I wouldn't have expected to be here."

"Problem?"

"No problem."

Claymore Richfield smiled. He was one of Yackley's loyalists. Why shouldn't he be? He had a free hand and free budget. His only complaints came when field agents rejected one of his devices. He had a James Bond idea for an exploding briefcase that had cost the hands of one of the field agents in Japan. He had complained the Japanese agent did not know how to use it properly and that the briefcase was perfectly safe. The agent in Japan had sued R Section for $4 million.

"I kept things tidy," Claymore said.

"Yes."

There was no encouragement to further conversation.

She waited at the keyboard.

"Well." Richfield seemed put out. "I suppose I'll be going."

"Yes," Mrs. Neumann said.

"Nice to have you back," he said.

"Nice to be back," she said.

When he was gone, she closed the door. She went back to the screen. She tapped Tinkertoy to life again.

At the fourth approach, in the fourth add-on level of security, she moved very far and it was frightening. She existed in a world of secrets, those kept and those stolen.

Secrets have their own familiarity, like the furniture in
a room you know well. But to stumble in the dark in a
strange room and not to know where the room is or when
there will be light to see the way makes for fear.

She nearly stopped. She was in a country without maps.

For a moment, she paused. She thought of Hanley in
St. Catherine's. She thought of Margot Kieker, overcom-
ing her own fears and uncertainties.

She thought of November, in clerical collar. And that
made her smile and she plunged in.

The computer was very quick to respond this time. The
numbers tumbled out.

NUTCRACKER:

CODE 9, PRIORITY ULTRA:

NUTCRACKER: 22 APR: DIRECTOR GORKI RESOLUTIONS
COMMITTEE;

EXCHANGE OF PERSONNEL: JANUARY, NEWMOON,
EQUINOX, JUNE, AUGUST, VERNAL, WINTER; EXCHANGE:
ALEXA, ANDROMEDA, SATURN, MERCURY, HEBRIDES,
GORKI.

KEY: GORKI FLUTTER ONE; ALEXA IN BLACK:
ANDROMEDA TO GREEKSTATIONFIVE; KEY: VERNAL IN
BLACK; WINTER IN GREEKSTATIONFOUR; JANUARYX;
NOVEMBERX.

She used a Number 2 pencil to write down all she saw
on the fluttering green screen. The screen held the message, waited patiently.

She understood it only a little but it would take too

long—perhaps be too dangerous—to press the file inward for CLEARSPEAK CONDSPEAK (for condensed version, the version on screen) would have to serve.

But serve whom?

Noon on Sunday. The fog was gone from the capital. The streets were wet and warm under the sun. The churches spoke songs and the bell tolled in the National Cathedral. From his apartment a block away, Hanley had often listened to that bell. But Hanley had not been in that place all this spring.

The gray Mercedes sloshed through puddles along Massachusetts Avenue. The car followed the gentle circle beneath the U.S. Naval Observatory and down across Rock Creek Park and down into the bowels of power. At DuPont Circle, the automobile leaned slightly into the curve and continued south along Connecticut Avenue toward the White House and the Executive Office Building.

The driver was a GS 9, cleared to Top Secret level for no other reason than that he drove an assistant national security adviser named Perry Weinstein.

Yackley had been on the phone at eleven. He had been contacted by Claymore Richfield, who had gone back through Tinkertoy after Mrs. Neumann left the DA building. Richfield had been merely curious and he had no way of understanding a damned thing that was going on. But Richfield was now a dangerous man.

Damnit. This was what you had to work with.

Perry Weinstein, in the back seat of the Mercedes, still had not repaired his horn-rimmed glasses. He wore a jogging suit that had never been sweated in. He sat back in the Mercedes and closed his eyes and tried to think.

It had only been thirty hours to Nutcracker, Yackley had shouted. It was April 18, the feast of Pentecost. Every move had been put in place. All the agents to be defected East were in place; Gorki had kept his bargain as well. But, perhaps, that was the way it was supposed to be. You didn't bargain with the devil.

Yackley, on the phone to Perry, had been very close to hysteria.

Hanley was snatched. By someone. Dr. Goddard said a nun was dead, as well as the security director, Randolph Finch. There had been two of them: A priest and a young woman.

Yackley had been babbling when Weinstein hung up the phone on him and made a second call. There was a scramble going on right now inside Operations Wing 3 of FBI. "The Sisters," as usual, didn't have a clue but they were the domestic intelligence agency and when it came to tracking people inside the citadel, they were the best at the game. So the FBI director kept explaining to the National Security Director who passed on his budget recommendations to the White House.

Now prove it, Perry Weinstein thought. Find Hanley and his abductors and do it in twenty-four hours.

He had allowed too much rope for Yackley. Yackley, in the end, was too stupid to know what to do with it. Weinstein had even had to prod the boob on electroshock treatment. Hanley was lingering too long; it was quite possible he could be legally rescued from St. Catherine's before he died. At least let his memory die.

He never said it in those terms to Yackley, of course.

Perry Weinstein was so careful and so close and it was not going to end badly. He had worked out a careful bargaining. Yackley had been assured he would have five enemy agents to show for the work and he would be more secure than ever. Even when this administration came to an end, Yackley would be included at the highest levels in the next administration—whatever the party. Perry Weinstein was a pragmatist and he promised practical things to people like Yackley.

And he would bring out Gorki. That was the key to the whole exchange. The master spy, the director of the Committee for External Observation and Resolutions— the Resolutions Committee of KGB. Gorki would come, kicking and screaming, because Gorki was the prize that Weinstein needed to make himself a "made" man in intelligence, one of the litmus tests to apply to others again.

And now some goddamn double-cross at the lowest level was being worked and two killers had snatched Hanley from St. Catherine's.

And a busybody named Lydia Neumann had somehow uncovered the digest of Nutcracker. She was being taken care of now.

The telephone was ringing when Weinstein entered his office. He popped buttons on the console and put on the speaker phone. He crossed to the window, hands in jacket, and stared down at the White House while he listened.

"Two chasers were put on Alexa ninety minutes ago," said the voice. There was a laconic charm to it. Ivers was the fixer from NSA; he had been part of Nutcracker from the beginning. Not that Ivers understood what Nutcracker was really all about. He was a good, loyal, conspiratorial, and limited man of action; his part in Nutcracker was just large enough to hold his interest.

"Where is she?"

"She is due to call in by one. We'll hold her this time, trace the call—"

"It'll be a pay phone—"

"That's in the movies, sir. We can trace anyone. Anytime. From any place." Ivers was sure and that amused Perry Weinstein. He pushed the glasses up his nose and smiled at the White House. The President was at Camp David. In a little while, the helicopter would clatter in and the ghouls from the networks would gather and wait for some word from the Main Man and the helicopter blades would keep rotating until the President had crossed to the south portico and entered the White House.

In two weeks, there would be the summit in May. But first, a crossing of swords called Nutcracker. A skirmish with spies and defectors.

Ivers rang off.

Dickerson at FBI was next. The Sisters had already found the abandoned Buick in Hancock. A second car had been stolen in that small town in western Maryland. "They're heading back this way," Dickerson said.

What a genius, Weinstein thought. "Do you have helicopter surveillance?"

"Yes sir, but it's a limited advantage today. The fog is really thick out on the Panhandle, I—"

"Roadblocks?"

"Yes sir, this is Division A emergency, we are moving—"

He rattled on in that dry disguise-my-accent voice. He offered reassurance like a telephone company salesman.

When the domestic business was done, Perry Weinstein moved to the other phone. It was colored red and it was safe and the numbers that it dialed were also safe.

He picked up the phone, waited, decided on the first block to be pushed over. Nutcracker was commencing in the morning because every block was in place now and the whole edifice could be tumbled.

Alexa had not slept at all.

She had followed the taxicab containing November all the way back to the hotel. Wisconsin Avenue was bright and unsuitable for the sort of direct hit she intended. And then the hotel had been wrong as well. She had lost him at the elevators and she suspected he had doubled back behind her. Watergate was so complex.

She had failed again. Everything else was an excuse.

She had not eaten for two days. She felt sick to her stomach all the time. She thought her breath smelled foul, for the first time in her life.

She dressed carefully, as always, but there was no joy in it. She was a woman who had delighted in all her senses, in feeling and smelling and touching. She was imbued with self-love but she never thought it was excessive. There had been much to love about herself.

How quickly it broke down, she thought.

A gesture from an old man with yellow skin in Moscow and suddenly she was a puppet on the stage with its strings cut. She had no action. She could not even save herself.

She pitied herself. And that was why she had not slept. That and the words of the man she had come to kill. So flat and soft in the darkness. He had known her. He had told her she was in danger.

She stood on Pennsylvania Avenue and the street was empty because it was Sunday and she looked at the White

House. She thought it should be more impressive, like the Kremlin. She thought she would kill the second November today and then kill herself. It would be far better than to be arrested by the Americans and put in cells for the rest of her life.

She dropped coins in the pay telephone and made the call to New York City.

The phone was picked up at the other end. There was no other sound.

She identified herself.

"You had opportunities. Why didn't you take them?" The voice spoke English; it was without any accent.

"I could not ensure my own way out," she said. She spoke as brutally as the voice. "Each time, there were difficulties. He knows me. He called me by name last night."

There was silence. She had silenced the pitiless voice for a moment. It was almost a moment of triumph.

"Is this true?"

The question was not meant to be answered.

"Do you have him?" Alexa said. "It doesn't matter now. I know what I will do. I will fulfill the mission." She closed her eyes and felt faint. She tried to think of the heroic posters thrown up in Moscow each May Day and in the fall, in celebration of the October Revolution. Men and women marched on banners hundreds of feet long, striding with Lenin toward the Revolution. But she did not feel heroic. Only sick and alone in this foreign, savage country. She would do her duty this last time.

"Yes. This time, without fail. Even at risk to yourself."

"Where is he?"

"There is a house on P Street," the voice began. "Go to the house on P Street and when you reach it, wait inside.

The key is under the mat at the door. Wait there for instructions." He gave her the address on P Street N.E.

She felt very afraid in that moment, more afraid than at any time since Helsinki when the agent there had directed her to "the second November in Switzerland."

"What will happen to me there?"

"Happen to you?" The voice seemed on the point of taking on coloration. But the voice paused and resumed in the same bland tone. "Nothing, Alexa. It is for instructions. This time, there will not be failure. There is no time for failure now."

And the line was broken.

She replaced the light-green telephone receiver. She looked around her. What a queer city of low buildings and Greek columns and shabby streets full of slums. There were trees everywhere and yet there did not seem to be gaiety to the city at all. She felt a sullen undercurrent around her. She was accustomed to the same thing in Moscow: But there was vitality in Moscow that came from within, from secrets kept locked in secrets.

Alexa thought there was no vitality in Washington on this Sunday afternoon. She felt alone and abandoned in the West.

She stared around her. Her eyes carried down to her soul. They were shining and black and dangerous. Her eyes could not be disguised and she would not die like a victim. If they meant to kill her, they would have to engage her.

She felt the pistol in her pocket.

She saw Lenin on the wall hangings, striding toward the Revolution.

She even felt the first stirrings of hunger.

29

FLIGHT AND REFUGE

W hy are we going back?" Margot said.

"The best place to hide is a city," Devereaux said. "Is he all right?"

"He's shaking."

"Give him my coat."

"You killed that nun?"

"Give him the coat, Margot." Softly, firmly.

"You killed her and that man—"

"Give him the coat."

She draped the coat around Hanley.

They heard the helicopter again. The copter swept low over the road but there was nothing to see. The fog was blinding. It was an act of desperation to fly in fog like this.

Devereaux drove very fast and very hard. His eyes were so fixed on the road—on the billows of fog—that it was painful to refocus them. The fog seemed to roll at the windshield. It was worse than it had been that morning. The day was warm and the ground wet. He rolled down the window and could smell the springtime all around, all hidden.

"His face is bleeding."

"Is it bad?"

"I don't know."

"For Christ's sake, Margot, wipe the blood away and see how badly he's hurt."

She shivered. She wiped the blood from Hanley's cheek and saw the wound. "No, it's not bad," she said. "You killed two people."

The copter blades sounded very close. That was the trouble with fog. It affected hearing as well as vision. It enclosed everything.

Devereaux had not intended to rescue Hanley that Sunday morning. He never thought that Hanley would recognize him. Or, if he did, that he would have been enough in his senses to keep quiet. It had been a surveillance, to see where they kept Hanley and how hard it would be to get him out.

Now it was a mess. There was no time left at all. Hanley must hold the key to whatever was going on in Section. But what help could he be?

The police car passed them and Devereaux saw the taillights wink in the rearview window. Turning around. It was a good idea to get back to Washington but this was a terrible road for it.

"Hold him, Margot," Devereaux said. "And get down."

She slid down in the seat and the car came very near behind them. The Mars lights were flashing. Devereaux slowed down as though to stop. The police car slowed down. The helicopter surged overhead.

Radio contact, he thought.

Nothing to do. He pushed the gas pedal and the Buick roared ahead and the reaction time from the patrol car was just a moment slow. There was no time to do anything else.

The Buick was going fifty miles an hour into blind fog. Devereaux could barely see the yellow line on the two-lane road; it was the yellow line that guided him. If he couldn't see the yellow line at all, they were finished.

Margot's voice was too loud: "My God, you can't drive this fast!"

He didn't answer. He held the wheel hard.

The cops had guts. They were following his taillights, scarcely thirty feet behind.

More guts than brains, Devereaux thought. He slammed the brakes, turning the wheels left to the wrong side of the road, and then rode the shoulder, controlling the skid.

The police car crashed into the right rear bumper and careened into a grove of trees that led down a gentle slope to a secondary road below. Devereaux never stopped. He pushed into the fog and Margot got up and looked around and guessed what had happened.

"This is insane, you're making me...an accomplice to...this is killing...you killed a nun!"

"Shut up, Margot," he said, never looking at her. "Hold him," he said.

"This man is dying," she said.

"He can die later," Devereaux said. The voice had no pity in it at all.

They made it to the edge of the city in a stolen car, swiped from a church parking lot in Fredericksburg. For a moment, Margot had forgotten her fear because she had been fascinated by the technology of stealing a car without keys in it.

In Bethesda, Devereaux said, "Change cars again."

"Are you insane? Are you just insane?"

"Margot, there are people after us. They are using helicopters. Just do what I say and don't ask me any more questions."

The car was a Rambler with the keys in it. It had patches of rust on the body and the tired look of a car that no one makes anymore. He pulled up the stolen Pontiac and got out. He helped Margot lift Hanley into the back of the Rambler.

The dude came out of the liquor store into the lot and watched them. He was in his twenties and looked scuffed at the toes. He had a worn leather jacket and he wasn't wearing a shirt.

"Hey, buddy," he said in an easy voice. "My car."

"I was just taking it," Devereaux said.

The kid grinned. "Why don't you steal something worthwhile? This is a shitbox."

Devereaux smiled. "I could buy it from you."

"Then I'd be stealing from you."

"Do you have scruples about that?"

"No. Do what you gotta do, you know? Been driving that old sucker all winter, though. Got me through. Have some affection for it."

"Are both of you crazy?" Margot was in the car now.

"Tell you what," Devereaux said. "I'll give you a hundred for it and I'll return it later. Just renting it."

"Ain't worth a hundred. Why don't you go to Avis?"

"What do you say?"

"Sure. That's what I say. Just give me a lift, will you? You going into the District? Drop me off down by the Huddle House over the line, will you?"

*   *   *

The Rambler coughed across the District line on Wisconsin Avenue shortly after two in the afternoon. The kid's name was Dave Mason and he told Devereaux to watch for the cop who always waited behind the supermarket on the south side of the line for speeders who wanted to push over the twenty-five-mile-an-hour limit.

Devereaux eased it down and was passed by a BMW. A better prospect. The D.C. police car shot out into Wisconsin Avenue with Mars lights flashing. They passed the BMW pulled over to the side of the road two blocks later.

"You got some idea where you're going?" Dave said. It was just a friendly voice. He smiled at Margot in the back seat.

"Some," Devereaux said.

"Ain't nothing to me, man. But I would like to get the car back."

"You'll get it back or I'll have one built just like it."

"Rust and all," said Dave. He smiled. He popped a beer out of the sack. "You want a beer, lady?"

"No," Margot Kieker said. None of this was real. It wasn't happening.

"You drop me off up ahead," said Dave. "I can hoof it."

"You working, Dave?"

"Not much. Do a little house-painting. Things are slow. Everyone with a job to offer wants you to work for two dollars an hour and clean out the toilets in your spare time."

"Gimme the address," Devereaux said.

Dave wrote it down on the paper sack and tore off a piece of the sack. He gave it to Devereaux. He looked him right in the eye and Devereaux stared back at him. Dave smiled. "Damn. You're gonna bring it back, ain't you?"

"Bet on it," Devereaux said.

The house was in Georgetown and it had occurred to Devereaux as they entered Hagerstown, an hour before.

The house was narrow and tall and elegant, with polished bricks and gleaming black iron. The roof was flat and ornamented with a copper façade. The Rambler seemed out of its class parked in front of the house. The Rambler would have to go. But first, there was the matter of Hanley. And the girl.

Margot had asked him after they dropped off Dave, "Why would he trust you?"

"He doesn't."

"He gave you the car."

"I gave him a hundred dollars."

"I don't understand. He didn't call the police or—"

"Why would he do that?"

"You were stealing his car."

"No one would steal a car like this."

"You would."

"Margot." Softer now. "You have too much belief in rules. There aren't any rules."

"Then it's chaos. No rules means it's chaos."

Yes, Devereaux thought.

That exactly described it.

He opened the door of the car. His arms felt heavy. His back was knotted with lumps of tension. He would have to shake all his muscles awake again.

He went first, up the three stone steps. The street was empty but it could be full of people if the sun came out.

He knocked at the ornate brass plate. The door opened and it was an old woman.

"Dr. Quarles."

"It's Sunday," said the old woman.

"Tell him it's Mr. Devereaux."

The old woman frowned and slammed the door. He waited. The afternoon was full of sweet smells and the fog. The wonderful fog that had covered their tracks all the way into Washington. Even the best agent needs luck; he had not expected the fog at all.

The door opened. Quarles stared at him. Quarles had large eyes and a red nose and his eyebrows exploded on a broad forehead. His hair was wild, long and combed in the absent manner of men who have better things to do than worry about how they look. He resembled an Old Testament prophet or John L. Lewis.

"What do you want?"

"I've brought you a patient."

"Just as well. I don't make house calls," Dr. Quarles said. He opened the door wide and stared at the car. "My God, I didn't know they still made those things."

"They don't."

"Well, get it out of here. You're driving down property values. Put it on M Street and let it roll down the hill and into the river."

Devereaux nodded at the car and Margot Kieker opened the rear door.

"Well, she's young enough. Knock her up?"

Then they saw the second man, emerging painfully, half-consciously, from the back seat.

"Goddamnit. He's wearing a hospital gown," Dr. Quarles said and he took a step down and then another and reached Hanley before Margot sank under the burden of the man.

Quarles was large and strong. He had the arms of a Welsh miner, which his father had been, and the manner of a Welsh preacher, which his father had opposed. Quarles had no time for foolish people or foolish notions. He was immensely successful. Seventeen years before, in Vietnam, he had been captured by a file of Viet Cong. Seventeen years before, he had been rescued—not for himself but for the sake of someone else captured that day. The second prisoner had been important for some reason of state. For some reason of state—neither Devereaux nor Quarles ever knew it—Devereaux had saved Dr. Quarles' life. It was a matter of a debt that could never be repaid and both of them knew it. And both knew that Devereaux was ruthless enough to exploit it.

Quarles picked up Hanley the way a child will pick up a bird with a broken wing. He carried him into the house.

He put Hanley down in an examining room, on a table covered with a leatherlike surface. He grasped his wrist, held his fingers to his throat, did all the things doctors do quickly.

"He ought to be in a hospital."

"That's where he has been."

"Why did you take him out?"

"Because they were killing him."

"Who is he?"

"It doesn't matter; you don't need to know."

"Need to know?" Quarles turned the face of the prophet on him. "Like that, is it, Mr. Devereaux? You'll roast in hell someday."

"But not right now."

"You wicked man and your wicked ways. Still playing at the game? Why don't you grow up and act your age and get into something important?"

"It's too late for that," Devereaux said. "What can you do for him?"

"What did they do to him, is more like it?"

"It was a mental institution—"

"A goddamn loony bin? You took this wretch out of a nut house? Well, you're not so far gone after all, you grave-robbing son of a bitch. Good for you."

Margot Kieker blanched but this wasn't the worst she had seen this day. She stood by her great-uncle, on the other side of the table, holding his hand because she didn't know what to do with her own hands. She was so amazed with herself—with her calm, with her actions—that she felt in a perpetual state of shock.

"Who's this? Your moll?"

"His niece."

"Niece my foot. I see Congressmen with their nieces prowling the joints on M Street. Those are nieces. This looks like a girl to me." He had such an odd manner of speech—as though he had learned to talk by reading old books—and the cause was precisely that: He had been nearly dumb until he was ten because he could not see very well and no one in that village in Wales understood it. He had taught himself to read by closing one eye and reading with the other.

Devereaux said, "There isn't much time."

"What? For him? He'll make it by the look of him. Just needs some beef. Heartbeat's slow but regular, pulse is— But then, why am I explaining this to you? I'm the goddamn doctor. If I say something, it's so."

Devereaux seemed to ignore the tone of voice, the glowering face, the posturing and theatrical gestures. He went to the window and looked out of the examining room at the street. "Bring him around," Devereaux said.

"What is this about?".

"Do you have a medical directory?"

The book listed surgeons in Washington, D.C., and environs and their specialities.

Devereaux found the name he was looking for. "I'll be back in a little while," he said.

"Where's your shirt, man?"

"It's a long story."

"And you don't have time to tell it."

Devereaux buttoned the black coat over his collar-less clerical shirt. He had no more time to waste with Quarles. Quarles owed him because of his own sense of debt; Devereaux would not have felt the same way. But if Quarles owed him, then let Quarles satisfy his conscience by paying the debt.

30

THE HOUSE ON P STREET

Alexa saw the man in the house on P Street. He was at the window. Alexa stood across the street and felt for the pistol in her pocket.

She thought she would shoot the man in the window. Then she would wait six more hours to see what the reaction would be when she called the number in New York.

Action was better than worry, she thought. If this was a trap, it would not matter. And if this was a mistake—well, then, she was being condemned for some mistake she could not even understand.

She drew the pistol out of her coat pocket and unsnapped the safety and drew the target in line.

And felt the muzzle on her neck.

"Don't even turn."

Said in bad Russian. But she understood.

He reached for her pistol and took it from her cold hand and pushed her ahead of him across the street and into the house.

There were three men. It was as she imagined it would

be. She felt something like relief. She had been on a tight-rope for so long. At least, this was the end.

The first man said it was necessary to handcuff her. For reasons of security. He said it as an explanation, which comforted her. He spoke fluent Russian but he was obviously not a Russian.

They cuffed her hands in front of her. The cuffs were attached by very thick and very heavy links of metal.

They searched her.

One of the men derived some pleasure from this. They removed her underpants and explored her body. They wanted to humiliate her; she understood that; she understood the techniques, all of them. It was preliminary to what would follow.

She hoped death would be easy. She had never dwelt on inflicting pain for its own sake or for her pleasure. She killed because she was a soldier in a war and that was what she was supposed to do.

Until the matter of the second November.

It had been a trap, all of it, and she had waited for the trap to be sprung on her with the timid courage of an animal that understands its impending doom.

They told her to sit down at last in a straight chair next to a wooden table in a room at the back of the house. One of the men went out. The second man sat at the table. The third man went to the window and looked out.

The first man—he was stocky, with rigid blue eyes and very blond hair—said, "We are United States agents."

"CIA," she said.

"Perhaps," the blond man said.

That confused her. She opened her eyes very wide and he seemed to stare straight into her, as though she had no secrets and no defenses. She felt the cuffs on her wrists. She was strong and she felt outraged—despite her training, despite her understanding, the search had touched an outrage in her—and she pressed her lips together very tightly. She had no intention of resistance, except in that moment of outrage. She had seen resistance shown by other prisoners and how that resistance was gradually broken down.

"My name is Ivers," the blond man said. "But how much do you know of this already?"

Again, she felt disoriented. She blinked and stared at him and tried to understand. She spoke in English now:

"I want to tell you what you want to know. I know that I am trapped in this. I have no way out. I realize all of this and I want to cooperate with you. My government has... abandoned me. I do not understand. But I do not want pain."

The one at the window said, "She doesn't want pain. You hear that?"

"I heard that," said Ivers. It seemed to give him pleasure to think about that. He said to the one at the window, "Why don't you go out and get some sandwiches. Some coffee and sandwiches."

"Oh," said the one at the window. "I get it."

Alexa stared at Ivers.

"All right," he said. The second one went out the door. "What do you know about Nutcracker?" It was what he had been told to say. Ivers was the fixer, the errand boy. He understood his status and it didn't bother him. No one else knew how important he was. Or who he reported to.

She stared at him without speaking. It was the wrong response. He got up from the chair and came around the table slowly. He hit her on the face. He hit her five times.

The blows were open handed and his hands were large and when they cracked her skin, the pain filled her head and clouded her vision. When the blows were done, the pain burned across her skin and filled her thoughts. She was crying but it was not self-pity; it was because of the pain. The tears came involuntarily.

"All right," Ivers said. He went back to his chair and sat down. "What do you know about Nutcracker, and who else was involved? Why didn't you do your contract, Alexa?"

"I don't understand you."

"Really? You don't really understand me? Dear, this is not a game. We have a loose cannon out there and it's up to you to help us haul it in."

"Please. Mr. Ivers. I will tell you. Please, I will tell you everything. I can tell you about the business in Finland five years ago, I can—"

"I'm not interested in ancient history. I want to know about November. Are you two in this?"

She felt she was sitting in the company of a madman.

"You didn't take out November. You were supposed to take out November. You had chances. Was he part of the deal?"

"I was to resolve him. Yes. But I did not resolve him because I saw this was a trap. If I resolve him, then I am trapped worse than if I am a spy. Yes, I am an agent."

"Oh, God, dear, we know that," Ivers almost laughed. "Everyone's known that. That's a given. You're a spy, he's a spy, everyone's a spy. So you tell me, dear, tell me if November was part of this scheme with you and...and who else? That's what we have to know, dear. Who else?"

She sat very still. She was locked in a room, in handcuffs, and she was speaking to a madman. Her head was ringing with pain. She felt isolated and alone and afraid. She could smell the fear in her breath.

"This is the way it is," Ivers said. "You are a Soviet agent in the United States. You were involved in the seduction of a security guard in California a couple of years ago. That's felony, dear. You have no diplomatic status. We could lock you up for the rest of your life."

"No," she said. "No." Softer.

"And think of pain, dear," Ivers said. "I have no aversion to that. I like my work. I do jobs for people and I do them well and I said, 'You can leave her to me, I can take care of her.' I saw your photograph. Very nice, all those photographs that Gorki took of you."

The photographs.

On a spring morning six years ago.

So inventive. Why would she agree to such a thing? Because he was Gorki and there was power in the glittering lizard eyes and the yellow skin was parchment to the touch and, in those moments with him, alone, he controlled her utterly.

And now he had abandoned her.

And thrown her to people like this man.

"Now, let's try this again," Ivers said.

The door opened.

Ivers looked up. It was too soon for sandwiches. Didn't the idiot understand anything?

Denisov said, "Will you take the handcuffs off?" The voice was as mild as a vicar speaking of children and flowers. The eyes swam behind rimless glasses and the right gloved hand held a Walther PPK.

"Who are you? This is government—"

"Shut up, please. Take the handcuffs off."

Ivers reached for the key.

"Slowly."

Alexa stared at him. He said to her, in Russian, "Why do you let yourself be trapped by dull people?"

She said nothing.

The wrists were freed and she felt for her face with her right hand. She felt the bruise.

"Who has sent you?" she said in Russian.

"I have come out of gallantry," he said. The approximate English could not explain the degree of mockery built into what he said in Russian.

"This is a fucking double-cross," Ivers said in plain English, without any subtlety at all.

"Perhaps," Denisov said in English. "Alexa, will you put him in the restraints? Behind his back, please?"

"There is no escape," she said.

"There is always escape. We are in America. There is always another way."

"I don't understand," she said.

"No. No one does at all. But that is the beginning of understanding, to admit you are ignorant." And Denisov smiled at his own cleverness.

Ivers learned to talk in a motel room outside of Arlington, Virginia, on a Sunday afternoon. It was amazing, Alexa thought. Denisov appeared so mild and the means were so brutal and direct. Ivers was eager to talk after only a few hours. Alexa thought it was the sense of patience that Denisov brought to the task; also, the sense that it did not pleasure him, any of it. Denisov was so powerful and controlled.

Alexa thought she was falling in love.

31

HANLEY'S SECRET

Devereaux found Dr. Thompson and Dr. Thompson agreed, after a lengthy explanation, and persuasion of short duration, to talk about part of Hanley's treatment. He was not so jolly when it was over. Dr. Thompson was left alive because Devereaux could not think of any reason to kill him.

The city of Washington was sunk into the calm of its usual Sunday.

The President had returned from Camp David in the mountains. He had an extraordinary ability to rest completely in a short period of time. He had shouted out answers to the hordes of photographers and newsmen awaiting his arrival by helicopter on the White House lawn. He had waved at them in that characteristic way and shrugged off those questions he did not wish to hear. The helicopter blades kept whirling until the President was inside the White House.

Across the city and into the suburbs, people dozed in front of their television sets, read the remains of the Sunday *Washington Post*, dined on sandwiches made with leftovers from the big dinner meal, sank into the torpor of the day.

Nothing was happening in the city. Even the police stations were unusually quiet. There was a small mattress fire reported on Eastern Avenue shortly after seven but no one was hurt and it was quickly doused. Washington was calm; therefore, the world was sleeping.

Hanley spoke rationally at nine P.M. He recognized Devereaux. He was able to understand the questions.

Quarles had said this might happen. Hanley was weak but the passages of clarity were frequent. The doctor had summoned Devereaux from downstairs.

Dr. Quarles, unchanged in appearance from the afternoon, sat at the foot of the bed in the spare room at the top of the narrow house. He said, "The body is free of drugs but there's been abuse. Definitely. They gave him tranquilizers in the last week but there's nothing active now."

Hanley said, "They gave me electroshock treatments." He remembered it so well. His voice was weak but the train of thought was clear.

He had been fed twice. The portions were small but the soup was very rich. The liquid had warmed him. He felt vague and weak, as one does at the end of an illness that fevers the brain.

"They were killing you."

"Yes," Hanley said. "I didn't expect that. Not that part of it. I thought they just wanted to get me out of the way. I really didn't think this was going to come to murder." The thought of murder—his own murder at the hands of others—was compelling to him.

Quarles stood up. "Time now for shop talk, is it? The evil you do is never worth the good it brings."

Devereaux said nothing.

Hanley watched Devereaux's face.

Quarles wanted some reaction and there was none. "Goddamnit. There should be rules."

"But there aren't. There never were," Devereaux said. It was the first time he had responded to the doctor's rages and sermons.

Quarles stared at him with the face of Moses for a moment. And then he opened the door, stepped out, and closed it. They heard his heavy tread on the stairs.

"I don't know how long I'll be rational," Hanley said. Very soft. "I think they've done some damage to my mind. I was quite rational in the last week. I was dying and weak and I was trying to think of a way to get out of that place. Or at least, tell someone."

"Why didn't you tell Mrs. Neumann when she came?"

"I wanted to. You see, the drugs, they had this effect on me. They must have drugged me all along."

"You were given medication by Dr. Thompson. When you were still functioning in Section," Devereaux said. And he told him everything Thompson had finally told him.

"So that explained..." Hanley trailed off. "I was trying to figure it out. And I thought about you and decided you must have been part of it, part of the trade. Or maybe, because I was drugged, I thought of you."

"You were reading Somerset Maugham. You were reading Ashenden. All set in Lausanne and Ouchy and across Lake Geneva."

Hanley blinked. "Yes. That's it."

"It was a mistake about me. I wasn't supposed to be

awakened. They tapped your phone and they made a mistake."

"There's a mole. In Section," Hanley said.

"Yes."

"You understand that?"

"Yes."

"I felt it for the last nine months. It's been terrible. It could have been anyone. It could have been Mrs. Neumann. My God, even her. I suspected her. I thought the day she called up, she called me at home, I thought she was setting me up. I suspected everyone. I was paranoid. We lost two agents—two damned good men and their whole networks—in three months last fall. They defected. Can you believe that? The networks were blown up. All that work wasted. All those lives... They defected to the goddamn Soviet Union." Hanley tried to sit up. He was exercised and his face flushed.

Devereaux held up his hand.

Hanley coughed. "And now I've got a goddamn cold," he said. He never swore. He was a man of propriety. "I feel like a fool."

"There are no spies," Devereaux said.

Hanley blinked. There was a silence that could be felt in the room. The house was shuttered for the night. Margot Kieker slept on a cot in the basement room. The whole house had been squeezed to find room for the three visitors. The housekeeper said nothing to any of them, as though it might be quite normal for three strangers to drop in on Dr. Quarles in the middle of a Sunday and stay for the night.

"I said that. I said that on a goddamn open line."

"What does it mean?"

"Yackley. Yackley said it to me. He attributed it to Richfield, our mad scientist. Richfield was very gung ho on this retrenchment program that was coming down from Administration. We had too many agencies, too many spies. It was involved."

"A lot of bureaucratic infighting," Devereaux said. "The same old thing. It had to be more than that."

Hanley's eyes brightened. "More. A lot more than that." The dry voice was drier still but the flat Nebraska accent emerged with clarity.

"Richfield was trying to sell Yackley on the idea of cutting back Operations, that the work of agents was now largely redundant because we had so many surveillance devices, computers, satellites... all the hardware. Yackley liked the argument. He used it against me. The cost could be shown so clearly as savings. I mean, he wanted to eliminate a bunch of agents to start, as an experiment, to see if the operation would suffer—"

"Who?"

Hanley frowned. "One of the things... specific memory. It's harder to fix times. This morning I woke up and I thought I was six or seven years old, the time I was in hospital with appendicitis in Omaha—"

But Devereaux had opened a sheet of paper. He read: "January. New Moon. Equinox. June. August. Vernal. Winter."

Hanley said nothing for a moment. "Yes. The names. The agents."

"They're all in the field—"

"Yes. No chasers or safe-house keepers. All watchers and stationmasters. They had networks. My God, I couldn't explain to Yackley that he wasn't talking about seven men. He was talking about hundreds of men. The links . ."

"I know," Devereaux said.

"It wasn't a matter of protecting our investment alone. It was all that work thrown away. And what good is the hardware without software? I mean, we get soft goods all the time from the Opposition. The hardware bona fides it for us. And the other way around. The satellite spies movement outside of Vladivostok. What's the good of knowing the SIGINT without knowing what the motive is? Software. Human contact. HUMINT. That's what you need. But the hardware doesn't have life or soul or judgment. It isn't human. You can't make it all on hardware, can you?"

"What did you do?"

"I didn't know what to do. I thought something was wrong. Yackley was positively demented on the subject. You'd think he was brainwashed."

"Yackley struck me as a man waiting for some stronger brain than his to tell him what to do. They call him a team player."

Hanley plucked at the cover for a moment. He was waiting but Devereaux said nothing more. Devereaux had made the contact with Denisov at five. It was the fallback point, derived from an old show business routine. Denisov called the lobby of the hotel and asked if there had been any messages for him. Then Devereaux called and used the same name and asked for messages. He then left a message for anyone who would call him. Denisov called again, asked for the name he had used before, and picked up the message Devereux had left. They made contact and the final message was: Ivers had talked.

"Damnit, man, what is going on?"

"What is Nutcracker?"

Hanley said the unexpected: "It was set up a year ago. We were collating information inside Operations. This was strictly Operations, Mrs. Neumann's division wasn't in on it at all. It was strictly software, strictly HUMINT."

"Go ahead."

"The idea came about because of what happened at the first summit. You remember the exchange of agents? It was all just coincidence. I thought it was coincidence at the time. I really wasn't paranoid."

Devereaux said, "In the trade, that might just be reality."

"But the idea took on some urgency." Hanley was going back over memory. "I mean, there was all this talk about cutting back Operations. Cutting back software. Field agents and Number Four men and station-masters and housekeepers and garbagemen. Even chasers. My God, you need chasers."

"My experience with chasers hasn't been all that pleasant. Section chasers," Devereaux said.

Hanley looked at the patterns on the wall. "A woman designed this room."

"The clever spy," Devereaux said.

Hanley said, "Sarcasm." Devereaux felt better at that. It was a trace of the old Hanley and not this weak man sitting up in bed in front of him.

"I'm so damned tired," Hanley said.

They waited for each other.

"Nutcracker. The idea was to find and identify three or four men from the Opposition. That wasn't so difficult. What we were going to do was to turn them. And if they wouldn't turn, we were going to muddy them up so that Opposition wouldn't know if they had been turned or not.

We decided early on it would be in Europe exclusively, because that's where the Summit was going to be held."

"Berlin."

"Exactly."

"This was for politics?"

"For survival. Of Operations. Operations is the heart of the Section. Operations is HUMINT. Besides, it was legitimate."

"We're supposed to gather intelligence, not play 'I Spy,'" Devereaux said.

"We're supposed to survive. That's the first rule of every game."

"This is crazy," Devereaux said. Nutcracker didn't turn out to be what he expected.

"It got crazier."

"How?"

"It was downholded."

"What happened?"

"I had my own file in Tinkertoy. On Nutcracker. Yackley didn't know about it, Neumann didn't know. Well, I thought Neumann didn't know; she's a smart cookie. I had the file to keep track of my own reports...we were moving along, setting up our targets, we had made contact with one..."

Devereaux waited. Hanley seemed to be seeing something beyond the room. He plucked absently again at the covers. His eyes were wet. There might be tears at times, Dr. Quarles had said. The body reacts in strange ways to the manipulation of the mind. Give him time, give him rest.

"In January, I came in one morning and I had...I had been feeling bad. I had seen Dr. Thompson a few times. He gave me pills. Iron pills or something. I don't know. At least, I thought they were." His voice was small. "I came in this morning in January. It snowed. You know what snow is to Washington. The office was half deserted. My God, people are babies."

Silence again. And then the distant voice resumed. "I went into Tinkertoy for the Nutcracker file. And Tinkertoy stopped me. 'Access denied.' It was my goddamn file. And I am the director of Operations. It was my file and my plan and it had been taken from me. I felt...so strange. I felt like I had gone through the Looking Glass. I had to know what happened. I went to Yackley and he looked at me like I was crazy.

" 'What are you talking about,' he said. 'I never heard of Nutcracker.' Of course, it was true. I mean, it was my operation. I hadn't shared it with anyone. I had used discretionary funds. I made it a secret and now someone had taken it away from me. I couldn't figure it out. It was making me... well, what happened to me? Did I go crazy or not?"

"I don't know," Devereaux said. "I'm not a shrink."

"They were going to kill me," Hanley said with wonder. "The first day at St. Catherine's, that bastard Goddard sprayed me. With Mace. He sprayed me in the goddamn face. That dirty son-of-a-bitch."

"You can get him later," Devereaux said. "Why did you write this? Why did you write Nutcracker and then list all our own agents? And my name?"

Hanley stared at the paper as though he had never seen it before. And then there was recognition.

"I was home. I was on fire all the time and so tired. I couldn't think what had happened to Nutcracker. It existed in Tinkertoy and I had no access to it. But if I went to Mrs. Neumann, what if it turned out that she was part of this...this thing that was happening in Section. She was the computer wizard. Maybe she wanted to destroy Nutcracker before it started. Hardware, she's in hardware. Software is old-fashioned. 'There are no spies.' It kept going around and around in my head. Everyone was against me. I went to Yackley a second time and then I thought that maybe Yackley was part of whatever it was that was going on."

"There is no file above you, is there?"

"My level, you mean? Yes. The Security file, the level of the National Security Adviser. And the President's file."

Devereaux said, "Why did you list the names of your own agents?"

"Because we had lost men and I got the idea—I got the idea that the Opposition was pulling a Nutcracker on me. On the Section. On our side. It just came to me like that. I thought I was crazy but there it was. It was logical. Maybe they—the other side—they were working against the Section. They could have access to my Nutcracker scenario and use it against me. Against the Section. They could let it go along and then, when the time was ready, turn it inside out."

"You called me," Devereaux said. His gray eyes shifted focus. He was remembering as much as he could. The room was as still as a confessional. "You said something about the highest levels. When you called me."

"I was babbling."

"But what were you babbling about?"

Hanley squinted, picked at the coverlet again and again. He sighed and tried to remember. It was so difficult to remember things. "I was out of my head most of the time. It was like being on fire."

"Remember," Devereaux said.

"The highest levels. The highest levels. It was like an itch inside my brain and I couldn't reach it. That's why I was writing down ideas. Like Nutcracker. That's it. The highest levels. I couldn't get through my computer to Nutcracker and that meant it was taken from me at the highest levels. But that didn't make any sense."

"Unless there is a mole," Devereaux said.

"A mole in Section." Hanley seemed to visibly collapse into the sheets. "A mole in Section." The horror of it clouded his face. He closed his eyes and felt like weeping again. He had said it before as though in a dream. And now, there was no dream. When he opened his eyes, they were wet. He loved Section. He had given his life to Section as you give your life to a bride or a cause or anything you love. The director of operations had become defined over the years by his job: He was the puppetmaster and, yet, it made him a puppet himself. And now the thought: There was a mole in Section and it would all come down and the play would be over, the stage cleared.

"Who committed you?" Devereaux said.

"Yackley."

"And supported him?"

"Richfield."

"And visited you at St. Catherine's?"

"Mrs. Neumann."

"Who else?"

"Perry Weinstein."

"Did Yackley ever come?"

"No."

"Yackley," Devereaux said, turning the name over in thought. "Yackley tapped your phone. Yackley knew you had called me. So Yackley must have sent the chasers after me."

"Yackley," Hanley said. "Are you sure?"

"In a little while," Devereaux said. "I need some things from you. Promises. And some money. Oh, and four thousand shares of stock."

"What are you talking about?"

"Expenses," Devereaux said. He tried a smile. "The only serious thing ever worth talking about to an employer."

"But you're not an employee anymore, Devereaux," Hanley said. He said it very softly.

"Yes. That's what I prefer." He listened to himself as if he might be detecting a lie. But then, that's what words were for. "I might come back. On active duty roster. But let everyone know so there are no more mistakes, no more independent contracts against me from the other side."

"Why?"

"Protection. If I come back, then Section is behind me." He said the words without any feeling in them.

He had given up his trade because he did not love it anymore and because he loved Rita Macklin. He had thought all along what he could say to her if he went back into the trade, back into the cold. The conversation in mind never had a conclusion but now, in a little while, it would have to be played out for real.

"I was set, I was anonymous, I was asleep. Only three people knew in Section—you, Mrs. Neumann, Yackley. And then one day, a Soviet courier kills Colonel Ready and it is neat and finished. Except someone told the Opposition they had killed the wrong man. That the real November was alive in Lausanne. So they sent a hitter down and two other hitters and pretty soon, it was like a comic opera. Every move that everyone made was orchestrated; everyone knew everything about everyone else. They couldn't have such good information unless it came from us. Came from you."

"I'm not a traitor—"

"I came back to kill you, Hanley," Devereaux said.

They let the silence support the words.

"You have to carry me on the books," Devereaux began again.

"But you won't come back."

"No. Not in the way you think. That's the way it has to be. I need my bona fides back. The badge and the gun." Said with bitterness. "You said you can never quit."

Hanley closed his eyes. He was weak but without pain. It was not an unpleasant feeling.

"I was so tired. At the end. Maybe I did have a breakdown. It was hopeless. If I went to the security adviser, what could I tell him but the raving suspicions of a paranoid? And if I did nothing, the Section was finished."

"The Section may be finished in any case."

"I gave my life to the Section."

"You nearly did."

"Who was it? Who is the mole?"

"In a little while," Devereaux said. "Mrs. Neumann was arrested at two. Right in the Department of Agriculture building. She must have penetrated Nutcracker. It must be very close, whatever it is."

"My own plan turned against me. But how are they going to do it? And why did you trust Mrs. Neumann?"

"Because I had to."

"You put her at risk."

"Yes."

"She's a woman."

And Devereaux smiled at that. "Are you a male chauvinist then?"

"That woman saved my life."

"Be quiet. She's in Section. What do you think they're going to do with her? Execute her? They took her to Fort Meade."

"My God, I can't stop whatever it is that is happening because I don't know what is happening. And no one knows."

"So think about it."

"I can't. I'm too tired."

"You were pushed about agents. Too many agents. The talk in Europe is about a major Soviet coming out. It's too much talk, too open. Gorki in Resolutions Committee— Denisov's old boss. It doesn't make any sense."

"Why?"

"Because everything is made so easy. Everyone knows everything about everyone else. 'There are no spies.' Who told you that?"

"Yackley," Hanley said.

"There are no spies," Devereaux repeated. "So what does the loss of a few spies mean? If they really don't exist. If we know all their secrets anyway?"

"But what is Nutcracker turned into? What's going to happen?" Hanley said. His voice was dry.

"I think I know." Devereaux stared through Hanley, through the walls of the room, to a schematic in his mind reflected on a blank screen. Like a sheet of white paper with names on it.

"I think I know," Devereaux said.

And began to tell him everything that would be done.

32

NUTCRACKER

The operation called Nutcracker commenced thirteen hours after Hanley began to explain the procedures to Devereaux. Nutcracker had been too imminent to stop.

The Soviet agent identified as Andromeda was drugged and slipped into the western zone of Berlin at 1945 hours. When he was awakened, in an American hospital in Frankfurt, he demanded to know what was going on. Two officers of the Defense Intelligence Agency said he was Andromeda, a Soviet agent who had just "defected" to the West. One of the agents was a little smug about that. It had been so slick a maneuver, without any trouble at all. The man called Andromeda said over and over that he was a Lutheran minister in Potsdam. No one believed him. Not at first.

At the same time but in a different time zone—1845 Greenwich Mean Time—the Soviet agent identified as Hebrides was picked up by two SIS men from Brit-Intell and hustled to the safe house outside London off the Great Western Road that leads to Oxford. Hebrides was clearly bona fided; his description had been confirmed by Washington. He was questioned, rather harshly, about his network. He explained, just as harshly, that one did not treat a British subject and the second tenor in the Warwick Light Opera Company in this manner. The SIS men were not very gentle and the CIA men looked the other way.

In three hours, Saturn and Mercury fell into the orbit of the West as well, the first in Tokyo, the second in San Francisco.

Nutcracker appeared to be functioning smoothly. Everyone was pleased. Quentin Reed phoned Perry Weinstein twice with a happy tone in his cultivated voice.

But Perry Weinstein was not so happy.

There were problems, all sorts of problems.

But nothing to tell Quent about.

There had been a definite fuck-up in Athens. The agent there for R Section, codenamed "Winter," reported to Athens police an attempt to kidnap him as he sat in Plokas Café on the sidewalk in Constitution Square. Only the chance that he had been dining that day with four business associates—all heavily armed—foiled the plot. Two men were dead.

By midmorning in Washington, D.C., the word from Athens was that the two dead men were Soviet commercial attachés with the embassy in the Greek capital.

Weinstein broke a pencil as he heard the report from Yackley by phone. Yackley was quite happy about it. Yackley did not understand.

Weinstein dropped the broken pencil in his wastebasket.

By noon, the watcher in Helsinki for R Section told police there his apartment had been broken into and ransacked.

Again, the R Section agent had not been harmed. Yackley had phoned Weinstein with that bit of news as well and now he was not happy, merely puzzled.

Weinstein saw what was happening.

He thought about it as he stared out his window at the White House. There was still a way to salvage things, he thought. If only—

He reached for the phone and pressed the button to connect him with Yackley.

Yackley could still be used.

Weinstein heard the phone ring and ring and ring. And then Yackley's secretary was on the line, explaining that Mr. Yackley was at lunch at an undisclosed location and expected to be out of the office until late in the afternoon.

"I don't believe this," Weinstein shouted. He never shouted. "I don't believe that idiot is out to lunch! What the hell does he think is going on?"

But the woman at the other end of the line said nothing and Weinstein slammed down the receiver so hard that the phone jumped on the desk. The white room was suddenly wrapped in silence.

What was going on?

Perry Weinstein considered himself a man of intelligence and calculation but there was a third part to him in that moment. He could not identify it. It began in his stomach and made him nauseous and built up through his organs until it reached his throat and made him dry and hoarse.

It was fear. For the first time, he felt afraid of what was going to happen.

He crossed the quiet room to the outer office.

His secretary was gone; well, it was lunch hour. He

stared at her desk and at the two television monitors connected with the security lobby.

He pulled his eyes away and started back into his own office and stopped.

He turned again.

On the black-and-white screen focused on events at the security desk he saw the man cross the lobby and flash an identification to the guard. The guard put the ID card into a machine and looked at the machine and at the man before him.

Weinstein knew the card. It would be gray and featureless, like a blank and unused credit card. The machine would read the message buried inside the card, between the twin layers of smooth plastic bonded together.

He stared at the monitor screen and the man looked at the camera.

He knew that face.

His mind swept memory, clicking over files implanted in brain tissue, connected to life with electrical impulses.

He knew the face from a 201 file he had read carefully before beginning everything that was now happening.

Perry Weinstein retreated into his own office and went to the desk. He opened the upper right drawer and removed the old, heavy .45 caliber Colt army automatic. It was the type designed at the turn of the century to kill a horse—literally, because there was still a cavalry in those days. It was replaced in service now by a light Italian handgun. Weinstein had a fondness for weapons and for antiquities. He was a very good shot and no one in the building knew he had a weapon in his drawer. It would not have been allowed, this close to the White House, across the street.

He sat down at his desk and waited. He waited for a telephone call to break the silence, to tell him the fortunes of Nutcracker were reversed. He didn't see how the blame could come back to him in any case.

But the door to his office opened anyway.

Perry Weinstein almost smiled in relief. The pistol in his hand was very heavy and felt good to him. He held it up so the other man could see the pistol clearly.

"Bang bang," Perry Weinstein said.

"You're dead," Devereaux said and stepped into the room. His presence filled the room. Weinstein held the pistol easily in his big right hand. He propped his elbow on the desk top to steady the grip.

"Bang bang," Perry Weinstein said again, like a child who finds himself very clever.

Devereaux waited by the door.

"The TV monitor. I was in the outer office and I saw you in the security lobby," Weinstein said.

"It doesn't matter."

"Why?"

"Nutcracker is off. Dead in the water."

"November," Weinstein said. His eyes glittered in the dull light of the room. "Our man November."

Devereaux stood very still.

"Come into the room a little more," Weinstein said.

Devereaux took a step.

Weinstein waved the barrel of the pistol in welcome.

Devereaux stood before the desk.

Weinstein came around the desk carefully. "I am very good with pistols. Very good. In case you think I'm one of those desk-bound bureaucrats who doesn't really know anything about anything."

He pressed the pistol against Devereaux's head, behind the left ear. The barrel felt cold on the scalp. Devereaux said, "In the belt, left side."

Weinstein reached and removed the pistol from the clip.

"Hands on head," he said. He pointed to a straight chair by the north wall. Devereaux went to the chair and sat down. Weinstein pushed the chair back on the rear legs so that it balanced Devereaux back against the wall. "Is that comfortable?" he said.

Devereaux did not speak.

Weinstein went back to the desk and sat on the edge of the desk. He stared at Devereaux with owlish curiosity. His eyeglasses were still held together by a paper clip. He had a rugged and tired look to him. It really had been a lot of work and now it was over.

Devereaux said, "You should have let sleeping agents lie."

"I couldn't do that," Weinstein said.

"I was curious about Hanley's calls. But it was only curiosity."

"I couldn't be sure of that. It was difficult for me to maneuver." He said this with a slow, funereal cadence. He wanted someone as smart as himself to understand.

He went on: "I was succeeding. In getting Hanley out of the way. In another year, I would have R Section stripped down, discredited."

"How long have you worked for them?"

" 'The other side,' you mean?" Weinstein smiled. "It's old-fashioned to think in those terms, don't you think? There is only one side: Stability. A sense of order. Real peace. The enemy is the terrorists and they're nothing more than nuisances. Who cares greatly that eight or nine people are killed in a Rome airport? I mean, beyond the eight or nine and their families? There is death like that every day, in every city of the world. No. There's no 'other side' anymore; just as there are no spies anymore."

For the first time, Devereaux smiled. He seemed at ease and that annoyed Weinstein. "You're the author of that nonsense."

"Yackley is my messenger, my agent. Yackley is an empty mind waiting to be filled. I gave a talk, actually, at Yale three years ago, before this assignment. I was trying to make an intellectual point that is true in practice. Eighty-five to ninety percent of our intelligence is hardware. It comes from things. It comes from satellites, skyspies, automatic listening devices. ELINT. PHOTINT. SIGINT. You know. There is so much information we can't process it all. The information is like a constant avalanche that just never ends, never runs out of snow, never fills the valley below. On and on, year after year. There is too damned much intelligence and we are drowning in it. So what is the use of agents in the field? Are they going to steal the drawings of the Norden Bombsight? Or a copy of the Enigma Machine? My God, no one grows up. HUMINT is passé." He became agitated and got up, walked around his desk, dropped the .45 heavily on the desk top. He sat down and Devereaux was very still.

"This is modern times. There are no spies and spies are not only a drain upon the resources of the government—an argument, November, that flies well in budget-making circles—but a positive detriment. Spies generate spies. We spy on one another like kids. We misinterpret information because we are limited in intelligence; we hold up important analysis of real intelligence because we have our doubts or we are fed disinformation by our opposite numbers…"

"And then, there are times when there are moles in government and it takes a spy to catch a spy."

Devereaux's words were not expected and the room was quiet now. The man at the desk with the gun stared at Devereaux with something like hatred.

"You caught me? I caught you," Weinstein said. "You're a renegade to Section. You crashed a crazy old man out of St. Catherine's. You killed a nun—or it looks that way. And you killed a state policeman pursuing you. He died in the crash."

"He was driving too fast for conditions."

"You are a killer. You are out of control."

"I am licensed again." Very softly. "In the old trade."

"Goddamnit. I can kill you right now and get a medal for it."

"Why work for them?"

"Work for them? Those midgets? I saw a way clear to do some good. Don't tell me you believe in that nonsense about recruitment in college and years of quiet dedication to the cause? I was in Czechoslovakia five years ago on a fellowship and I made the contact, not them. I told them I would do what I could. To make the world a saner place."

"How kind of you."

"I didn't even want any money but I had to take money or they wouldn't have believed me. I wanted to contribute to understanding."

"You're crazy, Weinstein."

"No. You are. And Hanley. Spies and spymasters. I was handed R Section practically as a gift by that idiot Yackley. He was a climber and a star-fucker. He wanted me to see what a good job he did. Liked to call me Perry just as if we worked out at the same club together. What a complete asshole."

"Most of them are," Devereaux said.

"Yes. None more so than Hanley. I wanted to get rid of Hanley but you can't just kill people, you know. Not at that level. I convinced Yackley, who convinced Dr. Thompson that Hanley needed calming down. Some sort of tranquilizer. Thompson is to medicine what Typhoid Mary was to cooking. Hanley was being blocked, going through some sort of career crisis—he doubted himself. And then, when I took Nutcracker away from him, he went off the edge. It was a clever enough bit of business, I think. I wasn't even suspected."

"What is Nutcracker?"

"Didn't Hanley tell you?"

"But that isn't what it is—"

Weinstein smiled. "You don't know. So you haven't blocked it after all. Nutcracker isn't finished, is it?"

"Only the parts I could understand. About the other side snatching our agents. Part of our pre-summit maneuvering in the field—we get a defector/spy and they get two—"

"That can't be." Weinstein picked up the pistol again and sighted Devereaux along the barrel. "That can't be." The voice was soft. "There are four hundred and fifty-three agents in field. They can't all be notified that quickly. I wasn't concerned when you escaped with Hanley that you could figure this out right away. And notify all the agents. You couldn't do it."

"No. You're right."

"Then what did you do?"

"I guessed which ones were the targets."

Weinstein blinked.

He felt his finger become very heavy on the trigger.

"You guessed?"

Devereaux waited.

"You *guessed? You don't guess! This isn't a matter of guesswork*."

"But it is. That's what it always is. All the information doesn't mean anything unless you can guess what the missing pieces are."

"How could you guess?"

"Hanley had a list of names. Of agents. Scheduled for early retirement to trim the budget. They seemed most logical. And it would be enough to begin wrecking the Section—"

"I gave Gorki all the information. I told him about you—that you were sleeping. I told him to take care of you. And that damned idiot Yackley had already sent out two Section chasers to talk to you. So we ended up with four dead agents in Switzerland. What a mess. What a stinking mess that was."

"You gave Gorki all the information. It was so good. He knew where to send Alexa. He wanted to get rid of Alexa."

"I know. She was an embarrassment to him. The old fool had photographs of her naked and dancing. Pictures of them together. Stolen New Year's Eve from his dacha. He has his enemies in the bureaucracy as we do. I had word that he was coming out when the matter was over. Voluntarily or not. My little reward. After November was dead and the R Section spies were defected, Gorki was coming out. He was tired and old and he had enemies."

"Which side were you on?"

"I didn't care about Gorki, except that I could get credit for his defection. R Section was going to be ruined by Nutcracker. Let CIA get credit, NSA, the Brits for pulling in some low-level Soviet flotsam...Gorki set that up as one of his bona fides, to show he was going ahead with the program. The grand prize was Gorki himself from Resolutions Committee. I would arrange the meeting myself—"

"You're a fool, Weinstein. Gorki gave you crap."

"They were low-level agents—"

"Gorki gave you a Protestant minister and an opera singer. He targeted innocents and turned them over to half a dozen intelligence agencies. Gorki isn't coming out. And Gorki was going to take credit for bringing in all the R Section people you were willing to betray. Gorki—whoever Gorki is—is a survivor. He got rid of Alexa—he was going to have her killed in Switzerland and put the blame on me—but it didn't matter if she killed me first and then you got her. In any case, she was no longer a problem to the man in Moscow. She wasn't going back to the Soviet Union to cause him trouble just by being alive. An old man learns to survive in a bureaucracy just because he's practiced all the tricks."

"We would have her. Ivers. It was pressure on him—"

"You're a fool in the long run, aren't you, Perry?" Devereaux's eyes seemed to glitter in the strong afternoon light. "I was asleep in Switzerland, dead to the world." For a moment, the two men were silent, considering the image of a sleeping agent, buried in a country at the edge of the world of spies. "You goddamn fool," Devereaux said at last. "I was on that ship in the Baltic as far as

Gorki knew—and then you let your contact know that I'm still alive in Switzerland, the real agent named November, because Hanley had called me, because Yackley had tapped his line, because you saw the transcript and saw that I had heard something about a nutcracker. One wrong conclusion and all the rest comes tumbling down and you had to believe that your masters would get Gorki out of Moscow, one way or another. Gorki must have a sense of humor, whoever he is. He played you the fool for so long you still don't understand that's what you are."

"Shut up," Perry Weinstein said. His voice hissed and a vein in his neck seemed enlarged. "Shut the fuck up."

"And I would have stayed asleep in Switzerland but you sent those chasers after me—"

"Yackley did. To talk to you. They were only sent to talk to you and you killed them and—"

"Killing and killing and everything came down because of it. Because you made so many smart moves that you couldn't move at all. And you forced me to come back into the cold, into the trade."

"There is no cold," Weinstein said. "Don't you understand a goddamn thing I tried to tell you? Are you as stupid as the rest of them?"

Devereaux dropped his hands on his lap. He was smiling.

A damned smile. A damned smug smile. Weinstein picked up the pistol and came around the desk. "Nothing matters," he said, regaining a tone he had lost in the last minute. "You're dead. The real November is dead. And I'll be more careful in the future. A little setback along the way. I can assure you that Hanley is finished in Section and that's a victory—one less HUMINT believer.

And we'll put a new man in for Neumann in CompAn and—"

"You won't survive," Devereaux said. He said it so certainly that Perry Weinstein paused. The pistol was fixed in front of him, pointed at Devereaux's face.

"I'll survive you. It's time to kill. End of the game, end of words."

He held the pistol in exactly the right grip, with the legs in a stance, the pistol in the right hand and the left hand around the right wrist to support its weight. Everything was exactly right.

Except for Devereaux's size. A petty miscalculation. His legs were longer than they seemed.

Devereaux's right foot reached the barrel just as Weinstein fired.

The shot singed his hairline and there was blood on Devereaux's scalp. He went down because the kick pushed him back off balance. His legs went flying. He rolled and Perry Weinstein brought the pistol down and fired again.

The shot destroyed a foot of plaster.

Devereaux braced, kicked out with both feet, making his legs points of a projectile. His feet slammed into Weinstein's left side. The pain crushed the breath out of Weinstein and the third shot went into the ceiling.

Devereaux was up again, seeming to spring up like a halfback from a tangle of bodies on the football field. He grasped the gun hand and the gun exploded a fourth time.

Devereaux brought Weinstein's wrist down hard on the edge of the desk and Perry gripped the trigger in pain and a fifth and sixth shot went off.

Devereaux cracked his wrist.

The pain went white, right up to Weinstein's eyes.

Devereaux moved in close, chopped at the damaged left side.

Weinstein was big and strong but very slow. He was taller than Devereaux. He grabbed the smaller man's face in his left claw and tore it. There was blood on the cheeks.

Devereaux stepped back.

Weinstein pushed him very hard with his whole body and exploded his body against the north wall. Devereaux hit the wall hard. He went to one knee.

The second pistol—a very light Walther—was on the desk top. Weinstein reached for it and the pain of his broken right wrist paralyzed him.

Devereaux pushed off the wall and slammed again into Weinstein, pushing his body against the desk.

Weinstein had the pistol in his left hand—not his shooting hand. He brought it around and the trigger wouldn't pull. The safety was on. It was enough.

Devereaux hit him with a very heavy right hand square in the face, breaking his jaw and sending his glasses broken and sprawling across the desk top.

Perry blinked with pain that engulfed him like fear. It rose in his belly and reached for his throat and blinded his eyes.

The room was all sounds without speech. The shots lingered in echoes that nearly deafened both of them. They grunted with pain and effort. Weinstein brought the pistol down hard against Devereaux's head and he went down.

Weinstein stood over the body for a moment.

He pointed the pistol at Devereaux's head and unclicked the safety. He went to the outer door and stood there and looked at the twin monitors on the desk.

And then he saw it.

Terror crept over his broken features. The eyes were wide. He saw the horror of it.

It was there, on the monitor, the second screen.

A picture of the room he stood in. A picture of Devereaux on the floor by the desk. The monitor had been turned to the room. Someone had put a goddamn spy camera in his private room. Recording everything he had said to Devereaux. He looked up at the ceiling and still could not see the camera that had recorded everything.

And now they were coming, all of them coming. He saw them in the lobby on the other monitor. He heard the machinery of the elevator whirring beyond his outer office.

It was so damned clever of them.

But there was one way to escape.

He put the barrel of the Walther PPK in his mouth and squeezed the trigger easily. The trigger, unchecked by the safety, slid back to the guard.

He didn't hear the shot at all.

33

EXILES

They sat in one of those coffee shops on Third Avenue in New York City that are full of old men and bored waitresses. The couple sat quietly in the corner. They ate and drank and talked. They talked Russian. It was good to talk Russian, for both of them.

They became lovers, as well.

Alexa disappeared from the game, just as Denisov had and by the same way of escape—through Section. She was a good defector but she knew so little about anything except killing. Gorki had gotten rid of her the photographs had been stolen from his dacha at Christmas and Gorki knew that his enemies intended to use them against him—and yet he had betrayed very little because Alexa knew very little. She was a disappointment to the Section but not to Denisov.

Denisov had cut off two of Ivers' fingers before Ivers learned to talk. To tell Denisov about his various errands for Perry Weinstein. Ivers had exceeded his authority and Ivers was in disgrace; worse, he was going to prison. The thought of prison terrified Alexa when Denisov explained what would happen to Ivers.

But Alexa had been drawn to Denisov that night in the room in the motel outside Alexandria. He had been utterly cold, ruthless, and without any compassion at all. He was cruel without pleasure.

It had given her great pleasure to see his power over Ivers.

She had slept with him. She had made love to him with great skill. She had done so many things to please him and he had come awake to her. She needed him so desperately because he was like her in this damned and strange and hostile world. She felt sadness because Russia was denied them and all the Moscow nights she had yearned for as a child—when she had wanted to count the stars— were over. She needed Denisov, the Russian words, the shared remembrances. If Denisov left her, she would be utterly alone and she could not stand that.

And Denisov, sitting across from her, his eyes mild and kindly behind the rimless glasses, understood her need. It very nearly frightened him.

34

CONVERSATION FINISHED

Rita Macklin unsnapped her seat belt when the plane hit the runway with a thump. The airlines all caution you not to do this. Old travelers always do. She was so damned tired of traveling. The story hadn't been in the Far East at all.

She reached under her seat for the travel bag that had been home, office, comforter, and dresser for four weeks. She thought she wanted a bath and then about three or four days of sleep. But she had only a day here and then it was back to Europe.

Back to him.

Because she was thinking of him being in a place that was not here in the bright and sterile concourse of Dulles Airport, she didn't see him at first. And then she realized what it must have meant, his being here. She felt a coldness rise inside her.

She crossed the terminal to him.

She stood apart from him for a moment. She was so damned tired and she didn't look her best. Her short red hair was mussed and she hadn't worried about lipstick.

Her wide green eyes took him in. Nothing ever changed in him, she thought.

"Where are we going?" she said.

"I got you a room."

"All right."

It was all they said. They had too much to say to each other. He wanted to touch her. He took her bag instead and led her to the waiting car.

"Are you back?" she said, getting in the car. Her voice was dull, tired.

"Yes. In a way."

"That's the end of it," she said.

"I want to talk to you," he said.

And she did not answer him.

Rita Macklin slept in the afternoon and into the evening. When she woke up, in the darkened bedroom, she was alone. She stumbled to the bath and took a long shower to ease the coldness that pressed between her shoulders. She held her sharply etched face up to the shower and let the water stream down on her. The water did not warm her.

She dressed in her "press conference" clothes. The skirt was washable—everything was washable and unwrinkleable—and so was the blouse. They were blue. He liked the way she looked in blue, though he never said these things to her.

She wasn't angry with him. She was just saddened.

She put on earrings. She brushed her hair. Her body was tanned by the Oriental sun. He had spoiled everything by being here, in Washington. She had wanted him so much. Not words, not tears, just touch and tasting. To be next to him when they slept. To have his arm draped over her shoulders. To burrow into him. To go to sleep with the smell of him next to her and awake and lick him awake. My God, she just had wanted him and not words and this stupid conversation that was going to have to be finished.

The note on the desk said he was sitting in the lounge off the lobby.

"Why?"

"Because they woke me up. Killers. Come to kill me in Switzerland. It was just a mistake. They made an error in judgment."

"I want a beer," she said.

She sat next to him at the end of the long, weekday-empty bar. It was nearly nine at night. She was wide awake.

He started at the beginning and told her everything. She didn't ask any questions. She drank beer and listened and after a while she looked at him.

"What about the girl?"

"Margot? She went back to Chicago."

"You used her," she said.

He waited.

"You're good at using people."

"When there's no other way."

"But do you know what everything means, everything you told me?"

"Yes."

"Nothing," she said. "It doesn't mean a damned thing. All that maneuvering, all the dirty tricks and betrayals and murders and all this booga-booga spy stuff you pretend you don't love . . . it comes out not meaning a damned thing.

I go halfway around the world and I hear the same leaders, the same revolutionaries, all the same words. The rhetoric never changes, the stupid lurching from one disaster to another. There isn't enough suffering to satisfy humanity. Death isn't horrible enough, there have to be varieties of death. Babies cry but it's not enough—we have to drop napalm on them to increase their tears. Someone I never heard of who's a ninth-rate bureaucrat becomes a Soviet agent and then gets found out by our man November— hurrah, hurrah!—and blows his face off and what the hell does it mean? Tell me one thing it means."

But he was silent. He watched her. He watched her eyes and saw pain at the corners of her pretty green eyes.

"Everything that happened didn't mean a damned thing to the world," she said at last.

Silence was a bond. They were the only people at the bar. She finished her beer and stared at the glass, at the foam coating the inside of the empty tumbler. She thought about the first time together, when she had slept with him in that old motel room on Clearwater Beach. He had slept with her only to use her and when she knew it, it wasn't enough to leave him. Use me. I'll do anything for you, Devereaux. You bastard.

Damnit, she thought. Why was there always pain between them?

"Is it finished? I mean, is it finished?"

"I can't finish it," he said.

"I thought you could do anything."

"I thought I could. I thought I could say no and walk away from it. With you."

"Make it finished," she said.

"I can't. Not anymore. Not in the way I wanted. The way we wanted it."

"Make it finished," she said again.

"I can't force you to agree to anything. I told you everything. I told you the truth."

"Is that right? Did you tell me everything? Did you tell me you love it? Tell me that. Tell me you love it. The trade, the business, whatever you call it. The spy who goes into the cold because it's the only thing that amuses him. Tell me." Her voice was bitter and her eyes were wet. "Tell me you love it."

"No."

Waiting. Quiet.

"I'm good at the trade, that's part of satisfaction, I suppose." He saw his face reflected in the mirror behind the bar. "No. I don't love it."

"Do you love any goddamn thing in the world?"

"You."

"What about Philippe? You saved his life. You took him off that island. What about that little boy?"

"No. I don't love Philippe."

"You cold son-of-a-bitch."

"I pitied him." He would not touch her. She had to understand him and the truth of things without tricks. "Perhaps I pitied myself. When I saw him. When I heard him plead. Pity is not such a small thing, Rita." He wanted to touch her, to smell her. But this conversation had to be finished now; it had been suspended between them for too long. "Pity is a good thing to feel as well."

"But you don't have pity for me."

He thought it was over then. He felt sick because the words were too brittle.

"I would have done anything for you," Rita said.

She got up. She stared at him as though fixing him in memory.

Her green eyes turned to liquid emeralds. And they were cold as gems. "Anything."

She turned from him and walked out of the lounge on the lush red carpet. Her steps were quiet and then she was gone, into the lobby.

The sickness overwhelmed him for a moment and then he saw his face again, in the mirror. He stared at the empty eyes.

He got up and dropped money on the bar.

He walked out of the lounge and saw her. She was heading toward the elevator bank. The lobby was bright with people who spoke in loud voices.

She waited for the elevator and he was behind her. She turned. She looked at him. The emerald eyes were still wet and the coldness in them was gone.

"More talk?" she said. "More facing the truth?"

"No more talk."

"We finished the conversation. I always knew we would have to come to the end of it," she said.

"No. It's not over."

"What's left?"

"I don't have arguments. Or words. I tried to show you."

"What?"

"I love you." He tried to say it right. The words were magic to him but they were so common to others. Everyone loved everyone else. No one else ever understood that Devereaux had not loved another creature in his life. He had existed on pity until he met Rita Macklin. But not pity for himself; it was the thing that kept him apart from the world. He could pity life and keep the cold thing inside himself to make him apart from everything he did or said.

"Don't I get to be happy?" she said. "Don't you?"

"No guarantees."

"There ought to be rules of behavior. There really ought to be." And she stroked his face then with one lazy gesture of her hand. Her hand touched his face as though it were no part of her words, her eyes, her thoughts. Her fingers raked gently across his cheek. "But there are no rules, are there?"

"No," he said.

"Dev." The hand lingered on his shoulder. The elevator door opened. The cage was empty. The bright lobby full of loud people was around them; they were alone in the middle of her gesture. He felt the weight of her hand on his shoulder and his hand touched her hand then, covering it, holding it. They crossed into the cage and the door closed on them and they were alone. He held her hand.

It was the end of a conversation that had been unfinished for too long.

35

RAMBLER

There was a tail car and a police car and then this thing. A 1973 Rambler.

Dave stared out the window of the rooming house and then rushed to the door and down the stairs. He paused on the first landing. What the hell was this about? If it came down to it, he could deny he owned the thing. But they had his name on the registration and the plates and—

He opened the door and crossed the sidewalk. It was a warm day in May.

The man in the tail car got out while the driver got out of the Rambler. The driver didn't seem too happy.

"David Mason?"

"What's this about?"

"Are you David Mason?"

"Yeah."

"This is your car."

"Maybe."

"It is your car."

"All right, it's my car."

"We found it."

"So, you found it."

"We're bringing it back to you."

"What are you, the tooth fairy?"

"Yeah, I'm the tooth fairy." He seemed bored. "Look, this is your car and here it is. Also, here's the bonus."

"What are you talking about?"

"The bonus for use of the car. Twenty-two cents a mile and forty-two dollars per diem. It comes to four hundred twelve dollars thirty-one cents." He produced a pen. "Just sign."

"Sign what?"

"Expense account form."

"What are you talking about?"

"Government. Got any objections to four hundred twelve dollars thirty-one cents?"

"Not one."

"Man who rented the car from you."

Dave caught on. "Yeah. What about him?"

"He works with us. Our...section."

"Yeah. What do you do?"

"We're spies," the man said.

"Is that right?"

"Yes."

"Okay, you're spies."

The man held the paper while he signed. He took back his pen and popped it into his shirt pocket. He looked at Dave as though he didn't like what he saw.

"Boss says I got to ask you."

"Ask me what?"

"You want a job with us?"

"You're spies, right?"

"That's right."

"James Bond? Cloak and dagger?"

"Yeah. And we all wear trenchcoats." In fact, he was wearing a trenchcoat, even though it must have been 85 degrees.

"Sure," Dave said.

"Sure what?"

"Sure, I'll take a job."

"Come on, then," the man said.

And that was that.

36

MRS. NEUMANN

By June, Hanley was back, a little thinner but still back. He was examined by three psychologists who said his mind was perfectly sound. Of course, if the Section had wanted to prove the other argument, it had three psychologists ready to testify that Hanley was deranged.

St. Catherine's federal subsidy was withdrawn because of certain abuses noted in a report filed with the budget office and the General Accounting Office.

Not noted in the report was the fate of Dr. Goddard. Hanley knew the signature. Dr. Goddard had been found with his throat slit. Hanley thought about it—and then put it from his mind. There was work to do. Operations was still...well, operational. Nothing had changed. Yackley was out of course, but quietly. Same with Richfield and the other division directors. The new boss of R Section was quite ruthless in the matter of personnel. Hanley understood that and appreciated it. Who could have appreciated Mrs. Neumann better than Hanley?

Even Quentin Reed, who had escaped any blame in the Weinstein affair, thought it was terrific. As he told the National Security Adviser, "What could be better? A computer whiz to put software on the right track and at the same time score points in the FBM derby?" It meant: Female, black, minority.

The National Security Adviser had trouble with that—with all of Quentin's jargon—but he understood the gist of it. Mrs. Neumann was the right sex for a change. And she'd ride herd on Operations, too.

37

SLEEPER

The tourists were in Copenhagen. It was summer and the air was filled with their English chatter. They all seemed to speak English.

They came by the trainloads into the quaint dark station in the center of Copenhagen, across from the Tivoli Gardens. They filled the streets and shops. They came in surging gaggles, they filled the sidewalks, they bought everything, and the Danes smiled with good humor at them.

The English language sounded good to the man at the table in the café on Vesterbrogade, west of the train station. The café was not a usual tourist place, but now and then a couple wandered in and spoke loud English and it felt good to hear it. The Carlsberg was very cold and he drank quite a bit of it every afternoon, reading the papers in the way of an exile with a lot of time on his hands. He had been waiting all winter and spring for the time to be spent, to watch the trail, to see who might still be on it.

He spoke Danish fairly well. They knew he was a foreigner of course but they appreciated him all the more for taking the trouble to learn that difficult language.

He read the *Herald-Tribune* and the *Wall Street Journal*'s European edition. He read the *Journal de Genève*, the French-language paper from Switzerland.

He was interested in Switzerland very much.

He was not an unattractive man. He had the scar, of course, across his cheek, from ear to the edge of his mouth. And he had the limp, inflicted on him one night by a gray-haired man whose name was Devereaux. He had taken a long time to overcome the perpetual pain in his ankle. Devereaux had cut his Achilles tendon. At least the pain reminded the red-haired man every day of whom he hated more than his own life.

He thought about Alexa sometimes. She had killed poor Nils on the *Finlandia*. Poor Nils.

Nils was a find. Nils had been attracted to him in one of those cellar clubs in Copenhagen where the smoke is very thick and the beer is cold and everyone talks too loud. They had sat at a booth together and shared secrets. Or Nils had shared secrets.

They were so much alike. They had reddish hair, both of them. Nils wore a beard and Ready was clean-shaven. He could not have grown a beard because of the scar.

They had shared their bodies with each other. Nils was fascinated by Ready. Ready always had that power—over men and women. He used Nils and Nils understood he was being used and accepted the position. It was a position of deference and some might have thought it was degrading. Nils attended to Ready's words and whims.

And then, as Ready listened at the trail for the sounds of those who followed him, he thought of the idea. Of using Nils to end the trail for once and all. To involve Nils in the job of being a spy. Ready's spy. Ready's goat. It would work because everyone would believe in it so thoroughly. It was too absurd not to work. Nils became Ready because he would do the things Ready wanted him to do; he would meet the agent on the *Finlandia*; he would seduce the agent and tell Ready about the seduction.

Except, of course, he would never live to tell a soul. The Soviets must have thought Ready very stupid to believe they would give him a second chance.

The trail was cold now. Ready slept and no one knew he was alive at all.

So, mostly, in the long lingering summer afternoons of Copenhagen where there is a smell of fish on the sea breezes and the chatter of tourists in the narrow streets and wide plazas, Ready thought about new things. About Devereaux and his girl. About the time to come when Ready would be awake again. And what he would have to do to Devereaux and to his woman to make up for all he had suffered.

38

November

Is this what being a spy is about? It's not so bad."

"There are no spies," Devereaux said.

Rita was bare-breasted because this was a very upper-class French resort called the Baie des Anges—the Bay of Angels—down the Riviera from Nice. The resort was formed by a series of enormous buildings curved around a very small harbor full of very large boats. The buildings resembled ocean liners with stepped decks. It was all very exclusive and monstrously expensive and he had taken her hand one afternoon, led her to a plane, led her here. She looked around her, to make certain all the other women had not suddenly slipped on their halter tops. All was well; breasts were naked. She wore a small red bikini bottom. Devereaux stretched on the chaise next to her; he had his eyes closed.

"I said this is a pretty good life."

"It's all right," he said. The sun was very warm and they were both dark now.

"I feel odd. Not wearing a top."

"You'd feel odder if you did."

"You like to look at naked women, don't you?"

"Yes," he said.

She closed her eyes for a long time and felt the sun on her breasts. With her eyes closed, she said, "Do you think it will be like this for a while? I mean, don't we get a breather?"

"Sure," he said. "This is the breather."

"But things always turn out bad in the end."

"There are no happy endings. I knew someone in New York once who wanted to believe in happy endings. It was the saddest thing you ever saw." And he smiled at her.

Rita waited for a while, feeling the sun on her body.

"This is the way it had to be." She frowned when she said it. She wasn't talking about this. She was talking about the matter they didn't really talk about anymore.

"I don't know," he said.

"Everything you told me. Everything you didn't tell me. It was supposed to save R Section. And nothing happened at all."

"Nothing." His voice was lazy in the sun. The babble around them was full of French voices and the occasional German grunt. The Mediterranean Sea beyond the pool was blue, deeper blue than it had ever been before.

"It turned out to be meaningless."

"If Perry Weinstein had remained, it wouldn't have been. Perry was moving up the ladder. He was that close to real power. This was a skirmish in the war. It could have been more than that. If Weinstein had won it."

"De Big Cold War. What is it, exactly, De Big Cold War?" She used an Amos 'n' Andy accent.

"Skirmishes. Little battles. It doesn't mean very much."

"People died."

"Yes."

"People always die." She was smiling at him because she was mocking him. It was what he might have said. His eyes were closed but he returned her smile. The smile came in her voice.

"It's a condition of life," he said.

"You're a philosopher."

"I wish I could promise you happy endings."

She said, "Would you like to go up to our rooms and make love?"

"You mean in the middle of the day?"

"Yes," she said.

He stood up and waited for her. She put on her top to walk back to the buildings. It was all so beautiful.

"You never want it to end," she said.

He said nothing.

They held hands as they walked back, among the half-naked bodies all around the pool. They looked exactly like what they were. Friends and lovers.

About the Author

An award-winning novelist and reporter, Bill Granger was raised in a working-class neighborhood on the South Side of Chicago. He began his extraordinary career in 1963 when, while still in college, he joined the staff of United Press International. He later worked for the *Chicago Tribune*, writing about crime, cops, and politics, and covering such events as the race riots of the late 1960s and the 1968 Democratic Convention. In 1969, he joined the staff of the *Chicago Sun-Times*, where he won an Associated Press award for his story of a participant in the My Lai Massacre. He also wrote a series of stories on Northern Ireland for *Newsday*—and unwittingly added to a wealth of information and experiences that would form the foundations of future spy thrillers and mystery novels. By 1978, Bill Granger had contributed articles to *Time*, the *New Republic*, and other magazines; and become a daily columnist, television critic, and teacher of journalism at Columbia College in Chicago.

He began his literary career in 1979 with *Code Name November* (originally published as *The November Man*), the book that became an international sensation and introduced the cool American spy who later gave rise to a whole series. His second novel, *Public Murders*, a Chicago police procedural, won the Edgar® Award from the Mystery Writers of America in 1981.

In all, Bill Granger published thirteen November Man novels, three nonfiction books, and nine novels. In 1980, he began weekly columns in the *Chicago Tribune* on everyday life (he was voted best Illinois columnist by UPI), which were collected in the book *Chicago Pieces*. His books have been translated into ten languages.

Bill Granger passed away in 2012.

Don't miss the other exciting books in the bestselling November Man series

**And look for the major motion picture
The November Man, coming soon!**